A NOVEL OF THE MARVEL UNIVERSE

SPIDER-MAN

FOREVER YOUNG

STEFAN PETRUCHA

A NOVEL OF THE MARVEL UNIVERSE

SPIDER-MAN

FOREVER YOUNG

STEFAN PETRUCHA

TITAN BOOKS

Spider-Man: Forever Young
Print edition ISBN: 9781785659867
E-book edition ISBN: 9781785659874

Published by Titan Books
A division of Titan Publishing Group Ltd
144 Southwark Street, London SE1 0UP

First Titan edition: October 2018
10 9 8 7 6 5 4 3 2 1

Spider-Man created by Stan Lee and Steve Ditko

Editor: Stuart Moore
Interior art: Humberto Ramos and Wayne Faucher
with Jay Bowen and Salena Mahina
Cover art by Ed McGuinness and Teo Gonzales
VP Production & Special Projects: Jeff Youngquist
Assistant Editor: Caitlin O'Connell
Associate Editor: Sarah Brunstad
Manager, Licensed Publishing: Jeff Reingold
Director, Licensed Publishing: Sven Larsen
SVP Print, Sales & Marketing: David Gabriel
Editor in Chief: C.B. Cebulski
Chief Creative Officer: Joe Quesada
President, Marvel Entertainment: Dan Buckley
Executive Producer: Alan Fine

A CIP catalogue record for this title is available from the British Library.

Printed and bound in the United States

Dedicated to Stan Lee, without whom…
'nuff said.

Brief as the lightning in the collied night,
That, in a spleen, unfolds both heaven and Earth;
And ere a man hath power to say "Behold!"
The jaws of darkness do devour it up:
So quick bright things come to confusion.

— A MIDSUMMER NIGHT'S DREAM
by William Shakespeare

PART ONE:
YOUTH

ONE

THE INSTANT Peter Parker's fingers lifted from his palm, he snatched the end of the thick strand shooting from the nozzle strapped to his wrist. The strand went taut, sending him curving through the air, leaving New York City a blur.

While his uncle's death had first motivated him, there was another big reason Peter fought crime as Spider-Man: He *liked* it. Swinging and diving, leaping and latching, moving from flagpole to building, scuttling along walls—it all felt good. Pretending to be an average Joe, on the other hand, made him feel like a runner forced to wear lead shoes. It wasn't that he felt more himself as Spidey…but he did feel *allowed* to be more of himself.

Tonight, though, his money troubles weighed so heavily that he couldn't even let go enough to enjoy the wild, roller-coaster whirl. Despite the sharp mind that created the web fluid and shooters—despite the proportional strength, speed, and agility he'd received from a radioactive spider bite in high school—Spider-Man kept thinking about all the things he *couldn't* do.

Can't believe I sold my scooter and still can't afford a lousy half-price matinee! Or books. Or food. Not to mention rent.

At the peak of the pendulum arc, he released his grip, felt a brief sensation of flight, and then landed flat on the white-brick surface of a pre-war building.

If water wasn't included with my apartment, I'd die of dehydration.

Sitting on a corner ledge, he tugged at an uneven fold in his mask that had been making the back of his neck itch.

Man up, Parker! Plenty of people don't even have clean water.

He scanned the silent buildings, the streets and sidewalks glowing from the lampposts, but there was nothing. He could usually count on a villain's pompous "I will destroy you" or a gasping mugger's "Oh nuts it's Spider-Man" to focus his chatty mind.

In the quiet, he had no one but himself to answer.

So now what? Hope *for a crime so I can snap some pics for the* Bugle? *Well…yeah…kinda.*

He listened carefully, in case the city din hid a cry for help. But even the traffic flowed free and easy. A recon of the area revealed nothing more than a few illegally parked cars. Otherwise, as far as he could tell, New York City was crime-free for the first time *ever.*

Eventually, the late shows ended, and the sidewalks filled with friends and couples.

Time to head home before Harry gets back from his date with MJ. Don't want my roommate and his girlfriend seeing me climbing in through our apartment window.

Picking the shortest path, he swung past the hulking warehouses of the garment district. As he passed a particularly old one, a small tingle ran from his fingertips and toes, up along his limbs, meeting at the small of his back. The spider-sense that warned of impending danger was usually more of a five-bell alarm, sometimes making him leap even before he knew what he was dodging. This was more like goosebumps from a cool breeze, a shadow of unease.

I'm so overeager, I'm jumping at nothing. Parker, when will you ever grow up?

○———————○

STANDING alone inside the decrepit building, 89-year-old Silvio Manfredi figured he'd left behind any need to grow up a long, long time ago. His street-name—Silvermane—said it all. He was the leader of the Maggia, the city's largest criminal syndicate. He was the silverback, the alpha male, and—for decades now—a target for anyone eager to take his place.

In his line of work, any sign of weakness was death. Silvermane couldn't just be on top, he had to make sure everyone saw him there—even when it came to fashion. The right business suit meant dominance. The right gun meant the guy carrying it knew how to use it. That was why—though he missed his old homburg hat, dark-gray striped suit, and two-tone shoes—he now wore the latest Brioni, and why, rather than his old tommy gun, he always carried a sweet little piece that could spray 420 rounds a second.

Experience had also taught him how to smell a threat. So when the pug-faced attorney Caesar Cicero had pleaded with him not to come to this warehouse without backup, his nostrils flared. Good advice? Yeah, sure, but lawyer-talk always had more than one meaning. Cicero, Silvermane's ambitious second-in-command, was probing for weakness, searching for signs the old man had grown feeble enough for him to make a move.

But Silvermane hadn't fallen for it. The city's crannies hid the bodies of hundreds of chumps who'd trusted important duties, like this face-to-face, to some lackey. He should know. He'd put half of them there.

So, despite his aches, a hip that creaked when he walked, and a bum heart that threatened to take him out faster than a hitman's bullet, Silvio Manfredi had showed up all on his own, refusing so much as a single bodyguard.

If it was a setup, he'd have smelled that, too.

But as the minutes ticked by and he remained alone, the cold making its way into his bones, he had to admit that, signs of weakness aside, death was death, too. Sooner or later there'd be a point where trusting his aging instincts might not be such a good idea. Three times, he'd forgotten the address. When he checked the flip-notebook he used for the special kind of info that only a fool would trust to a digital whatsis, he could barely make out his own scrawl.

Afraid the tremors had returned, he held out a hand. It was steady enough, but the fingers—once able to crack bones—looked so wrinkled, they reminded him of his grandmother.

Thinking of that sadistic witch sickened him. If one of his men were here, he'd have beaten him just to shake the memory. When his sainted mother had died shielding him from a Sicilian mobster with a vendetta, Silvio was sent to stay with his only living relative. That crone had never been young. She was already as calcified as a tombstone when they met, and she spat her first words to him:

"Se non fosse per te, mia figlia sarebbe ancora vivo!"

If not for you, my daughter would still be alive!

Too arthritic to make a fist, she'd beaten him with a wooden spoon.

But at night, when she thought he wasn't listening, she'd sing herself a lullaby, the tune half-remembered from the harsh countryside of her birth, where only the quick and strong survived, and survival was cherished above all.

> *They tell us that we're born to die*
> *But there's no sense in that—say I.*
> *Those of us who know the truth,*
> *Will drink, drink, the nectar of youth.*

When the wooden spoon cracked, she stole the few coppers his mother had left him and bought herself a new one made of steel. After a year of daily beatings, that one bent, too.

And his grandmother shook it at him, saying, "Anche sarai la mia morte!"

You'll be the death of me, *too!*

When she finally did die, from a massive coronary, he hoped it was true.

Silvermane was trying to recall the second verse when a cough made him spin. A hooded figure stood behind him. He must have entered while Silvermane was lost in his stupid reverie—a mistake he could not allow himself again. The newcomer was already too close for comfort.

Hiding any surprise, Silvermane sneered. "You're late."

The figure gave him a not-quite-disrespectful shrug that rippled through his bright green-and-yellow cloak. The costume was probably meant to distract from a face only partly concealed by the oversized hood.

The voice was husky, deep, its age difficult to place. "Word on the street was that you'd bring company. I had to be sure you were alone."

Manfredi feigned hurt feelings. "You thought I'd break my word?"

The contempt in the answer was clear. "From what I know of your history, part of the reason you've survived this long is because you only keep that word when it's in your best interest. I'm glad you understand that this time, it is."

Silvermane gave him a slight smile and stepped

a little closer. "Your info on the Kingpin's delivery schedule was golden. You've got nothing to fear from the Maggia, uh…what should I call you?"

"The Schemer."

To keep from laughing, Silvermane sucked at his teeth, dislodging a piece of chicken that'd been there since lunch. "Okay. Call yourself Lady Gaga for all I care. So now that we've bonded, what can I do for you, Schemer?"

"More like what I can do for you." The figure held out a thick file. "I know you prefer printouts."

The small print was difficult to read, but what Manfredi saw in the headings made him feel young again. "This is Fisk's entire distribution network! I could take him down for keeps if I play it right." Silvermane narrowed his eyes. "What's the Kingpin to you? He kill your sweetheart or something?"

"That's my business."

"Sure it is, sure. It's just that…"

Experience had also taught him not to trust anyone unless he knew their weaknesses. So, feigning an old man's dizziness, he stumbled forward, planning to yank away the Schemer's hood.

"…I don't *like* secrets!"

He'd either grown slower than he realized, or the Schemer was wildly fast. His fingers clawed air; the Schemer had already moved out of the way. Silvermane tensed, expecting a counterattack. But the Schemer, having quickly established a comfortable distance, waited for Silvermane to make the next move.

"That was foolish," the Schemer said.

He's right. I must've looked like an idiot. If this fool opens his yap about it at a bar, word will be all over the streets in an hour. If Cicero finds out…

Silvermane's finger twitched on the trigger of the piece in his pocket. Half of him wanted to whack the Schemer here and now. But the other half wanted to keep his pipeline to the Kingpin. What was the smart move? The indecision brought a sick, terrified dread.

Out of nowhere, it felt as if an invisible elephant had sat on his ribcage. Silvermane moaned, grasped his chest, and fell to his knees.

It wasn't until the agony made the Maggia leader pound at his own upper left arm that the Schemer came closer, convinced the heart attack was real. "Do you need help? A doctor?"

Enraged by the pity in his voice, Silvermane turned his tearing eyes to look up at the shadows within the hood. "Back off! What's it to you if I live or die?"

"Nothing." The contempt returned. "I only want to be sure the information is used. If not by you, then by your successor."

"Successor? There won't be any successor. *I'll* use it. Now, go on, get out. GET OUT!"

IN THE sleek office building rising above Hell's Kitchen, the Kingpin's conference room held both trusted advisers and hired muscle. By and large, the muscle knew that only advisers were allowed to speak here, but the newest hire, the high-cheeked Tommy Tuttle, had yet to learn.

"So what're we looking at here, boss?"

His train of thought interrupted, Wilson Fisk, a.k.a. the Kingpin, shifted to look at Tommy. As he did, his custom leather chair creaked like the hull of a New England schooner. Hoping his angry glare was enough to make his point, Fisk turned back to the image projected on the wall.

"The delicate carvings are beautiful, Wesley, even hypnotic. I understand your obsession with it. But how can this…artifact put my organization back on top?"

"It's a treasure map, Mr. Fisk, a key to the greatest secret of all time. Throughout the ages, men have died for it, but beyond some wild speculation no one knows for certain what that secret is, since no one's been able to decipher it."

The answer was obviously incomplete. No doubt the bespectacled man expected his employer to figure out the rest. It was one of the things Wilson liked about Wesley.

"And you believe you can?"

"Not on my own, but I've researched a number of candidates, and weeded it down to one. He should be easy to…procure."

Fisk's fingers pressed brief patterns into his chin. "Where is it now?"

"The National Science Foundation has been sending it to different universities, hoping one will be able to crack the code. Right now, it's on exhibit at Empire State University."

Tommy spoke up again. "It'll be easy to snatch it from there. What've they got, a bunch of bearded profs with padded elbows?"

Despite the second offense, Fisk kept his eyes on the tablet. The man's sad efforts to nickname himself Tommy "The Talker" had not helped. But something about the boy reminded Fisk's wife of their son, so he again tried to overlook the interruption.

Thankfully, Wesley stepped in. "Actually, sir, the college hired an outside security firm to guard it— Tech-Vault. On the surface, they look legit, but they're owned by the Maggia. They do a fine job for their clients 90 percent of the time, despite giving their owners a heads-up when items of singular value are being transported in the city."

Fisk's attention was piqued. "Go on."

"From what I can tell, the consigliere, Caesar Cicero, figures the tablet's too famous to have any black-market value. I doubt he's even mentioned it to Silvermane."

"But the Maggia has no idea how to translate it, and we do." Fisk's eyes twinkled. "Wesley, you've outdone yourself. I've been looking for a chance to make them look foolish. Snatching this from under their noses will send the perfect message. And if this legend turns out to be true, the world's greatest secret—whatever it is—will be an added bonus."

"Thank you, sir. Now we only have to…"

Wesley trailed off. All eyes turned to the door.

At first, the Kingpin was annoyed by yet another distraction, but when he whirled and saw the source, he felt his fierce expression melt into that of a vulnerable child. The presence of the tall, slender woman, the perfect black of her hair broken by a shock of equally perfect white down the center, was a completely appropriate reason for his employees to fall silent.

"Vanessa, my love…"

Vanessa Fisk returned a cooler version of his lovestruck look. "Forgive the interruption…"

Remembering his seldom-exercised manners, the Kingpin rose, his abdomen moving the table back an inch. "No. There will never be a need for you to ask forgiveness from me."

She was about to touch him, but did not. "I tried waiting, but I feel as if I'm going mad. I just heard from one of our son's former classmates. He said Richard was despondent before he left on his ski trip, and I can't stop worrying about it."

The intimate subject didn't surprise anyone. He and his wife often acted as if they spoke in private—not because the world didn't matter, but because they had the power to put it on hold.

"Is every college dropout a licensed therapist now?" He gave her a pleading smile. "Your heart is so large, I've seen you weep at the sunset. Richard's enjoying his leisure, that's all—taking time to think about the things that task all young men before they begin their adult lives."

The lack of an immediate response puzzled him. She looked as if she was wrestling with a dark cloud inside her, a fear…or a doubt.

"Wilson, is there anything you're *not* telling me?"

His eyelids fluttered. "Of course not. Vanessa. I would never lie to you."

Tommy the Talker mumbled, as if about to agree. Fisk gritted his teeth. From the corner of his eye, he saw Wesley grab the youth's wrist and squeeze it, hard.

"How can I be sure of that," she said, "when you lie so well to others?"

The words stung. "What? Because I love you. You and Richard are the center of my life, all that guides and drives me."

Frowning as if not entirely accepting his answer, she left. The way her gown flowed around her twirling form made him ache. As a girl, she'd been subject to depression. Now, her somber mood made her seem like a gray ghost who, after a brief visit among the living, must now retreat beyond the veil. He could lay the world at her feet, but he couldn't protect her from the depths of her own feelings.

o———————o

THE ROOM was so silent, no one could help overhearing Tommy Tuttle's whisper.

"Geez. She's like the only thing in the world the Kingpin's afraid of."

Spinning like a vast globe on its axis, Fisk locked his eyes on the youth. "I'll show you fear."

He stalked forward, effortlessly flipping the conference table aside.

Tommy, having seen hippo attacks on video, knew how deadly the heavy beasts could be. The Kingpin was twice as fast. Still, when the first punch didn't send him squarely into the bliss of unconsciousness, he hoped the beating wouldn't be so bad. Tommy knew he deserved a lesson. He'd never been able to keep his mouth shut.

It was only after the fifth blow began to flatten his high cheekbone that he realized Fisk was keeping him awake on purpose, so he would feel every second of the pain.

"No one mentions my wife. No one."

TWO

ALREADY late for the day's most important appointment, Peter rushed across the plaza at the center of Empire State University. He was concentrating on trying not to run *too* fast when a pat on the back startled him.

"You're Peter Parker, right?"

The face that greeted him was friendly, but unfamiliar. "Sure, if you're not a bill collector...?"

The stranger put out his hand. "Randy Robertson. Robbie Robertson's my dad."

Smiling, Peter took the hand, trying to remember whether the *Daily Bugle* City Editor had mentioned his son was attending ESU. "Right!"

"Dad said one of his freelance photographers was a VIP here."

"VIP? I can't even get arrested. It's great to meet you, but..." The *I'm-late* part stuck in his throat. Randy looked as new to the campus as his sneakers. Another minute wouldn't matter. "How's it going? Need help finding anything? Coffee house? Bathroom? Can't have one without the other, right?"

Randy shrugged. "I'm good, just wanted to put a face to the name. You're here for the protest too, right?" He tilted his head toward a large group preparing picket signs no more than a few yards away.

Wow. How'd I miss that? There must be a hundred people.

Activist Josh Kittling, the real VIP, stood at the center of the crowd. Zeroing in on Peter, his sonorous voice boomed from his thin body. "Parker, pick up a Sharpie. If you're not with us, you're against us!"

Peter felt like half the crowd stopped to stare at him.

"Uh…what exactly is it I'm for or against?"

"Way to stay on top of things." Kittling pointed across the plaza toward the Exhibition Hall. "That old rock on display isn't drawing the donations they hoped, so admin's planning to spend ten million to renovate the building. We want that money for needs-based scholarships."

Kittling was usually right, but not always. Afraid of whatever devil might be in the details, Peter hesitated to offer his full support. "I dunno, maybe fixing up the old place will bring in the money to help fund financial aid. Two birds with one stone, right?"

"We've been through the numbers, friend. It's time for action."

Sheesh. I like the guy, but last time we talked, I almost wound up on a pontoon boat chasing down leaky oil tankers. I'm all for the environment, but somebody has to stick around to fight the super villains.

"I want to hear more, Josh, but I'm running late."

"Right. I'm sure it's much more important than keeping corporate culture from destroying our education."

This time the crowd hissed at Peter, until Randy spoke up. "Ease up. You don't know what he's got going on."

Kittling's condescending headshake was infuriating. "All I need to know is that he's not standing with his community."

After years of being bullied as a bookworm, Peter was dying to tell everyone exactly what he stood up for as Spider-Man, but he couldn't. Trying to ignore the boos, he walked away, gritting his teeth.

As tight as his jaw was when he exited the plaza, it went slack when he saw Gwen Stacy. She was standing with her shoulders against the Coffee Bean storefront, her books pressed to her chest. The way her face brightened when she saw him made him suddenly aware of how nice the weather was.

"Hey, boo!" she called.

He trotted over. She put her cheek out for a kiss, which he happily provided.

"See the raging protest?"

"Yeah," he grumbled. "Sure you don't want to hang around and attend? By the time we're back from Queens, Josh and co. will probably take Manhattan, the Bronx, and Staten Island, too."

"And miss hearing you quote old song lyrics? Never. Besides, I already signed the petition and wrote to the dean."

"There's a petition? We have a dean?"

She slapped his shoulder and tugged him toward the subway. "Classrooms, too. I'll tell you all about them on the way to your aunt's."

The rush of the rattling train was too loud for talk, so Peter contented himself with looking at Gwen. Even without the platinum-blonde hair, doe eyes, and winsome figure, he'd be hopelessly in love. Being a police captain's daughter had given her a strong moral sense and an even stronger backbone when it came to standing up for what she believed. The only question about Gwen that ever worried him was: What on Earth was she doing with someone like him?

Of course, theirs wasn't the usual boy/girl dance. More like boy/girl/secret identity, with super villains cutting in on every step. The Meteor, the Rhino, the Molten Man, the Vulture, the Green Goblin, the Shocker, the Lizard, the this, the that. Sooner or later, he'd be facing some crook calling themselves the *The*.

Back when he'd slouched into his first ESU class distracted by Spidey business, everyone thought he was a snob. But the girl now cuddling with him had ignored Flash Thompson's advances and approached Pete first. Why? Maybe she'd also inherited a nose for mysteries. Still, whenever he "mysteriously" ran from an emergency, she dismissed him as a coward along with everyone else.

Halfway through the ride, the doors swished open. During the momentary lull, Gwen leaned in and whispered something.

"What'd you say?"

"I said, I'm glad to be with you."

He pulled her closer. "Yeah, I heard you the first time. I just wanted you to say it again."

In time, when MJ started hinting Gwen had more-than-friendly feelings for him, he couldn't wrap his head around it. Even when Gwen herself said she had a crush on "a bashful brown-haired biker," he thought she was kidding.

A nudge to the shoulder brought him back to the present. "Here we are, beautiful dreamer."

"Huh?"

"Thought you liked old songs."

"Yes. Right."

They exited onto the elevated platform at Forest Hills as lunch hour peaked. Peter tried to make a point of chivalrously clearing a path.

Not that he'd ever been a perfect suitor. On their first date, he'd forgotten she was a fellow science major. That time, though, when he returned after vanishing to fight Doctor Octopus, she didn't call him a coward—she wrapped him in a huge hug, genuinely afraid he'd been hurt.

That made him think.

Or, rather, it made him *stop* thinking for a change.

As they walked arm-in-arm down the tree-lined streets of his old neighborhood, he kept wondering why he didn't tell *her* all that. Chatter though they might about every other topic imaginable, he always held back, never letting her in all the way. The same distance he was forced to maintain with everyone now dogged his time with Gwen.

She sensed it, of course. His denial of the obvious had become a personal cliché.

"Penny for your thoughts?"

"You'd be short-changed, Gwen."

He could have said he was worried about Aunt May. It was true enough. When Peter left home to share a Village apartment with Harry, Anna Watson, Mary Jane's aunt, moved in with the woman who raised him. A few days ago, Mrs. Watson had reported that Aunt May was feeling poorly, and he hadn't had a chance to visit until today.

But that wasn't all he was thinking, and giving Gwen less than the whole truth would feel like an insult.

"Why do I always go for the silent type?"

"Huh?"

"Never mind."

When they walked up the path to the modest two-story home, his supposedly under-the-weather aunt opened the door before he could knock.

"Peter!"

Despite the well-earned wrinkles, her face was bright, her smile strong.

He pecked her cheek. "Someone's got her dancing shoes on, huh? Mrs. Watson said you weren't feeling so well."

"Nonsense, don't listen to her! I feel strong as a lion, especially when my nephew visits!" She looked from him to Gwen. "My, you two have been seeing quite a bit of each other!"

Gwen hugged her as they went in. "I hope you don't disapprove, Mrs. Parker."

Aunt May put her hand to her lips. "Disapprove? Sounds as if you're more serious than I thought. All I can say is you've made a silly, sentimental old lady very happy."

An oddly quiet Anna Watson joined them. Peter set his secrets aside for the next few hours. Sipping tea and eating cookies, he let himself enjoy the rare feeling of being part of something, of a family. That Gwen was part of it, too, made it all perfect.

Once they were outside, Gwen hooked her arm in his. "That woman's eyes are as bright as a newborn's. With someone like that raising you, it's no wonder you're ever so slightly special."

o————————o

AS SOON as Peter's only surviving relative closed the door, Anna Watson raced over to keep her from collapsing, then helped her to the couch to lie down.

When she finished settling her friend comfortably, Anna scowled. "May Parker! Why didn't you tell him about your test results? You can't protect him forever—he's an adult. He has a right to know."

May weakly waved her off. "I know, Anna, I know." She turned her face toward the afternoon sun shining through the window, revealing yellow traces in the whites of her eyes. "But Peter's always been so troubled, ever since he was a child, and he looked so happy with his girlfriend. I couldn't bring myself to spoil it."

Anna Watson *tsked*, but said no more.

THREE

BURYING the churning mix of rage, fear, and guilt that haunted his feelings for Vanessa, the Kingpin forced himself to focus on the news.

"...their numbers now over a thousand, we're hearing unconfirmed reports that the students may try to take over the Exhibition Hall. The occupation of academic buildings has been part of student protests since the '60s, but..."

Despite their naïve ideals, the protestors were admirably organized. Using real-time connections to support groups such as the ACLU, they'd achieved a wealth of media coverage in just a few short hours. Campus security, surprised by the size of the event, was barely equipped to control the *current* crowd—and it was growing by the minute.

It was as if the very sky had parted just for him. Events had moved so swiftly, he doubted that the Maggia-front security company, Tech-Vault, had had the time, let alone the interest, to increase its presence at the hall. After all, these children, despite their numbers, posed no real threat to the status quo, let alone the ancient tablet.

But Wilson Fisk did.

Using a satin handkerchief to wipe Tommy Tuttle's blood from his knuckles, he turned to Wesley. "It's almost too perfect. The time has come to strike. Gather the best we have and prepare my car."

Wesley stared at him. "Sir, you're not planning to go yourself?"

"Of course I am. You know how Manfredi thinks. He should have retired decades ago, but he still acts personally. If the point is to impress the Maggia, I have to be there myself."

STRESSED as he'd been lately, Peter managed to maintain the cozy feeling of home even after Gwen left the subway a few stops early to study for an evening class. He didn't even mind thinking about money, or the protestors.

May as well drop by the Exhibition Hall. I can grab some shots of that tablet for the Bugle, *maybe even try for a better conversation with Kittling.*

As he exited the subway in Greenwich Village, the feel of Gwen nestled in his arm lingered, like a sweater that had been warmed by a fireplace on one side. It was only when he turned the corner and saw the crowd that he felt the chill in the air.

ESU's grassy, open plaza was standing room only. Forced to the fringes, campus police were struggling to keep people from spilling into the street and blocking traffic. Satellite vans from the major new outlets lined a cordoned-off media area. NYPD crowd-control units were just beginning to arrive, but he didn't see how they could hope to contain things.

He loved the Big Apple, but just looking at the tightly packed throng made him claustrophobic. The crowd-control units nearby looked like they were sporting tear gas cannisters. And the students weren't organized, the way he'd seen in other protests like Occupy Wall Street. This felt more like an overcrowded concert where a stampede might get someone killed.

The mass, insofar as it had shape, centered on a small group passing out signs and pamphlets near the hall's entrance. Peter weaved closer, using his press pass to get onto the plaza and his student ID to get beyond the cordoned press area.

Turns out having multiple identities isn't always a bad thing.

The first face he made out was, of course, Josh Kittling. He was literally standing on a soap box, megaphone in hand. The second was Randy Robertson, who looked somewhere between impressed and overwhelmed.

His face brightened as he saw Peter. "You're joining us for the takeover?"

Takeover?

Before Peter could answer, Kittling wheeled the megaphone his way. "Finally decided to man up, Parker?"

"Josh, I totally agree about the financial aid. I

couldn't afford it here in a million years if it wasn't for my scholarship…"

"Exactly, bright boy. That scholarship makes you bought and sold, while the rest of us who scrimped and saved to get here are being forced to drop out left and right."

"Yeah, you're right, but I barely made it this far without getting trampled. If you start a takeover with this big a crowd, and someone starts shoving, there could be a panic. People could get hurt. Have you at least given the administration time to respond?"

"Time? You kidding me? We've got the eyes of the world on us right now. If we don't ride this wave, the press will be gone by morning, along with the biggest reason admin has to meet our demands."

"Look around, Josh. Is it worth the risk?"

"My answer's yes! What's yours going to be? You going to be part of the solution, or hide in the back like a coward?"

Peter knew Kittling was talking more to the protestors than to him. But the jibe still hit its own very special nerve. Especially when everyone booed at him, except for Randy, who looked confused.

Peter clenched his fists. Trying to get away before his rising temper made things worse, he shoved through the densely packed protestors. He all but popped into an empty space beyond a line of sawhorses that blocked the steps to the hall.

Two private security guards wearing riot gear stood at the door. Seeing Peter, one held up his hand.

"Back off. No students past this point." The massive crowd was clearly making the man nervous.

But Peter was still steaming. "Really? I thought the place was *built* for students."

One stomped toward him. Peter flashed his press pass.

"Look, I'm just here to take some pictures of the tablet."

With a simian grunt, the guard stepped aside.

Seeing this, some of the students came forward, pushing aside the sawhorses. Panicking, the guards raised their shields and batons. Peter tensed, but Kittling ordered the students back. "Not yet, not yet! We go in a small group, and *together!*"

Huh. Maybe he was listening to me about the crowd. Either way, the takeover will begin in earnest soon. What should I—what can I do?

Unsure of the answer, Peter went inside, marched down a long hall, and entered the main gallery.

At least I can get a look at what the fuss is all about.

Surrounded by four more security guards, the only thing on display in the huge marble-tiled room was the tablet. It was surprisingly small, maybe a foot across. Even the signs surrounding the case dwarfed it. He skimmed a few sentences. The legends about its origin were vaguely interesting, but after hitting the word "unknown" for the umpteenth time, he stopped.

Sure takes a lot of words to describe something they don't know much about.

As for the tablet itself, the ancient writing had a

nice swirly thing going for it, if you liked hieroglyphs. The fact it had survived thousands of years provided a passing sense of wonder. But ultimately Peter found the display more interesting—probably because he knew the molecular structure of its super-strong transparent polymer.

He aimed his camera, thinking of the notes Robbie Robertson had given him about composition (which were much more helpful than Editor in Chief Jameson's go-to critique of *This stinks!*). He took some shots he hoped would make the little rock look more impressive to an untrained eye—such as his own.

<hr />

OUTSIDE, Kittling and his small group of coordinators struggled to keep the protestors in check. "Feel that power?" he said to Randy. "It's like we're trying to hold back the tide! We'll go in with just the coordinators, but sooner or later we're just going to have to let go and let it all flow."

The mix of fear, awe, and glee on Josh's face made Randy even more uneasy. "But what about what Peter said? What if people get hurt?"

Kittling eyed the wildly packed plaza, then the relatively quiet entrance. He turned to Randy and lowered his voice. "Listen, if NYPD and campus security start in with the pepper spray and rubber bullets, yeah, people will freak, and yeah, there'll be damage. But they can't get to us because of the crowds. Right now, the only thing between us and the hall are a few rent-a-cops in over their heads. Want to make it quick and easy? I've got an idea. Once we go in for the takeover, I'll split off and grab that old hunk of rock. With that as a hostage, they'll *have* to back off and pay attention."

"That's not what we're about," Randy said "Besides, that thing's priceless. What if you damage it?"

"I say it's time to find out what we're about." He waved the crowd toward the steps and shouted, "Coordinators, follow me! We're going in!"

And the sea of people crashed forward.

A HORRIFIC pounding sent Peter running back toward the entrance. He was halfway there when the doors opened and about a dozen students swarmed in, led by Kittling. The two guards stumbled backwards into the hall, dropping their nightsticks and drawing their sidearms. Seeing the weapons brought the students to a halt.

Moving a bit faster than a human should, Peter raced toward the guards.

"Hey! Put the guns down! Those are students—they're just demonstrating!"

The guards turned his way. One shouted back, "I don't give a damn about their protest! We were paid to guard that tablet, and that's what we're going to do!"

They leveled their handguns at the protestors.

"Back out, all of you! Now!"

Though clearly frightened, Kittling held his

ground. "You shoot, and the people out there will tear this place apart!"

The steadier of the two guards aimed at the floor and nudged his partner to do the same. "No one wants to shoot anything. Just back off!"

"We're not going anywhere. You, stand aside!'

Peter relaxed slightly. *Stalemate, for now. I could switch to Spidey, but what good would that do? Wait a minute…*

He held up his camera and snapped a picture. Instantly, one of the guards covered his face. "Put that down!"

In response, the defiant students held up their phones. They took photos, began recording videos.

Not only am I making those guards think twice, I'm getting some great exclusive shots!

Kittling's admiring glance was cut short when a great roar rattled the building. The chanting outside turned into screaming. A glimpse through the window of rising smoke told Peter that something at the far edge of the plaza had exploded.

The crowd was panicking. The police were already rushing toward the blast site, taking them even farther away from the Exhibition Hall. Peter couldn't see whether anyone was hurt, but at least the crowd was thinnest there. Why this spot? Why this timing?

It's almost as if it was intended as a distraction—

A second blast, smaller and closer, made him turn him back inside. At the end of a long hallway, an emergency door tore loose from its hinges. Six armed men marched in. Though dressed like the protestors, they moved with military precision. Behind them, an oversize limo was visible in the service alley.

With the police focused on the plaza blast, they hit the side of the hall facing the street. Smart.

A larger shadow appeared at the fallen door. At first Peter thought it was three more men—but it was only one. Wearing a tailored jacket and vest more suitable to a gala than a heist, a massive figure stormed ahead of the gunmen. His bald head shone beneath the fluorescents like an oversized bowling ball. Each footfall boomed like a small explosion all its own, his diamond-topped walking cane making little ticks against the marble.

"To the main gallery, quickly. And keep those gas masks at the ready!"

The Kingpin! I've seen photos, but he looks even bigger in person. What's he doing here?

Before Peter could guess, Wilson Fisk's moose-sized shoulder hit him. To preserve his identity, Peter let himself be tossed aside, then watched as the Kingpin bulldozed a path through the students.

Before anyone could tell whether the two security guards were going to attack, the Kingpin's men fired, taking them down. Ignoring the screams of the students, the villains approached the entrance and braced the doors closed with telescoping bars that fit neatly through the handles.

Now locked inside, the dozen protestors looked to their leader, Kittling. He, in turn, stared numbly at the bodies of the security guards. "You can't just…"

Seeing the attention the others paid to Kittling's choked-off words, Fisk gripped the youth's shirt and wrenched him into the air.

In a flash, two of the protestors—linebackers from the look of them—rushed up. An angry Randy Robertson was right behind them.

"Randy, stop!" Peter tried to grab him, but before they even got close, the gunmen formed a tight line between the Kingpin, Kittling, and the students. A single shot fired into the air stopped Randy and the others in their tracks.

Wilson Fisk's thick lips curled. He grabbed Kittling's phone, crushed it, and then twisted his albino-bull of a skull toward the trembling group. Letting go of Kittling, he turned toward the cowering students.

"Stay out of our way, and you'll have an exciting story to tell your friends. But if any of you take the additional step of identifying me to the police, I'll find you. You don't have to lie, just tell them you were all frightened and confused. That always makes it hard to remember details."

All eyes on the Kingpin, Peter stepped back. Once he was behind the students and blocked from the mobsters' view, he ducked into an adjacent hall.

I may not be much with politics, but these jokers are definitely my speed.

He looked for a quick place to change but found only a locked supply closet. With a twinge of guilt, he broke the knob and wedged his way into the cramped space. Knocking over buckets, brooms, and pungent cleansers, he scrambled to remove his civvies, revealing the blue-and-red webbed suit beneath.

Mask in place, he bounced out, scuttling along the tiled walls. By the time he reached the lobby's high ceiling, only the students remained.

The Kingpin must be after the tablet!

Kittling, dazed and sprawled on the floor, pointed up at him. "First the Kingpin, now Spider-Man! It's like some crazy super-conspiracy is trying to bump our protest out of the news!"

Spider-Man fired a web and swung across the open space. "Stay out of this, all of you! It's not about the protest! If you want to be useful, go warn the police that gunmen are trying to steal the tablet!"

He landed on the ceiling of the wide hall leading to the main gallery. At his back, he heard Randy apologize to Kittling.

"I feel like a coward! I should have tried to stop them."

Kittling's response impressed the wall-crawler. "Forget it, man—the only way to stop a bullet is with your body. Let's pry those bars off and get these front doors open!"

Relieved to hear it, Spider-Man paused outside the main gallery. Before starting any fights, he wanted to give the students time to flee the building—and set up his automatic camera. Within, the Kingpin and his men also seemed to be taking their time. Half-hidden behind the tall signage, they were donning gas masks as the four remaining security guards braced for an attack.

That can't be good.

Still unseen, Spider-Man crawled along the ceiling, but before he could reach the crooks, the Kingpin hurled a handful of pellets toward the tablet. They shattered as they hit the case, releasing a curling green mist. The guards started gasping and clawing at their throats.

"Make sure those masks are on tight!" the Kingpin called out. "That gas is powerful enough to knock *me* out!"

As the guards fell, the Kingpin strode up to the display case and raised his walking cane. At first Peter was confident the polymer would withstand the blow, but it didn't. The diamond at the tip of the Kingpin's cane cracked its surface.

Is he hiding a jackhammer in that tux? Another shot like that and he'll shatter the case. The alarms are already screaming, but with the mess outside, who's left to respond? He planned this perfectly, except for one thing...

Spider-Man dropped from the ceiling. "'Scuse me, but you've got something on your chin..."

It worked well enough. The startled Kingpin turned just in time for Spider-Man's blow to connect with the hard bone of his jaw. "My fist."

Spider-Man's knuckles crunched under the impact. Thrown off-balance, Fisk took several staggering steps away from the case. Thinking the crime-boss was as good as out, Spider-Man shot out several webs, tripping up two of the Kingpin's men. Turning back to their portly leader, he was surprised and a little frightened to find him still standing.

"Uh…that was the part where you were supposed to fall down."

"Spider-Man?" The Kingpin crouched the way a tiger might before pouncing. "Perhaps you've heard that no one ever gets ahead by doing as expected."

By the time Fisk finished the sentence, Spider-Man had a third goon down.

When the Kingpin lunged, Spider-Man swung one of the inert gangsters by the shoulders, striking Fisk's chest with the man's heels. The maneuver barely delayed the Kingpin, but the follow-through sent the unconscious lackey hurtling into the remaining gunmen. In one move, he'd taken the last of them out of play.

But the Kingpin held another surprise: his speed. When Spider-Man came at him, Fisk likewise threw his considerable mass into the air. In an instant, he'd wrapped his arms around the wall-crawler's waist, and landed square on his feet. Unharmed, but disoriented, Spider-Man twisted for leverage.

"Many of my foes mistake my muscle for fat," the Kingpin said.

Still maneuvering to free himself, Spider-Man looked down at his foe's smooth, hairless scalp. "Really? Do they also mistake your head for a baby's butt? Because, you know, from here there is a strong resemblance."

"Angering me won't help you." Fisk puffed and drew his anaconda-arms tighter around Spider-Man's waist until he was able to clasp his own wrist. "I've read of your fabled spider-strength, but the man doesn't live who can endure my grasp!"

Peter pushed down against the elephantine forearms, but the Kingpin's grip remained locked. Any more force, and he might break Fisk's bones.

"Fabled, huh? You'll make me blush."

The Kingpin squeezed tighter. "Good. That will be the first sign of your impending death."

The air forced from his lungs, the only comeback Spider-Man managed was, "Ungh!"

Certain he could take the Kingpin by surprise, if only he could catch his breath, Peter went limp.

Besides, Jonah always pays more for the pics where it looks like I'm losing...

But rather than simply let go, the Kingpin lifted his foe overhead and hurled him into the floor's hard marble tiles.

Okay, that hurt. But now that I'm free, all I need is a couple of deep breaths—

An earnest, youthful cry echoed through the gallery. "Back off of him!"

Who the heck...Randy?!

Sneakers squeaking on the tiles, the teen hurled himself onto the Kingpin's back. "Somebody's got to tackle you. Might as well be me!"

Holding onto the prodigious neck, Randy tried to ride the mobster like he would a mechanical bull.

"Trust me, lad, you were far better off beneath my notice."

As if shaking off a fly, Fisk tossed him into the nearest wall. Randy's body slammed into the tile and crumpled to the floor. The cracked marble façade shed flakes onto his limp form. Spider-Man caught his breath, but after a few seconds, he saw Randy's shoulders lift.

He's alive! But hurting bad. Have to settle for a half-breath, then.

Spider-Man bolted to his feet, drawing the Kingpin's attention away from the fallen youth. "Any of your foes ever mistake your muscle for a punching bag…like this?"

With blistering speed, he unleashed a barrage of blows, leaving the larger-than-life crime lord no time to respond. When Randy managed to crawl a few feet away, Spider-Man slammed Fisk into the same cracked wall, not once, but again and again. Each time, he let the big man fall forward just far enough for the next punch to maximize the damage.

"It's not like you're easy to miss!"

Spider-Man continued to pummel the Kingpin, beating and battering every inch of his body, but he would not fall. Plaster came down in bigger and bigger chunks. The support beam began to buckle.

"What? No comebacks? Like how your foes confuse your lack of responses for stupidity?"

Peter could see the fury in the man's eyes, a deep rage not only at his foe but at his own helplessness. Peter kept punching until finally, finally, the odd animal grace that had informed Fisk's movements was gone. His cannonball knees buckled. He fell forward, his face landing ignominiously flat on the floor.

Phew! He's down!

He rushed to Randy's prone form. "You still with us?"

"I think so."

Randy managed to sit halfway up, but the way he favored his shoulder meant it was probably dislocated. Spider-Man took a few seconds to fashion a sling from his webbing.

When he glanced back, he was shocked to see the Kingpin up on all fours. Like a rampaging albino hippo, Fisk rammed his head into the damaged wall.

Peter blinked. *What the…? Did the beating leave him crazy?*

The weakened support beam snapped. The wall collapsed, shedding chunks of marble large enough to split a skull. Catching one, the Kingpin used it to finish cracking the display case open.

The fracture spread along the wall and into the ceiling, sending more rubble falling. The Kingpin's dazed gunmen staggered out on their own.

A well-placed web angled a portion of the falling wall catty-corner so it shielded the unconscious guards. Now Peter only had to get out fast enough to keep both himself and the wounded teen safe. It meant leaving the Kingpin with the tablet, but the choice between saving a life or the artifact, even if it was priceless, wasn't a choice at all. He grabbed Randy under one arm, fired a web, and swung out of the crumbling gallery.

They're sure going to need that renovation money now!

He set Randy down in the lobby. He was out cold, but breathing. Afraid the damage might be worse than it looked, Spidey tapped his cheek.

"Wake up! The party's over!"

Randy's eyelids fluttered. "What happened? Did the Kingpin get away?"

This guy has enough guts for a regiment, but what was he thinking?

Several boys in blue were pushing open the doors, reinforcements visible behind them. Satisfied the police would see to Randy, Spider-Man took it as his cue to exit.

The path to the main gallery was blocked by debris, so he headed down the access hall to the door the thieves had blasted to get in. The limo and Kingpin were of course, gone. Spider-Man scrambled to the roof, feeling, for the first time, his own bruises.

Probably from the falling marble, but I doubt getting hurled around by the Kingpin helped. I feel like I've been wrestling a roller coaster!

Other than his aches, the first thing he noticed was the plaza. The crowd hadn't exactly thinned, but it was grouped in smaller pockets. The closest was right below him, in front of the hall. There, under the watchful eyes of the press, dozens of student protestors—Kittling among them—were being led by police into paddy wagons parked along the concrete paths.

They're pressing charges? For what? Hold on. They don't think the students are responsible for the bombing, do they?

A man in a white shirt and tie had pushed beyond the press cordon to question the police. Even from a distance, Pete recognized Robbie Robertson, no doubt worried about his son. An officer took him to Randy. Despite the sling, the wounded youth was in line for one of the wagons—not for an ambulance.

Geez, that's a helluva first semester at college.

The best way he could help would be to catch the real bomber and bring back the tablet. The service alley was still empty, but in the distance, a delightfully conspicuous limo sped along Sixth Avenue. It was just big enough to carry someone whose muscles could be mistaken for fat.

Like the man said, someone's got to stop you. It may as well be me.

FOUR

ASIDE from the white noise of spinning tires, the soundproofed limo silenced the sounds of the city. Wesley's voice over the speakers sounded clearer than if he'd been there in person.

"I've erased the hall's security tapes, as planned, but, I assume, sir, you're aware you're leaving a trail a mile wide?"

Fisk settled back into the cushioned seat. "Of course. The police are busy at the campus, and the car's low-intensity lasers are scrambling the traffic cameras as we pass. The students will be too terrified to identify me, and the four guards we left alive never saw me. As for our last witness, that twitchy crusader, I *want* him to follow. Why expend the energy to hunt him down later when I can destroy him in the comfort of my home?"

"As you say, sir."

The question had been answered, but the connection remained open. "Some other curiosity I can satisfy, Wesley?"

"Apologies, Mr. Fisk. I know I'll be seeing it shortly, but...what's it like?"

The Kingpin saw no harm in indulging his assistant. He ran his finger-pads along the stone's intricate writing. Each pictograph was so uniform, it was as if they'd been engraved by machine.

"It's strong, Wesley—like me. I'll want to secure it in the vault upon my arrival. Only a temporary precaution. You should be able to begin work in a few hours."

"Thank you, sir."

Wesley hung up, but the Kingpin continued to stare at the tablet. Holding the "greatest secret in all the world" made him think of his own secrets. Sooner or later, Vanessa would learn the truth: Richard was dead. She would leave him, and without her love—without an heir—whatever he was would fade in time.

This rock held an advantage: It had existed for eons and would exist for eons more. By doing nothing other than simply being, it had bested him.

Well, if nothing else, luring the spider into his web would provide a distraction.

○———————○

CLINGING to the smooth, windowless face of the Hell's Kitchen luxury building, Spider-Man watched the private garage open to admit the limousine.

Don't want to say this was easy, but...

His torso nearly flat against the surface, Peter's hands and feet propelled him upward in that special, spidery way. It was second nature to his body, but still freaked him out a bit if he thought about it too much.

An egomaniac like the Kingpin wouldn't take

anything less than the penthouse, no matter how obvious it makes him. And speaking of obvious…

Every window on the uppermost floors was dim save one, right at the top. Steel shutters covered it, but the light escaping along the seams glowed invitingly. Spider-Man didn't *need* his spider-sense to warn there was imminent danger on the other side. All the same, as he drew closer, it tingled nice and loud.

Those shutters won't keep me out for more than a few seconds, but if the Kingpin's the cheese, then I'm the rat. Let's see if I can grab a peek before I step into the trap.

He leaned upside down over the shutters, peering through the same seam that let the light out. Inside and below, in some sort of huge private gym, was the big man himself. The Kingpin sat in an oversized chair that looked like a cross between a throne and a Barcalounger. Armed flunkies stood around him in a semicircle, craning their necks up as if the closed shutter was the best TV show ever.

The men were tense, uncertain—first aiming their guns up at the window, then lowering them, then snapping the barrels back up a second later. They looked like mutts who'd thought they'd seen a squirrel, realized it was only a leaf, but still wondered whether they should chase it anyway.

Just to mess with them, Spider-Man used his web to yank a shingle from the roof above and send it skimming sideways against the wall next to the window. The nervous minions practically jumped out of their skins.

"Boss?"

Fisk remained motionless. "Steady! Show some patience, and I promise you won't be disappointed."

Frankly, I'm already disappointed. To think he respects me so little he'd try such a cheap trick. Not that it'll stop me from using his lame ruse against him...

Shortly, the steel shutter tore open with a pained, earsplitting squeal. After a melodramatic pause, a figure flew in, bearing the familiar Spider-insignia on its back.

"Look!"

"There he is!"

"You were right, Kingpin!"

The gunmen opened fire. As the form writhed and twitched with each bullet impact, they cried out with boyish glee: "We finally got him!"

The Kingpin was far from delighted. "Hold your fire! Are you all deaf? The point was to keep him in check while I faced him myself!"

Smoke still curling from their guns, they approached the body. It dangled limply in the air, not falling.

Shoving his minions aside, Fisk finally noticed the web-line that kept the body suspended in air. The decoy itself was made of a gooey mesh that drooped from its sleeves and waist. Seething, wordless, Fisk turned back to the window while his men kept their eyes on the dummy.

"What is it? Some sort of mannequin?"

"He must've made it out of his webbing."

A few quick *thwips* of webbing yanked several

weapons from their hands. As the guns sailed out, a shirtless Spider-Man sailed in.

"Brr! It's cold! Someone leave a window open?"

As he dropped, he kicked the two nearest thugs. They flew across the room and collapsed into the Kingpin's empty throne. Before landing, Spider-Man drove his fists out to either side, smashing two more in the face.

Furious, the Kingpin howled. "You think you can make a fool out of me?"

"Gonna have to go with 'yes' on that one."

Getting his goat is almost too easy. I had no idea someone's face could turn that red.

One mob-soldier aimed, about to fire; another rushed forward, hoping to catch the wall-crawler off balance. Spider-Man brought down his fists on both and used their heads to propel himself back into the air.

"Given that cheesy trap, I have to ask: Do your foes mistake your *brain* for fat, too?"

He landed in a crouch and waited for the irate Kingpin to make his move. Not bothering to remove his tailored jacket, Fisk lumbered toward Spider-Man. He shoved his own remaining men out of the way with such force that one slammed into another.

"Sheesh! If that's how you take care of your employees, no wonder mommy and daddy never got you that puppy."

Expecting the fuming Kingpin to keep coming straight at him, Spider-Man leapt to meet him halfway. But Fisk somehow stopped short, defying the physics of his own forward momentum. One second, the wall-crawler was sailing through the air—the next, both wrists were caught in a viselike grip, his spider-sense screaming *Too late.* The Kingpin had reached out faster and farther than Spider-Man believed possible.

Pivoting at the waist, Fisk hurled him straight into the web mannequin.

No! Stupid, stupid! I handed *it to him.*

With no time to maneuver, Spider-Man felt his arms sink into the gummy sludge.

Angry at himself, he pulled and tore, but only entangled himself further. His web fluid could assume three forms: swinging strand, webbing, and thick globs. The adhesive quality faded fast when exposed to air, but the globs he'd used for the dummy had a sticky, gooey center.

Dammit! How many times have I made fun of some struggling crook tightening my web? Here I am, doing the same thing! If I could just relax, I'd get free in seconds.

But seconds were all the Kingpin needed. His trunk-like right arm pulled back for the first punch. Still stuck, Spider-Man managed to swing the hanging mannequin, and himself, out of the way. The ham-sized fist caught the exposed edge of the meshed web, sending the ensnared wall-crawler into a dizzying spin.

"Look at you now! Your mannequin put up a better fight!"

The next attack came with startling speed, but Peter's spider-sense told him when to move. The Kingpin's fist flew through empty air and down into a heavy oak desk, cracking it in half. Taken off-balance by the strength of his own strike, Fisk had to reach backward to keep from falling.

"How long do you think you can keep dodging me?" the Kingpin asked.

Arching his back against the mannequin's exposed surface, Spider-Man wrenched his legs free. "At least until you change your mouthwash."

Spider-Man's left leg kicked out awkwardly, allowing the Kingpin to grab it by the ankle. He didn't see Spidey's right leg coming, though, until it was too late. The kick sent the Kingpin tumbling backwards over the broken desk.

With more of the mannequin's goo exposed to the air now, Peter pulled himself and his shirt free. Unrestrained, he tucked the shirt into his pants, hopped to the wall and scooted across.

Rising, the Kingpin tried to swat him off with a contemptuous backhand. But thanks to his spider-sense, Spider-Man was already jumping back to the floor.

That was close! I'm still underestimating him. Fortunately, he hasn't seen everything I can do, either.

Executing a midair flip that would break a normal person's spine, Spider-Man wrapped his legs around what he could find of the Kingpin's neck and pulled him down hard, doing his best to ensure the thick head would take the bulk of the impact.

When they hit, the floor shook and the paintings rattled.

"Did that hurt? Sorry, must've mistaken your fat for muscle."

Unfazed, the Kingpin grinned. "Actually, it didn't hurt at all." His hand wrapped around Spider-Man's wrist. "This will, however."

Again with the squeezing? If he thinks he can crush my bones, he's got a...

A thumb thick as a hammerhead found a spot and pressed.

"Combat isn't just about raw strength, bug. It's about knowing the right pressure points."

Peter tried to use his free hand for a counter-strike, but a searing pain shot from his wrist across his back and shoulders, causing his arm to seize up. The agony collided with his screaming spider-sense. Black spots swam before his eyes.

SOMETHING more than the night air hovered outside the broken window. Unnoticed, held aloft by silent rotors, a drone was relaying images of the gloating Kingpin and his helpless foe to a black armored car below. The vehicle resembled an SUV, but longer and lower to the ground.

At the wheel, the Schemer watched the built-in screen, tapped his chin, and thought a moment. Then he placed a call.

"Silvermane? Are you aware of the theft at the Exhibition Hall?"

Manfredi's croaking response was so loud, the

Schemer had to hold the phone away from his ear. "Of course—it's all over the news! What do you…?"

Hoping the Maggia leader would do the same, the Schemer lowered his voice. "The Kingpin is currently under attack by Spider-Man. It's left his defenses seriously compromised. Should you notify the police and give them the address I'm sending, I'm sure they'll have no trouble finding him—and the evidence they'd need to charge him for the crime."

The aged mobster growled some expression of gratitude.

The Schemer hung up and went back to watching the fight.

FIVE

ON THE second floor of a venerable brick precinct house a few blocks from ESU, City Editor Joseph "Robbie" Robertson turned away from the window to face his son. The group outside was a fraction of the mob that had occupied the plaza, but he worried it was about to grow. News of the arrested organizers' location had yet to spread.

"I know how badly you want to help, but how is getting a criminal record going to do that?"

A few months ago, Randy had been a high schooler eager to start college. Now he looked more angry than eager. Robbie admired the passion, recognized and remembered it from his own youth. But as a father, he was more afraid than angry.

Randy picked his eyes up and glared. "How has working for a racist like J. Jonah Jameson helped you?"

Robbie stiffened. "Racist? Is that what you think? The man can be a complete ass, but racism is one of the few flaws you *can't* pin on him. Do you understand that if I wasn't his City Editor, and didn't know the people here, you wouldn't be sitting here with me?

You'd be locked up with the others."

"*His* news editor? Like he owns you?"

"No!"

"So I'm supposed to be grateful for the privileges some rich white guy bestows on you? And let everybody else be damned?"

"That's not what I meant. I…"

He turned back to the window to take a few breaths. Below, there was some sort of argument going on among the students. A flash of platinum blonde hair told him Gwen, Captain Stacy's daughter, was one of the participants.

He wondered what issues Stacy had with his daughter, but doubted it was the same as his own problems with Randy.

Either way, looks like everyone has something to be angry about tonight.

HOPING to see how her father was doing, Gwen Stacy found herself facing off against 20 steaming peers. Backing down would be the easy thing to do. But years of worrying whether her dad would come home safe had taught her that the easy thing was seldom the right thing.

When the group's tall, lanky spokesman got all puffed up and in her space, she climbed up a step to respond eye-to-eye. "Look, I understand why you're here, but protesting at the precinct keeps the focus on the theft, not on tuition! It isn't helping."

Listening, he nodded. "Okay, I get it. You're sticking up for what you believe. That's cool."

She thought it was over, but then another voice called, "Where's your runaway boyfriend, Parker? He hasn't got the guts to make *any* stand!"

Gwen walked up to a smug junior in a vaguely fashionable crewneck and raised her finger at his chin.

"Was that you? You said Peter Parker doesn't have any guts?"

Unlike the other protestors, he had liquor on his breath. "Yeah, I did!"

He was an idiot, not worth the effort. But she still found herself slapping him. The sharp crack made the others stare.

"He could be half the man he is and still take 10 of you!"

He rubbed his cheek, shocked into silence.

Gwen stormed up the steps to the door, the protestors' childish chorus of "Ooooh!" hot on her back. Officers Fenway and Huntington, who'd known her since she was a child, let her by without question.

Peering beyond Sgt. Murphy at the front desk, Gwen spotted her father's snowy white hair. His sharp blue eyes were glued to a printout, but, seeming to sense her presence, he looked up and greeted her with a gentle smile.

"I didn't think you'd be here."

She folded her arms and hissed out a breath. "Why not? I'm a student at ESU, aren't I?"

Captain Stacy's smile waned. "Of course you're

concerned about the protests—I wouldn't expect any less of you. But you're shaking. What's got you so riled up?"

She pursed her lips and eyed the floor. "Some loudmouth outside."

Sgt. Murphy aimed a thumb at the door. "Fenway says you socked that kid good. One hand, hey, good for you. Other hand, be careful you don't get accused of assault."

When her father's brow furrowed, his thick eyebrows almost met. "Did someone get rough with you?"

In a flash, the anger drained, leaving only embarrassment. "Nothing like that. He just…said something about Peter."

He studied her with the keen eyes that had analyzed a thousand crime scenes. "I can see getting annoyed, but striking someone? Are you worried that whatever he said might be true?"

Gwen loved her father more than anything, but no one liked having their mind read—especially before you were ready to read it yourself. Her thoughts raced back to all the times Peter had vanished at the first sign of trouble, how once she'd hated him for it. But hadn't that changed? Hadn't her doubts vanished yet?

Or do I still think Peter's a coward?

IN HELL'S KITCHEN, Wesley watched his boss grapple with the impressively brave Spider-Man. Seated comfortably in the security office, with cameras covering every inch of the penthouse save the private quarters, Wesley had a perfect, and perfectly safe, view.

He'd been wary of the brash decision to lead such a powerful enemy here. Between the Maggia pushback and his strained relations with his wife, the Kingpin was facing some unusual challenges that might cloud his judgment. But it looked as if his instincts had been correct, as always.

Wesley might have held the wall-crawler longer, but when the Kingpin did let go, Spider-Man slipped weakly to the floor, barely able to curl into a fetal ball. The hero was probably stronger pound-for-pound, but he was young, overeager, and inexperienced. Mr. Fisk had taken full advantage of those facts.

As for the unconscious mob-soldiers strewn across the gym, replacements were already on the way. Wesley's bigger concern was the crushed desk: If the dealer was to be believed, Al Capone had once owned it. But Wesley was sure he could find a suitable substitute.

Perhaps Silvermane's desk would work.

As the Kingpin gloated, Wesley indulged in a rare bit of his own reveling. The tablet he'd spent years studying was here, and while its physical attributes might belong to his boss, the task of unlocking its strange script fell to him.

Not that he wanted to use its secrets himself. Wielding power struck him as garish, but the thought of cracking the ancient code, when so many others had failed—well, that gave him a heady tingle.

On screen, Fisk raised half the broken desk and prepared to bring it down on the helpless Spider-Man.

Despite the apparent victory, Wesley decided to heed his own paranoia. That was his job. He checked the other camera feeds, then scanned the police bands for unusual alerts.

One came up at once: "We have a 10-34s on 46th and Ninth Avenue, Hell's Kitchen. All available units report. The Kingpin and the stolen tablet are believed to be at the scene."

Wesley seized up. That was their address. A 10-34s meant an assault in progress, shots fired. How could the police know? Besides being carefully soundproofed, the penthouse was so far above the loud streets that the Kingpin had once fired a missile launcher without anyone blinking an eye. Even if the handpicked tenants below were to hear something, they'd be too terrified to contact the police.

Some sort of breach? An informer?

There was no time to figure that out now. The law was on the way. Wesley slammed the intercom button: "Sir?"

The line was dead, perhaps damaged by one of the bullets fired when the wall-crawler had first entered. Just as Wesley shot to his feet, things got worse. On the screen, the "defeated" Spider-Man sprang up into action. The web-slinger's speed reminded him of a jumping spider, of the *Salticidae* family. He didn't seem to move from the floor so much as vanish and instantly reappear in midair, his fist driving deep into Mr. Fisk's abdomen.

"If playing dead's all it takes to surprise you, I get why you thought that window-thing might work."

Wesley watched, assuming the Kingpin would strike back immediately. But Fisk fell over backwards.

"Mr. Fisk!" Wesley's cry was pointless in more ways than one. He could hear the combatants, but they couldn't hear him. Worse, microphones in the the sound system were picking up a high-pitched wail.

Sirens? So soon?

Thanks to the recent setbacks, Wesley had managed to broach the subject of a police raid with his boss. Thinking it would be madness to confront the cops head-on, he'd advised Fisk to let himself be arrested, at least temporarily, and allow the legal team to handle any charges. By the letter of the law, Mr. Fisk was innocent until proven guilty.

And unless they found proof, Spider-Man was the criminal here, breaking and entering private property.

That might work, save for one piece of incriminating evidence: the tablet.

○────────────○

PRESSING his advantage, Spider-Man advanced on the prone Kingpin. "No wounded college kids around this time, baldy, so you've got my full attention."

But the mobster's assault on his pressure point had done more damage than he'd thought. His wrist and right arm were completely numb. He rubbed them to get the blood circulating.

A kick from the Kingpin's heavy foot caught him off guard. It was weaker than the earlier blows, but it still pushed him a few yards up and away.

He's either rattled, or he's finally getting tired.

Spider-Man landed lightly near some thick curtains. The Kingpin rose, lowered his head, and charged. As he came, Peter tore the curtains from the wall and, with a bullfighter's flourish, whipped them in the Kingpin's direction. "Olé!"

The cloth twirled around Fisk's legs, tripping him into what seemed a vulnerable sitting position. But Peter's spider-sense suddenly sent him leaping away, clinging to a high spot on the wall. He didn't understand why—until he noticed that the Kingpin had grabbed a fallen AK47.

"Have you ever actually been to a bullfight, insect? I can tell you it's far more enjoyable when the bull wins!" Fisk spun around, but before he could engage the trigger, Spider-Man fired a thick glob into the barrel.

The gun didn't explode, as it might in a cartoon, but it did split open—and the unexpected backfire slammed the stock into Fisk's gut. Wincing, he tossed it aside and raised both arms to strike.

Spider-Man tensed, ready to leap as soon as there was an opening. But then he noticed something else.

"Uh…KP, is that green smoke coming out of your pocket, or are you just glad to see me?"

Confused, the Kingpin looked down at his sweat-stained jacket. The rifle butt had shattered a gas pellet—apparently he was still carrying some in his pocket. Cursing, he frantically tried to tear off the jacket.

As Spider-Man crawled a bit higher to stay out of the way, the wafting smoke reached the Kingpin's head.

"I will…!" His eyes swam in his skull.

"Hold that thought."

He fell.

Once the gas dispersed, Spider-Man hopped down. He was about to wrap the mobster in webbing when the sound of scurrying footsteps caught his attention. He turned and spotted a hallway entrance the curtains had previously concealed.

Probably one of Fisk's stooges, making a beeline out of here.

But when he poked his head into the hall, he realized that the exit was in the opposite direction.

Or maybe he's after the stolen tablet?

Fisk *looked* down for the count, but Peter had already been wrong about the guy more than once.

I need that thing to prove Fisk, not the students, was behind the bombing. What to do? Stay here, or go after the tablet?

o———————o

SECONDS later, the panicked Wesley reached the vault where the tablet was stored. Purchased from a savings-and-loan bank before its demolition, the classic steel-reinforced concrete door was secure enough. But once the police knew it existed, they would get a warrant and demand entry.

Panting, he entered the code only he and Wilson Fisk knew. The bolts disengaged at once. Wesley pulled at the thick handle. He strained and yanked, but it wouldn't budge.

Mr. Fisk had talked about reinforcing the door with additional composite metal. The extra weight wouldn't be a problem for someone with the Kingpin's strength. For Wesley, it might as well have still been locked.

Why had Fisk contracted for the work without consulting him? The thought rankled. Given events, the extra precaution made some sense, but Wesley had never given his employer any reason to doubt his loyalty. Now he'd need three men to budge the thing—and thanks to Spider-Man, they were all unconscious.

The sirens grew louder—so loud he could feel them in his jaw. An almost forgotten sense of self-preservation kicked in. Wesley turned to run.

"Hey, pal. Where are you going?"

There was a short whoosh—like a thin, high-powered spray—and Wesley felt an odd pressure just below the nape of his neck. Something yanked him upwards, his knees coming up to press against his chest. A sticky mesh crisscrossed his field of vision, and he found himself dangling in a sack of webbing.

"I won't tell you anything!"

"Fine by me. Stay right there, and I'll see if I can guess what you were up to, okay?"

Twisting, he spotted the smug wall-crawler standing on the ceiling. Tapping a finger to his chin, Spider-Man looked around, then pointed at the vault door.

"Tablet's in there, right?"

Briefly, Wesley hoped the door would hold. But once Spider-Man hopped down and braced a foot against the wall, it opened easily. Seconds later, the prize tablet was in his hands.

Wesley moaned. "No! You have no idea what you're holding!"

"Again, lemme guess. Is it...the mysterious tablet whose undecipherable hieroglyphs are believed to contain the greatest secret in history?"

As if things weren't bad enough already, the infuriating philistine sounded like he was reciting from the insipid signs at the Exhibition Hall.

Spider-Man lifted the tablet. "Time to get this back to the hall." He cocked his head. The sirens were louder. "Or better yet, the police."

Wesley clenched his fists. "Wait! You can't just leave me here!"

He thought he caught a smile beneath the mask. "It's not every day I find such a great straight man—but to answer your question, sure I can. Don't worry. I'll let the boys in blue know you're hanging around up here. I'm sure they'll find you before you get too lonely."

○━━━○

THE KINGPIN awoke surrounded by police. His dry mouth tasted of bile; his sense of helplessness infuriated him.

They'll never be able to hold me, but now is not the time for a fight. I have a better idea.

"Gentlemen, come in—I have nothing to hide."

The lead officer whistled at the unconscious men. "If you say so."

Fisk held up his wrists. They handcuffed him—with

oversized cuffs, he realized. The cops hadn't responded to some nuisance call. They'd expected to find him there.

Someone had given them inside information. A traitor.

It took three straining officers to force their "collar" to his feet. As they read him his rights, he congratulated himself for managing to protect what he held most dear.

Thank heavens I sent Vanessa to Long Island. I'm used to dealing with vermin, but she should never have to deal with such indignity.

The lead detective finally asked the obvious.

"Where's the tablet, Kingpin?"

Fisk smiled at the man's predictability. "If I had it, do you think I'd be foolish enough to keep it here where it could incriminate me? Perhaps it was that very issue that caused the little disagreement with my web-swinging ally."

"Spider-Man's your partner?"

The grin he gave in response wouldn't be admissible as a confession, but it spoke volumes.

The officer at his back, still holding his wrist-clamps, sighed. "Jameson was right: That guy's a menace!"

Their disappointment was charming.

The bedraggled detective grabbed a walkie-talkie. "Anyone spots Spider-Man in the area, I want him taken in for questioning."

That was almost too easy. Loathe as I am to admit it, I owe that vigilante-obsessed publisher J. Jonah Jameson my thanks.

○────────○

LEAVING the crook dangling behind him, Spider-Man found the nearest window and sailed into the night. The cool air felt good against his bruises. As he snagged the side of the luxury building with his web, the wide arc of his swing provided a great view of the flashing squad cars surrounding the front entrance and garage.

Excited, he scrambled down the side of the building.

I'd know that shiny dome anywhere. They've got the Kingpin!!

As soon as he was close enough for the officers to hear him, he pulled the tablet from his back and held it aloft like a trophy. "Hey, boys in blue! I've got something for you!"

In retrospect, given his history with the law, their reaction shouldn't have surprised him. But it did.

"It's Spider-Man!"

"He's got something in his hand!"

"Could be a bomb!"

"Wait—a what? Are you guys—"

Bullets sparked against the building façade.

"Geez, I'm only trying to—"

"Watch it! He's probably out to free the Kingpin!"

The bullets drew closer. He leapt from one spot to another to keep from being hit.

"Why the heck would I free him? I just *caught* him!"

But the sound of gunfire drowned out his words—

and the odds that a lucky shot would get him were growing by the second. The more pinned he felt, the more his far-from-ordinary body flushed with adrenaline.

Catching the high-rise with another web, he swung up and out. At the peak, he let go. A second web, anchored to a water tower across the street, carried him far from the line of fire.

Losing the police among the rooftops was easy; letting go of his outrage was not. The long day had taken its toll. By the time he landed on the asphalt surface, he was grinding his teeth and sweating.

Is it too much to ask for a thank-you now and then? Just something small, like having the police not *try to kill me while I'm trying to return a priceless artifact. But no, no matter what I do, nothing changes. Nothing!*

More distance from the cops would be good. But when he shot another web, he yanked it so hard that the flagpole at the other end nearly broke in half.

Instead of putting myself in harm's way like a sap, I could be earning a decent living! Decent? Hell, with my powers, I could be rich and respected, not a starving photographer with a rep as a coward.

At the apex of his swing, he yanked at the web. This time, the flagpole did break. Part of him hoped the rush of the freefall would snap him out of his rage.

It didn't.

A second web steadied his path, but not his mind.

Fine. Screw it. If the world's going to be against me, I'm done being too stupid to fight back. Call me a menace? Treat me like a menace? I might as well be *a menace.*

SIX

PETER lay in bed staring at the ceiling, his heart hammering. Every now and again he glanced at the tablet, thinking how ridiculous it was to have the greatest secret in history sitting half-hidden under his dirty laundry.

Something had to change. He didn't know what, he wasn't sure how, but something had to change.

He'd tried giving up being Spider-Man before, but it hadn't stuck. When the only father he'd ever known, Uncle Ben, had died at the hands of a mugger Peter could have stopped, he'd promised to use his powers to help others. But he'd been doing that for years now, and it seemed as if none of his good deeds had gone unpunished. He was sick of it.

Maybe I could just stop fleeing muggers that happen to run past me?

His head filled with the faces of taunting enemies. His boss, Jonah Jameson, laughed alongside super villains like the Lizard, the Green Goblin, and Doctor Octopus. His loved ones—Aunt May, Gwen, Harry, and Mary Jane—looked down at him in pain and disappointment. They were so real, Peter didn't even realize he was dreaming until he heard Uncle Ben say, "Calm down."

In his mind, Peter sat at the old kitchen table in Queens, working on a middle-school science project. It was a crude model of the polymer that would eventually become his webbing. He'd cut his finger twice carving the small pieces, but still couldn't get them right. Finally, in a fit, he smashed the whole thing.

"Calm down, Peter!"

"Why bother? My stupid teacher probably doesn't know what a polymer is anyway!"

His classmates certainly didn't. He was a nerd, harassed daily by Flash Thompson, ridiculed by the others. It all felt pointless.

"Take it slow. You'll get there."

Peter snapped back, "I can't! I don't know *how* to slow down."

As he woke, he realized he still didn't.

It was morning. He felt hungover, partly from the bruises, but mostly from the mix of anger and guilt still roiling his gut. The night's phantoms clung to him like strands of his own web. He robotically made breakfast, managed two bites, then trudged to ESU.

The morning sun partly melted his funk, but it was only when he saw Gwen that his spirits began to rise. She was crossing the street, walking toward him, hair tousled in the breeze, her sharp, wonderful eyes locked on him.

And then she opened her mouth.

"Peter! I've been looking all over for you! Where've you been?"

He was used to the accusing tone, but not from her.

"Sorry, Gwendy. Been a little tired, I guess."

"Too tired to answer your cell?"

"Uh…sort of…"

Her hand went to her hip. "Really? Well, maybe you *should* be exhausted from running out whenever it's time to take a stand!"

"Wait? What?"

Here it was again. The same old questions, the same old insults—even from the one person who he thought cared enough to trust him unconditionally.

"Where were you while the protestors were getting arrested?"

Getting the snot kicked out of me while trying to prove their innocence! Not that I can say that out loud.

"The least you could do is fumble for an excuse!" After a beat, she hissed. "Okay, stand there chewing your cud. There must be a reason for your disappearing act. Maybe I should have my head examined for not writing you off, but I'm going to wait until you level with me."

"Gwen…are you crying?"

She was. Trying to choke it back only made the tears well up and curl down her cheeks.

She turned away. "Forget it. It just stinks losing your heart to someone who always acts like a coward!"

Again, that word: *coward.* The sickly feeling that

had barely started to fade came rushing back. Mute, face flushing, he stood watching as she walked off.

"I'm going to the precinct house to check on the students. *They* at least stood up for what they believed in."

After a few steps, she broke into a run.

IN THE precinct's walnut-paneled conference room, a stoic Dean Corliss met the glares of the tired protest organizers. Though there were no armed officers present, Captain Stacy watched from the sidelines, accompanied by Robbie Robertson.

Bleary-eyed from a long, sleepless night in the basement holding cells, Josh Kittling refused to sit at the same table with Corliss. "Bad enough we're facing jail terms. Are you here to expel us?"

The gray-haired dean's sigh communicated both his ease with his own authority, and a lack of patience. "No, Mr. Kittling. The police have determined that your student group had nothing to do with the bombing. And, despite the YouTube video in which you personally threaten to steal the artifact, ESU is dropping all the charges. I'm also here to tell you that the money initially earmarked for the hall has been reallocated to needs-based financial aid."

He waited for the news to sink in.

Randy blinked. "Then…we won?"

"If you'd like to think of it as some sort of contest, yes."

Kittling's brow knitted. "Why didn't you do that in the first place? Why refuse to meet with us?"

The second sigh was more irritated. "I never *refused*. I delayed the meeting because I was trying to arrange additional donations that would've made both expenditures possible. Admittedly, I should have shared that with your group before things spiraled out of control, but our biggest donors didn't want to be seen as rewarding your protest."

Kittling sneered. "So you kowtowed to the two-percenters."

"Again, if you like, yes. But they *are* the ones with the money. In any case, we're past that now. The structural damage the thieves caused is being covered by insurance, giving us ample funds for the renovation. That's all I came to say." As the dean rose, Captain Stacy handed him a cane that was leaning against the table. "I hope in the future we'll all be able to continue this dialogue in a more productive manner."

When he limped toward the exit, Robbie held the door open. His father's relieved "Thank you" earned a killer stare from Randy.

ONCE the release was processed, Robbie walked his son out, trying to figure out the best way to talk to him. If now was the time to talk at all.

They paused on the steps to enjoy the sun. Randy looked exhausted. What he needed most was rest and a home-cooked meal. But Robbie still couldn't quite believe how difficult it had become to reach the boy he'd raised for 18 years.

He opted for an attempt at humor.

"So, Rand, which bugs you more: that the dean you were blaming turned out to be an ally, or that sometimes the system *does* work?"

Randy scoffed. "The way I see it, Josh was right. The system only works when it doesn't have a choice. If Corliss really was on our side, he'd have communicated with us in the first place. He's part of the problem."

"He's been limping half his life because his hip was broken during a protest that *did* turn violent. I know the '60s are ancient history to you, but you have no idea how much worse things were then. You have to put things in perspective."

"Perspective? So, because Jim Crow's dead, I should shut up and trust whoever's in charge?"

His father wanted to say, *No, of course not. But you still have so much to learn. You have to rein in that temper so you can pick your battles.*

But he didn't, and the two walked on in silence.

o————o

BEYOND the basement windows, half-below the pavement, stood the dank holding cells that now contained Wilson Fisk, his captured bodyguards, and a glum Wesley.

"Get me out of here!" the Kingpin yelled.

He wasn't truly angry, but he needed the police to

think him a mindless fool. To Fisk, the officers guarding him were little men—not in stature but in mind. Whenever he shouted, two of them kept professionally silent, as if hoping that good behavior would one day provide a better assignment and higher pay.

The third was an utter lout. "Quiet down in there, tubs."

He sat with his feet up on a desk, reading the *Bugle*. Noticing the Kingpin's stare, he held up the paper. The headline declared:

Spider-Man Wanted!

"According to Jameson's editorial, your buddy Spidey's run off with the tablet and left you to rot. But don't worry, the wall-crawler's going to be in there with you pretty soon."

Fisk had to suppress a grin at how quickly everyone had bought into his lie. But for the sake of appearances, he reminded himself how much he *did* have to be angry about. Spider-Man had the tablet. Fisk's operation had been hit hard. Worse—his defeat, however fleeting, would give Vanessa more reason to doubt him.

He gripped the bars. "You'll see—I'll be out of here soon enough!"

The oaf in uniform laughed. "You're right about that. You'll be gone just as soon as they find a prison suit big enough."

It was probably the first time in his life the loudmouth even *thought* he was in a position to gloat. But he was right: The clock was ticking. Within hours,

Fisk would be transferred to Ryker's, where maximum security was far better equipped to hold him than this century-old building with its 1920s fixtures and quaint iron bars on the cells.

Wesley had advised trusting the attorneys to have him released. They were the best money could buy, but Fisk was hardly the only rich criminal they represented. If the Maggia had managed to plant a spy in his own organization, why not among his lawyers, too?

So, rather than trust anyone on the outside, the Kingpin had been gripping the same two bars all night long, shouting invectives at the guards and the heavens—all the while twisting the old, brittle iron. He gave the bars a little quarter turn. They weren't ready to break yet, but soon.

"Come a little closer, and I'll make you eat that paper," he growled.

The fool actually got to his feet. "Yeah, big shot? This paper right here?"

The other officers stiffened. "Frank."

He waved them off. "It's okay. I got this."

When "Frank" was close enough to smell, Fisk pretended to reach for him, knowing full well that his arms wouldn't fit between the bars.

As they glared at each other, the lout sneered. "Just another gorilla in a cage, now, huh? You got nothin'."

He looked as if he might withdraw, but instead he leaned in close, whispering so the others wouldn't hear. "Silvio Manfredi sends his regards."

Adrenaline flooded through the Kingpin. He

didn't have to twist the bars again—he simply snapped them. Pinning the startled guard's neck between them, he stepped from his cell.

The others reached for their weapons. "Don't move or we shoot!"

But Fisk kicked the desk up on end, shielding himself. A second kick sent it flying into the guards.

He lifted the squirming Frank aloft, keeping the man's skull scissored between the bars. The bright-red shade on the choking man's face delighted him.

"Please, I don't want to die!"

The Kingpin *tsked.* "Then I'm sorry to say we're at cross purposes. But perhaps you can change my mind. Tell me how Silvermane found out about my plans."

Blood dripped down the crooked cop's neck, the rough iron scratching his skin. "Don't know, but word is he met some guy in a hood calling himself the Schemer. He's the one you want. He's…"

His eyes fluttered up into his head, then closed. Frank had fainted, more from fear than the pressure of the bars. The Kingpin let go. There would be little satisfaction in killing an unconscious man.

His captured men called to him, "Get us out!"

Even Wesley. "Mr. Fisk, I can help you."

The others were a dime a dozen, but Wesley he owed a response. "My apologies. The basement will be flooded with police any second. There isn't time. Once I've found our traitor, I'll see to it that the lawyers get you out."

He charged the length of the narrow hall and

slammed into a fire door. As he stumbled up the steps toward the sidewalk, a bullet passed by his ankles, sending up a spray of shattered concrete. Apparently one of the officers had already recovered from his collision with the flying desk.

Avoiding the streets, where he'd be an easy target, Fisk sped along a narrow vacant lot next to the precinct house. A takeout restaurant on the opposite side had left it strewn with garbage, thick with the worst of the city's stench. His haste, coupled with a desire to avoid the trash, had him brushing against the precinct wall, tearing and staining his white jacket.

The cop puffed behind him in pursuit. Another shot came from a window above. Ahead, a squad car emerged from the motor pool, hoping to block Fisk's escape. Scratched and filthy, he leapt onto the car's hood and vaulted over a barbed-wire fence.

He landed hard on the sidewalk, scuffing his shoes, tearing his pants. Though loathe to flee any fight, at least now he had the room to do so. His powerful legs carried him through side streets and parks. But the police cruisers on every wide avenue told him it would be foolish to remain on foot.

Finding a safe spot behind a wide oak, he withdrew the small phone he kept concealed in the leaden heel of his shoe. He flipped it open, then hesitated. His organization had been compromised by the Schemer. Who was there left to call?

There was only one option: Vanessa, his raison d'être. It would make him look weak. Still, it was fitting that his emotional salvation would become his physical salvation, as well. She would understand. Of course she would.

"My love, I am…in trouble. The coded GPS in the phone will take you to me. It has to be just you, alone. I'll explain why when you get here."

In less than 10 minutes, he spotted her SUV, its tinted windows darker than most. He slipped inside, relieved to see her, but afraid of how she might react. When she didn't even turn to greet him, that fear grew.

"Crosstown, my darling, then head north."

Nary a police car in sight. He exhaled a little.

Her eyes were fixed on the road. He turned to her, about to caress her arm. He saw a dark dirt-smudge on the sleeve of his jacket and stopped.

"We've been betrayed. This…this…worm calling himself the Schemer has been feeding information about my business to the Maggia. I don't know how much he's told them, but it's best we go into hiding as a precaution."

When her expression remained distant, his fear turned to panic. He touched her shoulder, marring the sleeve of her dress with the muck on his hand.

"It's only temporary. I promise you, I can fix this. Everything will be as it was."

He tried to wipe off the dirt, but only made it worse. When she pushed his hand away, he felt as if he'd been stabbed in the chest.

"Vanessa, I'm sorry I was weak. I'm sorry I didn't know…"

When she turned to him at last, he saw, for the first time, disdain in her eyes. "You think I'm angry about the collapse of your business? Or that you're covered in the filth you swore we would stay above? No, my love, my *one* love, none of that could break my heart. But this did."

She handed him a printout. The quickest of glances told him it was a document from his private server—one that contained the details of his efforts to quash the press story about their son.

He felt the knife in his heart twist. He fumbled for words, any words at all, that might remove it.

"They don't know for certain he's been harmed! They're only guessing…"

"Guessing? Our son went missing after an avalanche! He's believed dead!"

"I…I wanted to save you the pain."

She pressed down on the gas. The tires squealed as she took the next turn. He wanted to remind her it was important they not attract attention, but he kept silent.

Her eyes were wet, but anger seemed to keep the tears from falling. "You swore this was all for him. That was how you justified it: for him, something better in the future. This means you did it for nothing. Nothing!"

She hit the brakes so hard that the Kingpin, still turned sideways to face her, struck the dashboard with his shoulder. The door popped open.

"Get out."

He clasped his hands. "Vanessa, you must forgive me. You must!"

"Get out!"

The command seemed to carry physical force. He half-fell into the street, landing in a puddle. She didn't even wait for the door to close before she sped off, didn't even slow down as he bellowed her name.

"VANESSA!"

As he rose—clothes wet, torn, and stinking of garbage—he realized the depths of his failure.

He couldn't save her from the pain.

He couldn't even save her from the smell.

A small crowd gathered, like flies drawn to rotting fruit. Thanks to the *Bugle*, Fisk's face was as well-known in the city as the wall-crawler's mask. The crowd kept its distance, treating him like some feral beast. He managed to stumble off before anyone could record him with their damned, ever-present phones.

He would hide, but not for long. And when he emerged, he would have his revenge—on this Schemer, on the Maggia, on Spider-Man. On everyone.

SEVEN

PETER was still afraid he'd punch someone if they looked at him the wrong way, so he skipped class and headed off campus. He reached the end of the plaza and kept going, not even seeing Harry wave, or hearing Randy's friendly, "Hey, Pete, where you off to?"

Determined to keep busy until the foul mood passed, he returned to his empty apartment and slid the tablet out from beneath the pile of clothes.

I could just leave it somewhere, let it become someone else's problem. But the Kingpin wouldn't want it so badly without a good reason. If that "great secret" turns out to be for real and it falls into the wrong hands, I'll be doing more harm than good, and I've already got all the guilt I can handle.

Turning its rough exterior in his hands, he stared at the incomprehensible symbols.

Yep, that's writing all right. At least I think it is. Might be doodles for all I know. But hey, this is New York. Find a plumber on the weekend? Forget it. Eminent hieroglyphic experts, why not?

Sure enough, a quick search turned up several local names.

Dr. Jennifer Collier at the Met looks like a good bet. Hope she has office hours.

He slipped into his red-and-blues, webbed the tablet to his back, and exited through the window. As he arced toward the top of the office building across the street, he hoped the exercise would put his head back on straight. With Gwen's hurt face fresh in his mind, though, kept him remained distracted. As he came in for a landing, he planned to propel himself skyward again. But his toe nearly missed the corner, and he wound up scrabbling on hands and knees across the roof.

Cripes! Another inch, and I'd be eating air. If I'm going to be up here leaping around in my underwear, I've got to get a grip.

But that's the thing, isn't it? Why am I out here in the first place? I'm taking my life in my hands every time I squeeze into this corny suit.

Exasperated, he swatted an air vent. The gesture felt offhand, the way someone else might slap a newspaper against their desk. But in his case, the pipe bent in the middle.

Focus on the tablet, Parker, before you do some real damage.

Chastened, but still champing at the bit, he forced himself to take more care and reached Fifth Avenue without further incident. Perched atop the terra-cotta roof of a cupola crowning a luxury apartment building across the street, he looked at the Metropolitan Museum of Art.

Science and natural history were more his thing, but being a city kid, he'd toured the Met more than once during school trips. Most places he revisited from his childhood tended to look smaller than he recalled, but the museum looked much bigger. For some reason, the figure of 2,000,000 square feet stuck in his head.

Should've thought this through. Sure, Dr. Collier's in there somewhere, but which window do I tap? If I remember correctly, that full-size Egyptian tomb is in the northeast wing. Maybe the offices are nearby.

He climbed along the tall front windows, but they were either blocked by shades or opened to the exhibits. Meandering lower along the more humble windows, he hoped to see something that said *office*—cubicles, desks, anything. No luck.

He turned the corner for more of the same until he saw the ancient temple standing in a huge open gallery area. That indicated the end of the Egyptian section. Hoping a better idea might strike, he squatted halfway up a stone column.

Can't just walk in. I'm wanted by the police. Should I buy a cheap burner and call? But how do I convince her she's talking to the real Spider-Man? Man, this idea sucked.

Before he understood what was happening, his spider-sense had him springing 10 feet to the next column, barely avoiding a bullet. Clinging by one hand, he looked down. He'd been so preoccupied with his search, he'd failed to notice that a patrol car had pulled onto the curb along East 84th. The stiff-lipped young officer who'd fired at him stood outside the passenger side, both hands on his weapon, legs planted apart.

His spider-sense was no longer tingling, which meant the guy had already realized his bonehead mistake. Knowing that did nothing to improve Peter's mood. "What the hell, man? Don't I even get a 'Hold it right there or I'll shoot'?"

"Fine. Hold it right there, or I'll shoot. Again."

By then his older partner had raced over from the driver's side. He wrapped his hands around the weapon and forced the rookie to point the barrel down.

"Joe, are you freaking insane? There's people all over!"

"He's way up there. What else am I going to hit, a bird?"

"Holster that weapon, now!"

Joe grimaced, but obeyed.

Still irritated, Peter couldn't resist blowing off some steam.

"Let me guess: good cop, stupid cop?"

The senior partner grimaced. "His mother's in the hospital, okay? Look, we're not going to shoot you off that building, but SWAT's on the way and they're already cordoning off the area. You'll make it easier on everybody if you turn yourself in."

"Why? I didn't steal the tablet!"

The officer made a face. "Spidey, I can see the freaking thing stuck on your back from here!"

At least they couldn't see him frown under the mask. "Oh. Right. But it's not what it looks like!"

The rookie scoffed. "Give me a break. You're probably taking it to the Kingpin right now."

"Yeah, that must be it. I was gonna bake it into a cake and sneak it to him at Ryker's."

Both stared at him. "Where've you been? He busted out an hour ago."

"What?"

The air filled with the promised *chuk-chuk-chuk* of helicopters. Fortunately, the Met abutted Central Park and its 800-plus acres of tree cover. The perfect place to get lost.

His web stuck fast to an oak tree's high branch. He swung down low, trying to make it look as if he were headed right for the police. They dropped to the ground.

"Appreciate your leveheaded handling of the situation, officers, but I've got to go find him." As his feet sailed over them, his web snagged a second tree. "To catch him! Because we're *not* partners, okay?"

By then he was off, facing the sky. He doubted they'd heard him—or that they'd believe him if they had.

If Baldy's out and about, he gets the Bigger Threat Award. I'll figure out what to do with the tablet later— but as long as I've got it and he wants it, I bet I can make him come to me.

Hiding from the police in Manhattan was an old game. He waited a few hours and then scoured the city's seamier areas trying to get some attention from the *other* side of the law. During the daylight, he managed to stop a few muggings, but it wasn't until sunset that the real pros came out to play. In short order, Spider-Man fouled up a break-in, crashed a meth lab, and mopped the floor with some musclemen collecting protection payments. He even entered a few downtown bars where the hired guns hung out, just to put every crook on notice. Each time, he made sure they all got a good look at the tablet webbed to his back.

The rush of city-swinging usually cleared his head. Today, whenever he took a breather, he was still fuming about Gwen. If she'd cooled off, she'd be wondering where he was. Plus, he'd missed all his classes—again. It was late. By rights, he should've been exhausted by now, but the bubbling anger made him feel like he could keep going for days.

For the third time, he hit the more desolate sections of Hell's Kitchen. The Kingpin wouldn't dare go near his home turf—there were still police parked outside his building. But his boys on the streets still had their jobs. Spidey could get lucky.

And he did.

The first thing that drew him to the short, lonely avenue was the fact that all the streetlights were out save one. The second was the tractor trailer backed into a space that could barely hold it. Coming in for a closer look, Spidey spotted the driver backed up against the truck with his hands up. He was surrounded by gun-toting criminal types. A black van idled nearby, waiting.

Landing in their midst brought a satisfying cry of, "It's Spider-Man!"

He scanned the worried faces, wondering which cheap hoodlum he'd let go. "Wow, a classic hijacking? These days, you don't see as many as you used to."

Before he could choose, his spider-sense thrummed. The van's rear doors flew open, and a familiar figure appeared.

Spider-Man cracked his knuckles, and the gunmen ran off. "Well, pierce my ears and call me drafty, it's Mr. Fisk! Just the guy I wanted to catch! Why is it that seeing you always makes me think of 'Night on Bald Mountain'?"

The Kingpin stepped into the cone of light formed by the lone streetlamp. Being a fugitive, even for a day, had taken a toll. His clothes were mussed, and he was panting.

"You didn't think I'd abandon you to the police? No, I'll beat you myself, and I will have that tablet."

Spider-Man crouched and twisted, showing his back. "This old thing? Oh, it's just something I throw on when I don't have anything nicer to wear."

Fisk charged, but Spider-Man kept twisting, turning the move into a spinning high-jump. Coming back down on the mobster's broad shoulders, he slammed his fists into the sides of his skull.

"Or is aspirin more the kind of tablet you should be looking for?"

While the Kingpin staggered, he jumped again. Pulling the artifact free, he tossed it up and pinned it high on a building with a glob of webbing—safely out of reach.

He landed, one hand to the ground, ready to begin the battle in earnest. Fisk circled, looking for an opening. As they squared off, Peter felt...*relieved*.

"I don't know about you, Stay Puft, but I've been looking forward to hitting something that really deserves it all day."

A half-smile took Fisk's face. "My sentiments exactly."

They came at each other swinging. Remembering the Kingpin's speed, Peter blocked Fisk's thick arm and slammed a right hook into his cheek. It was like hitting a fireplug. Fisk kept his skull pointed straight ahead, not even turning to absorb the impact. Wrapping his arms around the wall-crawler, he tried to tackle him. Spider-Man held his ground, put his hands against the wide shoulders, and pushed.

Each man strained, trying to force the other back. Neither would bend, but Spider-Man's superior strength soon had the soles of the Kingpin's oversize shoes scraping along the asphalt.

Maintaining his grip, Fisk hurled them both sideways, bringing them crashing to the ground. He rolled, using his greater weight to force Spider-Man beneath him. Holding his enemy in place with one elephantine arm, he pounded away with the other.

"No one defeats me! No one!"

The first punch caught Spider-Man's nose and bounced the back of his skull against the ground. It only made Peter angrier. After that, each time a fist came down, Peter twisted his head out of the way and jabbed. Alternating his left and his right, he connected four times for every one of the Kingpin's glancing attacks.

When Fisk picked up speed, Spider-Man matched him. Finally, that stiff fireplug skull started to give, turning this way and that.

"You know if you were *really* shaped like a pin, your head would be almost as wide as your waist, right? Kingpin, pin-shaped. Get it? Oh, never mind."

Realizing he was losing, the Kingpin tried attacking with both hands. Seizing the opening, Spider-Man folded his knees to his chest and shoved his feet into Fisk's abdomen. It felt more like lifting a truck than a man, but the hefty torso rose. He tried to toss Fisk to the side, but the Kingpin's uncanny sense of balance allowed him to settle back onto his feet.

Free of the weight, Spider-Man managed a backwards somersault. Before Fisk could raise his arms to block, Peter landed a solid roundhouse. But Fisk kept coming forward.

He's a wreck. I can see the bruises welling. What's keeping him on his feet?

They went at each other like boys in a playground brawl—punching, kicking, no longer caring what they hit as long as they hit something. Losing his advantage, Wilson Fisk succumbed to the beating and dropped to one knee. A final roundhouse left his eyes spinning. His huge form rocked one way and then the other, until he crawled into the middle of the street and landed along the double yellow line, face down.

Finally!

But it wasn't over. Through his bloodied lips, the Kingpin mumbled something that sounded like *contessa*—and rose again.

It can't possibly take much more to finish him off!

Peter jumped toward the roof of the Kingpin's black van to gain some height for a flying slam—but he instinctively shifted in midair, his spider-sense screaming.

The *Daily Bugle* satellite van sped onto the scene, narrowly missing him. It screeched to a halt in the worst possible spot: right between Spider-Man and the Kingpin. The door flew open, and no less than J. Jonah Jameson himself stepped out, barking orders at the man behind the wheel.

"Get a live feed up, Leeds! I told you that witness tip was hot! Now the whole world is going to see this!"

Peter had once thought the publisher's face was prematurely wrinkled, until he'd caught him napping. Resting, Jonah looked 20 years younger. The guy was just perpetually angry.

Well, I've had a crappy day, too.

"Get out of the way, both of you. Leave the Kingpin to me!"

Jameson shook his fist. He was always shaking his fist. "And let the two of you escape again? Not a chance! Leeds, where's my feed?"

In the van, reporter Ned Leeds gaped at the rear-view mirror. "Mr. Jameson, another car's pulling up!"

"So what?" Jonah howled. "This is the story of the year! Stop being a…"

The rest of his sentence was swallowed by the sound of the SUV's arrival. Tires squealing, it swerved around Fisk and stopped. Jonah was shouting and waving, blocking the stunned Spider-Man's path. When the rear door popped open, the Kingpin, with what must have been the last of his strength, threw himself inside.

Before the hatch closed, the Kingpin gasped two words, but Peter couldn't make them out. It sounded like *eye glove*—but the tone was strange, not like a mob boss commanding an underling. More humble, almost pleading.

Is that a woman at the wheel? And…wait. Did he say…my love?

Between his confusion, the simmering anger, and the lunatic screaming in front of him, Spider-Man didn't know how to react. The SUV's engine whined as the driver hit the gas.

I've got to calm down! They'll be easy enough to follow, and with JJJ ranting, getting out of here sounds like a great idea.

He pressed his palm, but nothing came out.

Empty! Seriously? Tell me I've got another web cartridge, please tell me…

As his hands fumbled with his belt, the car picked up speed. The distance between them was increasing. He braced himself for a long, standing leap.

It'll be close, but even if I can't reach it, I'll be able to toss a spider-tracer on it.

"Leeds! Spider-Man's trying to get away, too! Block him with the van!"

Leeds obediently gunned the engine. The satellite van lurched ahead of the leaping Spider-Man. It wasn't much of an obstacle, but it was enough to check his momentum. Completing his perfect round of misfortune, Spider-Man landed behind it.

The SUV carrying the Kingpin screeched around the corner, out of view.

Aghast, Spider-Man wheeled on Jameson. "You hysterical nut! I was trying to *stop* the Kingpin. You let him get away!"

Jonah roared back. "You don't fool me! You're pretending to be enemies, but I know you two planned the whole thing together. This time, you're finished. I'll keep the public clamoring for your hide! I'll dog the NYPD in every editorial until they've caught you. I'll…"

Furious, Spider-Man flitted to the wall directly above the publisher.

"You'll what? Go on. You'll what?"

Jameson choked. "Leeds! Stop him! He's attacking me!"

Spider-Man inched closer. "You know what? That's the first time you've been right in a long time. You've been attacking me for years. Now it's my turn."

He grabbed Jameson by the lapels of his overcoat and lifted. Nose to nose with his nemesis, Jonah sputtered, "No! No!"

Leeds popped out of the van. "Spider-Man, don't!"

Spider-Man took a few steps higher so that Leeds couldn't reach the publisher's dangling feet.

"Take a hike, Leeds. This is between me and the hate machine."

Jameson's eyes were popping out of his skull. The veins in his temples throbbed.

"Do you have any idea what all your stupid lies have done to my life? Do you even care that…?"

But then the eyelids fluttered, and his form went limp. As Jameson's head slumped forward, Spider-Man saw all those wrinkles disappear.

He shook him a little. "Jameson? Hey, Jameson?"

The body wriggled like a marionette.

Below, Leeds was already calling for help. "What did you do to him?"

Climbing down, Spider-Man gently lowered him to the sidewalk.

"I just wanted to give him a scare!"

Stunned, he allowed Leeds to push him out of the way and grab Jonah's wrist.

"You gave him more than that. I don't feel a pulse!"

Shaking, head swimming, Spider-Man climbed to the nearest roof. His body begged him to keep going, to run and hide, but he ignored the impulse. He waited in shadow for the ambulance to arrive, then watched the EMT crew load the still-unconscious Jameson inside.

This can't be real. It has to be some kind of nightmare.

Hoping he would wake up, he kept watching. Long after the twirling red-and-white lights disappeared into the night, he still hadn't moved.

EIGHT

LATE the next morning, Peter kept playing the scene over in his mind, hoping to recall some sign of life in Jameson that he'd missed. It was pointless. He couldn't even be sure whether the look of terror he remembered on the publisher's face was accurate, or a guilty exaggeration.

Does it matter? Whether I meant to hurt him or not, if he dies, I'm every bit as bad as he thinks. I said it myself: If they keep calling me a menace, I may as well be one. Even if only for a few seconds, that's what I was.

His mind circled back to the crushed science project. The powdery remains of the Styrofoam on his fingers mixed with the feel of his publisher's lapels.

A double rap on his door, followed by a turning knob, raised his head in alarm.

"Hey, Pete!"

Harry.

As the door began to open, he realized he'd forgotten to remove the pants of his spider-suit. He yanked the blanket above his waist so fast, a pen lying on the bed flew across the room and lodged in the plasterboard.

He couldn't tell whether Harry had heard the pen. At least the tablet was safely out of sight beneath his laundry.

Fortunately, as he entered, his gaze remained on Peter.

"Haven't seen you in a while, so I thought I'd check in."

Assuming his friend was hinting at some shirked responsibility, he went for the obvious. "Harry, man. Sorry about the bills…"

The curly haired youth raised his hands in surrender. "Hey, don't turn me into *that* guy. Pay up when you can. What's the point of being a two-percenter if you can't cut your brilliant pal a little slack? This is more of a general 'Are you okay?'"

I should have known better. Not wanting to mooch on Harry is more about me. He doesn't think that way.

The wealthy heir had been Peter's first college friend. When others dismissed Harry as a snob, Peter listened to his worries over his dad's weird behavior. Of course, Peter never mentioned that a chemical concoction had temporarily turned Norman Osborn into the villainous Green Goblin.

Harry wavered on his feet. "I tried saying hi yesterday, but you looked like you were practicing for a zombie walk. Then you were gone for the rest of the day. What's up? Is your aunt okay?"

"She looked fine when I visited." His brow immediately furrowed. "Did you hear different? Is she okay?"

"No, no. Just fishing. Things cool with Gwen?"

Gwen. He'd almost forgotten about that problem.

Seeing his reaction, Harry nodded. "Ah. Got it. Look, whenever you're ready to talk, I'm here."

"I know that, Harry. I'm okay. I think at least half my funk is this flu I'm trying to duck. My body can't decide if I should get better or worse."

His fake cough sounded especially unrealistic, even to him. Harry clearly wasn't buying it, but he bobbed his head. Smiling, he let it go. "Then take a stand already. Either come down with it, or get the heck up."

Knowing Harry didn't mean *take a stand* the same way Gwen had, Peter offered a weak farewell wave. Harry closed the door and left him alone. Again.

When I don't take a stand, I'm a coward. When I do, I put Jonah in the hospital. It was better before I got my powers, back when I was Flash Thompson's victim. At least then I knew I was getting batted around for nothing.

A few feet below the pen he'd embedded in the wall, his camera sat on the bureau. Remembering he'd set it up in the Exhibition Hall, he powered it up and clicked through the jpegs. Seeing himself tackle the bad guys and save Randy made him feel better.

Not much, but a little.

Even Jameson would admit some of these are pretty good. But with him out of the picture, I don't even have anyone to sell them to. Or do I?

Showing up at the *Bugle* would also mean getting the latest on Jonah. He wasn't sure he was ready for that. Convincing himself he had to find out sooner or later, he managed to dress and head over to 39th and Second. But when the *Bugle* building's ancient elevator opened on the editorial floor, he had to drag himself out.

The floor plan—reporters' desks surrounded by windowed staff offices with old-style windowed doors—had been unchanged for years. Their crusty leader was too cheap to update anything: Peter had once seen him duct tape a broken keyboard together. Surprisingly, it had worked for another six months.

The reliable mess was home, in a way. An abusive home, perhaps, but a home. Now it was frighteningly quiet.

Is everyone grieving, or is this just what's it's like without JJJ caterwauling?

Jonah's assistant, Betty Brant, was at her desk in front of his office, with Ned Leeds leaning in for a quiet conversation. Their faces were too neutral for him to guess what they were talking about. He swallowed and walked over.

"I heard Jonah was in the hospital. Is he…?"

Leeds picked up his head. "He's fine."

Peter felt a rush of relief.

Leeds continued. "When Spider-Man grabbed him, Jonah had what they call an acute stress reaction, but that passed quickly. He's only still there because of his blood pressure. The doctors have been telling him to take a break for years. Now they're insisting on some hospital bedrest. He'll be back screaming at everybody in a week."

"That's amazing!"

When Leeds furrowed his brow, Peter realized he'd sounded a bit too excited. Before he could offer a fake explanation, the door marked *City Editor* opened and Robbie Robertson waved him inside.

"Peter, a word?"

"Uh…sure."

Closing the door, Robbie gestured at a chair. As Peter sat, Robbie looked out the window, took a sip from his very old coffee mug, and said nothing.

Peter broke the silence. "So…what's it like being in charge?"

Robbie sighed. "Quiet. I'd forgotten what that was like. But that's not why I wanted to talk to you. I know you've met my son. I hate to ask you about this, but Randy barely talks to me, and I'm worried. Sure, he's an adult now, and don't get me wrong, I'm proud of who he is. But he was nearly killed by the Kingpin, and I haven't slept since. How do I get him to understand that next time, he may not be so lucky? That the kind of change we want doesn't happen overnight?"

The City Editor leaned against the paper-strewn desk. It was then Peter noticed the faded words on the mug: *World's Greatest Dad.*

"Uh, Mr. Robertson, I barely know the guy, and I have no idea what it's like growing up black. I do think I get what it feels like to believe the whole world's against you—how sometimes it's so frustrating, you just want to hit something. While he was around, my uncle always tried to keep me grounded emotionally, telling me what worked for him, what he felt was right. I didn't always listen—heck, when I remember him, sometimes I still don't listen. But I always heard him. With a dad like you around to steady him, I'm sure Randy will find his way."

A wistful, pleasantly surprised smile came to Robbie's face. "Thank you. Your uncle sounds like he was a wise man."

Clearing his throat, he pivoted to the next subject. "I'm guessing you didn't just come here to check on Jonah. Have you got something for me?"

Couldn't ask for a better opening. "Well, there are these…"

As he scanned the images, Robbie's eyes grew wider and wider until he laughed and slammed his intercom button. "Betty, call the press room!"

"So…pretty good?"

"Good? The hall's security system was erased, but these show beyond a shadow of a doubt that Spider-Man tried to stop the theft! If you'd gotten here sooner, you could have saved the wall-crawler a lot of trouble."

Figures.

Not wanting to take advantage of Robbie's good mood, Peter tried to think of a reasonable price. But before he could name one, the City Editor was writing in a ledger so dust-laden it didn't look as if Jonah had paid a single freelancer since the Clinton administration. With a sharp snap, he tore a check free and handed it to Peter.

Peter blinked, narrowed his eyes, and blinked again.

"What? Isn't it big enough?"

"Big enough? This is the most money I've seen in years! Jonah would have gnawed off his own hand before signing something like this!"

Robbie gave him a paternal chuckle. "Don't expect it every time, son, but those pics are going to double our circulation for at least two days."

"No, sir. Yes, sir. Thank you, sir!"

Waving the check over his head, he raced out—laughing so loudly that Leeds and Betty stared as he passed by.

"I thought he was being a little weird about Jonah, but maybe he's just in a good mood," Leeds said.

"Yes," Betty mused. "He does look happy for a change."

———○———————○———

AT HOME, after adding up the bills three times, Peter let out a whoop of joy. He not only had everything covered, there was enough left over to send Aunt May to Florida for some well-deserved sunshine.

An hour ago I thought my life was over. Man, things can change fast.

His eyes wandered over to the tablet.

Some things, anyway. Don't know what made me think I'd know what to do with that thing, but the talk with Robbie gave me a good idea who would.

Spidey's still wanted, though. As long as I'm trying to be smart, I should lay low until my pictures are out. That should help clear me with the police.

He spent the afternoon trying to catch up on schoolwork and hoping for a call from a certain blonde coed.

I'd call myself, but she was so angry.

By late afternoon, the photos were all over the internet. With no word from Gwen and no official declaration of Spider-Man's innocence (did they even *make* official innocence declarations?), he decided he'd waited long enough. He donned his uniform and headed out. After slipping some overdue papers into the mailboxes of his ESU professors, he made his way to the precinct house. Despite the quiet surrounding the building now that the protests were over, he perched in the shadows of an overhanging elm and waited.

His patience was rewarded when a trenchcoated figure exited and looked in his direction. Spider-Man worried he'd been spotted, but after briefly admiring the few visible stars, the figure covered his white hair with a fedora and nodded a farewell at the officer standing by the door.

"Good night, Captain Stacy."

I trust Gwen's dad as much as I do anyone. Just want to be sure we're alone first.

When Stacy turned onto an empty tree-lined street, Spider-Man followed. Catching up, he lowered himself in front of Stacy, upside down on a web-line, and held out the tablet.

"I hear the police are looking for this."

The semi-retired detective looked more pleased than surprised. "Spider-Man?"

"You know it. I've been trying like crazy to protect this thing. The Kingpin's got a lot of informers, but I figure if anyone can get it into the right hands, it's you."

Stacy took the stone, but kept his eyes on the web-slinger. "Why not come in yourself? The *Bugle* photos made your role plain, but there are a few things I'd like to speak with you about."

No. I don't even dare talk for long or he might recognize me. He's too sharp.

"Sorry, Captain. My relations with the police haven't exactly been cordial."

"You have a point. But that works both ways. Obviously I can't stop you…"

"Thanks!"

As he swung off, Peter swore he could feel the detective's gaze on his back.

CAPTAIN Stacy wasn't the only one keeping his eyes on Spider-Man's departure. The dark car parked at the corner looked empty, but the Schemer sat at the wheel.

When the web-slinger was out of sight, the Schemer turned his attention to the man with the tablet. Stacy took off on foot—headed away from the precinct house. It was a smart move. If the captain hadn't already suspected that some of his officers couldn't be trusted, the slow response from certain units during Fisk's escape would have given him pause. In fact, the Schemer knew that the Kingpin had one paid informer on staff at the precinct. The Maggia had two.

The Schemer knew a lot of things.

Once Stacy crossed the next avenue, the Schemer started the engine. He circled the block, spotting him again on the other side. Keeping his distance, he followed as the captain strolled along, turned onto a street of townhouses, and entered one.

He's brought it home. A perfect hiding place—if no one else knows it's there.

○———————————○

IN THE upper floors of the gothic-revival Galby building, in a plush office large enough to hold a small army, Silvio Manfredi grabbed the ringing phone. Recognizing the number, he waved everyone out of the room. The hired guns left at once, but Caesar Cicero lingered. Hand on the old-style receiver, Manfredi glared at him until he got the idea he wasn't welcome.

"I'll be right outside, if you need me."

"I won't," Silvermane croaked.

"Suit yourself."

When the door shut, he removed his palm from the phone. "Schemer, no one's seen the Kingpin since he tangled with Spider-Man. Tell me you know where he is."

"I don't, but I may have something better."

"There ain't nothing better, but I'll bite. What?"

"The ancient tablet he was after? Spider-Man just handed it to Captain Stacy. Seems the old detective doesn't trust the precinct house anymore, so he brought it home. He's probably calling the feds now, so it won't be there for long. If you want it, you'll have to move fast."

"Want it for what? A paperweight? You can't move something that hot unless you've already got a buyer."

The Schemer's contemptuous sigh immediately soured Manfredi's mood. *Soon as this arrogant cafone outlives his usefulness, he goes missing, too.*

"This isn't about money—none of it is," the Schemer explained. "It's about the Kingpin. He stole the tablet to make himself look good. Once it's in your hands…"

"Yeah, yeah, I get it. It'll make us look better."

He cut off the line, tapped the phone to his chin and stared across the cool dark of the empty space.

Where the hell is everyone? Oh, right. I ordered them all out.

"Cicero!"

The lawyer appeared so fast, he must've had his ear pressed against the door.

"You read the Arts Section. What do you know about that tablet the Kingpin stole from ESU?"

The squat man shrugged. "It's supposed to hold some kinda great secret. But hey, the dirt under my fingernails holds some great secrets, too."

Silvermane nodded. It seemed like a waste of time. Still, the Schemer had been right so far—and if Fisk was so interested, maybe *he* had a buyer set up.

"What kind of secret? Like a magic incantation that makes unicorns fly out of your butt?"

"That's the thing: Nobody knows. They only ever

managed to translate a couple of words."

"Like what?"

Googling the question on his phone, Cicero skimmed the entries. "Let's see. 'Those who know the' something-something 'will drink the' something-something. Smart quotes before Those, after the, before will, and after the. That's it." He laughed. "I know I could use a drink of something."

Silvermane's eyes clouded over. All at once, he was a weak, terrified child, hiding in the shadows and listening to a song his grandmother thought she'd kept to herself.

> *Those of us who know the truth,*
> *Will drink, drink, the nectar of youth.*

"Get Michael Marko up here now."

○———————————○

SITTING in the cozy bedroom above her father's study, Gwen Stacy tried to get down another few lines of her biophysics paper on her laptop. It wasn't due until next week, but she preferred having time to revise her work. It helped clarify her ideas and clear her mind.

And her mind certainly needed clearing.

After all, it was better than staring at the phone and debating whether to contact Peter. After her blow-up, he'd done his usual vanishing act, leaving her feeling like the magician's pretty but befuddled assistant.

Why doesn't he call? Probably because he thinks I'm still angry.

I am still angry, aren't I?

Sure she was, but at some point that anger had been joined by the nagging little worry a police captain's daughter always had for her loved ones. It was the same concern that made her so thrilled whenever Peter did finally turn up, that helped her realize how deep her feelings for him were—and that led her to forgive him again and again.

With her father safely in for the night, Gwen's missing boyfriend became the sole focus of her concern. As her anger ebbed, the worry grew. She looked at her phone, trying to convince herself she was being ridiculous for not calling him first.

He's probably off sulking somewhere. Sulking? More likely celebrating.

She'd seen his byline on the photos of Spider-Man battling the Kingpin. It was probably the high point of his career. Why hadn't he called to share the news?

Because I called him a coward.

The photos made her as confused as she was proud. Peter would walk through fire to get a good picture. Why wouldn't he make a stand on real issues? Why couldn't he open up to her? Was what they had together *that* frightening?

And what, exactly, *did* they have?

She was about to give in and call, when a crack and thud rattled the floorboards. It sounded as if something heavy had crashed through the window of her father's study. Grabbing the Taser she kept by her bed, she raced downstairs, but stopped short of the study door. She knew better than to rush in—if there was a break-in, she could just as easily become a hostage as a rescuer.

Crouching, she crept toward the sliding double-doors.

Her father's loud voice brought some comfort. "If I were you, I'd get out now. Even though you cut the alarm system, I'm sure the neighbors have already called the police."

Realizing the words were meant for her, Gwen hit the number on her cell that transmitted a silent alert to the precinct house. They'd be here in minutes—but a lot could happen in minutes. As she moved closer, the crisp smell of outside air reached her nostrils. It was so strong she figured the intruder hadn't just cracked a window pane—they must have completely broken the frame.

The doors were open slightly, allowing a narrow view of broken glass and splintered wood along the carpet. She saw her father: grim, tense, but thankfully unhurt. Given the intruder's size, Gwen wasn't sure how long that would last. At first she thought it was the Kingpin, but this man had a head of thick, black, curly hair. His muscles were more clearly defined, nearly bursting from his ill-fitting clothes.

"Neighbors, huh? Then I'll explain things quick."

With disturbing ease, he lifted their old Bridge-water sofa, the one they'd owned since she was a child. Since her mom was alive.

"This is going to be you, unless you hand over that tablet!"

He broke the sofa in two.

Her father responded evenly. "I already told you, it's not here."

"I hear different."

The trespasser moved toward Captain Stacy. Gwen armed the Taser. She doubted it would have much effect on that giant, but the Stacys weren't going down without a fight. She was about to rush in when the man veered toward the wall. He pulled away a portrait of Teddy Roosevelt, revealing the small locked safe behind it.

"Safe behind the only picture? I'm no college grad, but that was obvious even for me."

He was right. Her father had talked about replacing the safe, but had never found the time.

"Combination?"

"You won't get it from me."

"You got guts, but I don't need it. I was only trying to save you some repairs."

The thief grabbed the handle of the safe and pulled. With a grunt and the loud creak of snapping wooden beams, he tore the safe right out of the wall.

Afraid as she was, Gwen was also relieved. If the robber got what he wanted, there'd be no reason to harm her father. But old instinct made the veteran police officer grab at the safe. For a moment, they were all surprised. Then the giant back-handed the older man, sending him sailing across the room.

He crumpled atop the remains of the sofa, motionless.

Gwen burst in screaming. "DAD!"

Sirens wailed from the street. The attacker looked at Gwen, at her father, then at the hole in the wall where the window had been. With another grunt, he jumped out through the hole.

Tossing the Taser aside, Gwen knelt by her father. His quiet moan told her he was alive. His effort to rise to his feet told her there probably weren't any broken bones.

But the way his eyes swam in his skull told her he was not all right.

"Easy. Rest. Help's on the way."

Rallying, he put a shaky hand to her shoulder. "I'm fine, Gwen…just had the air knocked out of me. Make sure they know. That was Michael Marko, works for the Maggia. They call him Man Mountain Marko. If they're involved, I'm afraid we're in for a world of trouble. Right now, I have to close my eyes and catch my breath, but don't worry. You worry too much…"

She wanted to ask, *How can I not?*

Instead, she patted his hand. "Okay, Dad, okay."

NINE

IN THE morning, Peter stretched, showered, and put on clean clothes. As he did, he felt more and more off, as if something important was missing. When he caught himself humming while he made breakfast, he realized what it was.

Tension. I'm not tense. Is this what being well-rested feels like?

He glanced at the clock. There was plenty of time before Aunt May's train was scheduled to leave. So rather than rush off as usual, he sat and ate with his bemused roommate.

Harry sprinkled sugar on his cereal. "You know, Pete, handing money over to the electric company doesn't make most people this cheerful."

"Are you kidding? It's like a weight's been lifted off my shoulders. I can't wait to tell…"

There was that old twinge.

"You didn't see Gwen yesterday at all, did you, Harry?"

His roommate answered as he chewed. "I think she headed home early to get some work done. You two make up yet? No? Man, why haven't you called that girl already? Or at least texted?"

Undaunted, Peter wiped his lips. "I'll do better. Soon as I see off Aunt May, I'll track down Gwen and talk to her in person. The mood I'm in, I could charm the clouds from the sky."

"Bring an umbrella just the same. They're predicting a downpour."

Outside, Peter didn't understand for the life of him how such a dull, gray Manhattan sky could look so beautiful.

HE WAS at Penn Station five minutes early, waving eagerly as Aunt May's cab arrived. Grabbing all her bags in one arm, he almost forgot to pretend they felt heavy.

"Yeow! Didn't we talk about not bringing along *all* your barbells?"

Still sitting in the cab, she laughed. "Don't hurt yourself, dear. Rent one of those caddies."

"No, no, I've got it. I won't drop a thing."

Moving to stand, Aunt May wavered, as if she was about to fall backwards into the seat. He quickly set down the bags and reached inside to catch her.

"Easy, Aunt May! I've got you."

He let her rest a bit, then helped her up and out of the cab, watching her carefully before letting go of her shoulders.

"You're sure you're okay, now?"

She pinched his cheek hard.

"Ow!"

"See? Strong as an ox. You just have to be careful about getting up too quickly at my age."

She marched with him toward the departure tracks, smiling all the way. "Peter, dear, those pictures made me so proud. But you're certain you can afford this?"

"With the money Robbie gave me, I could send you to the moon, but I figured Florida was warmer."

Once she was secure in her seat, he kissed her forehead. "Remember the sunscreen, and be careful not to overdo the skateboarding."

"I'll be fine. Don't worry!"

As he straightened, he noticed a vaguely yellow color around the edges of her eyes. As the train pulled out, he wondered how fine she really was.

Back outside, a cold autumn rain trickled, then picked up, making him feel even better about being able to send his aunt someplace warm. Sunshine would be good for her. Right?

Finding Gwen was easier than he thought. Arriving back in the Village, he spotted her walking toward the Coffee Bean. Getting her to notice him was another matter.

He called and waved. "Gwen?"

Nothing. He tried being louder. "Gwen!"

But she kept walking.

Huh. How many times have I done that to people myself?

Not giving up, he trotted up next to her. "Gwendy,

what's wrong? Are you too miffed to even talk?"

She looked up. Her pale face held no anger, only vague surprise. "Peter. I'm not, not right now anyway. I was so busy thinking about what happened to my dad last night, I didn't even hear you."

"Your dad? Is he all right?"

As he walked her into the college dive, she described the attack. With every word, his muscles grew tighter and his heartbeat sped up. Captain Stacy had treated him like a son. Worse, Gwen was involved.

If she'd been hurt because of my carelessness...

She was still shaking. "Dad's trying to brush it all off. He keeps insisting the doctor ordered bed rest for him just to calm *me* down. He didn't earn all those medals sitting behind a desk, but he's not as young as he used to be."

I knew the tablet was dangerous. If I'd only followed Captain Stacy, I could have done something!

"Hey, beauty and the bookworm!"

The deep timbre of the familiar voice pulled Peter back into the present. Across the café, Flash Thompson rose from his table and headed toward them. Between the self-assured gait and his pristine military uniform, he looked like sunlight against the gray day.

Arrogant, annoying sunlight. The kind that gives you a headache.

Ignoring Peter, Thompson fixed on the young woman at his side. "Gwen! I *hoped* you'd come by here. Man, are you a sight for these eyes."

Brightening, she leapt up and pressed her lips

hard against Flash's cheek. "Soldier-boy! Why don't you tell a girl when you're stateside for leave?

Thompson's eyes twinkled. "How come you don't write me more often?"

"I thought Mary Jane was taking care of that department. And…" Still beaming, she turned toward Peter. "I've been seeing a lot of Mr. Parker here."

Flash barely gave him a glance. "Have the pickings been *that* slim since I've been gone?"

Peter knew it was idle ribbing, but he was already tense. He rose to his feet, ready for a fight.

"I thought the Army had changed you. Last I saw you, I swore you were almost human. But if you think that outfit gives you the right to treat me—"

Chuckling, Flash pointed a dismissive thumb at the door. "Screw off, brainiac! When I need a civilian, I'll ask for one."

"This isn't high school anymore," Peter shot back. "I'm not going to let you put me down in front of Gwen—"

Gwen's hand flashed in front of his face. "Peter! What's gotten into you? He was only kidding!"

The good cheer vanished from Thompson's face. "Maybe I'm the one who was wrong about *you*. Maybe you're still the same uptight nerd I always thought you were."

But Flash's sneer was lacking its old haughtiness. He actually looked a little hurt, so Peter lowered his hands. "Okay, maybe I overreacted. But no one likes to see some other guy make a play for his girl."

Flash backed away. "Look, pal, any hetero-normative guy that doesn't make a play for her is ready for embalming. But don't let me interrupt. I'll bounce. Thanks for the warm welcome."

As soon as his sharp uniform disappeared in the rain, an abject Peter turned to Gwen. "I…I was all fired up after hearing what happened to you. I'm sorry…"

Her anger was back in full force. "You should be. For a boy who's always missing when there's trouble, it's strange how hostile you can be to a man who's been in combat!"

She turned her back and headed out, too. The Coffee Bean's brass shop bell gave a little tinkle as the door closed.

Peter slumped into his chair.

I heard her. I'm a boy, he's a man. I'm a coward, he's selfless. If I'm being honest, I wasn't just revved up from hearing about last night. I was jealous, afraid of losing Gwen to Flash. And stupid rants like that are exactly what'll drive her away.

THE PRECINCT'S basement windows provided at least a little natural light. With the ceiling fixtures sparse, Wesley found himself in the shadow of the dozen guards present since Mr. Fisk's escape.

New York State required an arraignment within 24 hours of arrest. If they were too busy to get to him before that, it could provide grounds for his release.

But Wesley's heart sank as the cell door opened with a half hour to spare.

Instead of a judge, though, he was taken to a particularly severe-looking officer behind a security window. She gave him his things and asked him to sign for them.

"I'm being released? What is this, some trick? Are you planning to have me followed?"

The woman gave him a world-weary look. "I wouldn't know. They don't let me in the room where the tricks get planned. I hear it's hidden in the sewers with the mole men."

Wesley sniffed. "I don't appreciate the sarcasm."

"I don't care. Door's behind you. Unless you'd like to go back to holding?"

He stiffened, grabbed the thick envelope awkwardly stuffed with his belt, wallet, and sundry personal items, and headed out. At the front entrance, his hands full, he waited for another officer to hold the door for him, but the man just laughed. Tucking the envelope under one arm, Wesley shoved the old oak slab open himself and stepped into the pouring rain.

A limo was parked at the curb. A chauffeur in full regalia trotted up and flashed open an umbrella over his head. "May I take your things?"

Increasingly suspicious, Wesley refused both the offer of help and the umbrella. Though the seconds it took him to reach the limo left him soaked, he hesitated to enter. Instead, he leaned down for a look at the occupant.

"Caesar Cicero? What is this about?"

"Why don't you get out of the rain so we can talk more comfortably?"

Wesley didn't move. Cicero rolled his eyes.

"You know that thing they always say in the movies, about how if I wanted you dead, you would be already? Hey, you've probably said it yourself, right? Get in."

Once the door closed, the rush of rain disappeared, leaving only the drip-drip-drip of the water falling off Wesley onto the plush leather seats.

Cicero looked out his window. "Funny how fast things change. One minute your friend's leaving you to rot in jail, the next your enemy's calling in favors to get you out."

Wesley did his best not to squirm, but every movement of his damp clothes squeaked against the leather. "If you think I'll tell you anything about Mr. Fisk, you're sadly mistaken."

Barely listening, Cicero buffed his nails against his coat's fur lapel. "Yeah, yeah. I get it. You're not gonna leave your man until the day you die. Nice song. Good for you. Don't sweat it. These days there are probably a few things I could tell *you* about Wilson Fisk. But this ain't about him or his dying operation. It's about an old rock someone swiped from the Exhibition Hall."

Wesley's eyes widened. "The tablet?"

Cicero smiled. "You'd be lousy at poker, you know that? We should play some time. Anyway, yeah. It's ours now."

Tired, disoriented, Wesley let his shoulders slump. "It's worthless to you. You have no idea what it means."

"Worthless, priceless, I hear all kinds of things. Fact is, you don't know what it says, either. That's the thing about the really good secrets. They're secret." The attorney tapped the partition. The limo pulled so smoothly into traffic, Wesley barely realized they were moving.

"What I do know is that the very thought of figuring out that secret makes your geekhood tremble. How do I know? Because we have access to all the Kingpin's servers. Every document, every email, no matter how private—yours included."

Cicero tossed a printout into his lap. As Wesley read, his hair dripped onto the paper. Cicero waited for him to finish, rubbing a stubby index finger adorned with a gaudy ruby ring.

"Get the picture?"

Slack-jawed, Wesley nodded.

Smiling, Cicero nudged him playfully. "Good. Denial can be a mother. Personally, I think it's a waste of time, but I don't gotta tell you what it's like indulging a boss's eccentricities, do I? *Marone a mi*, the things I could say about that fossil." His wide face went stone-cold sober. "But I won't. Not ever. I'm not only loyal, I'm on the winning team—something you and I do *not* have in common. I can prove to you a dozen different ways there's nothing left for you to betray. The Kingpin is over. On the other hand, here's your big chance to translate that stone."

Reaching an oddly ominous Gothic Revival skyscraper, the driver took a sharp right. Just before the limo disappeared into its private garage, Wesley recognized the Galby building. They came to a gentle halt before an elevator.

"If I refuse?"

"Then you die—which, sure, we all have to do eventually. But in your case, you die without solving the puzzle that's been eating at you."

This time, the driver was less than polite. He yanked Wesley from the car and pulled him to his feet. Cicero reached up to straighten Wesley's collar and pat him on the cheek.

"We're not barbarians. You don't have to decide right now. The elevator ride's a good 30 seconds."

The elevator was as smooth as the limo; without windows it was impossible to tell whether it was moving at all. Trapped in the small confines, Wesley's nostrils flared at Cicero's cologne.

The Maggia attorney nudged him again. "If it helps, tell yourself that if you play along, you can still somehow turn the tables and help out your old boss. Dead, you're no good to anybody."

Wesley had thought Cicero's gruff mob-speak indicated a second-rate intellect, but now he knew it was a facade. The man was a master manipulator. Wesley *had* been thinking along similar lines.

The doors opened. Cicero swept his arm like a maître d' showing a diner to his seat.

"And hey, if you live, let's have that poker game sometime."

The office was so large, its shadows held more than a few somber, silent guards. A mahogany desk stood, tastefully lit, at the far end of the room. Idly, Wesley reflected that it would make a perfect replacement for the original Capone desk destroyed in Mr. Fisk's gym.

Behind it sat another original: Silvio Manfredi, last of the old-time Maggia leaders. He was likewise carefully maintained, but with less success. His skin tone nearly matched his gray suit. The shirt and tie, clearly meant to complement his blue eyes, brought out their jaundiced yellow instead. The trimmed, perfectly combed white hair made him look like a corpse about to be laid to rest.

In fact, Wesley wasn't quite sure the man *was* alive. The body was motionless. Then Manfredi blinked. His eyes focused on Cicero, who deferentially removed his hat. When Manfredi blinked again, he was looking at Wesley.

Silvermane flicked a finger at his second-in-command. "He thinks I'm a doddering old fool for bringing the Kingpin's pawn to our headquarters. But he's also hoping it'll make me look stupid, so he can move in. I can smell it on him—every foul, treacherous thought."

Cicero's lips twitched. "Not even you can talk to me like that."

Silvermane either ignored him or hadn't heard. "On your way out, tell Marko to come in."

Cicero kept sneering as he exited, leaving the door open. As they waited, Wesley realized his back still felt damp, but a stream of hot air in front of him had already dried the rain on his face. The lights weren't only for illumination—they were there to keep the old man warm.

A moment later, someone nearly as wide as Wilson Fisk, but taller, appeared in the hall. As he entered the office, he had to duck to avoid hitting his head on the door frame.

Manfredi pointed at the giant. "I like big dogs. The dumber the better. A pat on the head and they'll defend you to the death."

Wesley wasn't sure who Silvermane was talking to, or what point there was in insulting his own men. Was it dementia? But the newcomer didn't seem to mind. If anything, he looked happy he'd been allowed into the office.

"You got it, Marko?"

"Yes, Mr. Silvermane." The man held up the tablet, half-wrapped in an old cloth.

"Good boy. I knew you wouldn't fail me."

Marko placed the tablet on the desk with a thud that made Wesley wince. Thankfully, it didn't seem damaged.

"Go on, take a closer look. Make sure it's genuine."

As if from nowhere, one of the mob soldiers in the shadows brought out a chair and handed Wesley a high-powered magnifying glass. To his later embarrassment, Wesley's every thought of Wilson Fisk vanished as he scrutinized the finely chiseled glyphs.

"It's real. I'd know it anywhere."

As soon as he said it, he felt guilty. For the first time, he was confused about his loyalties. However sarcastically Cicero's advice had been offered, he was correct: Wesley would be no good to the Kingpin dead. And here was the tablet, in his hands.

Silvermane gave a faint smile. "All those other translators thought it was a recipe, like from a cookbook. But you think it's a chemical formula."

"That's my theory."

Manfredi's eyes had a faraway look, as if his spirit was barely tethered to his body. As he spoke, they grew more distant. "No. Not a theory. Don't ask me how I know, but it's true."

"You understand, there's not much I can do on my own."

Silvermane nodded. "I know. You wanted that biochemist to help with the translation—Dr. Curtis Connors. He'll be here soon, too."

o———o

GEORGE Stacy lay propped up in his big wood-frame bed, faded blue pajamas mostly covered by thick blankets, as his daughter arranged pillows of various sizes. Spider-Man watched from a branch outside. He was close enough to the slightly open window to see and hear everything without being seen himself.

Eavesdropping made him feel guilty, but shocking Gwen with his sudden costumed appearance was out of the question, so he'd have to wait until she left. He'd hurt her enough already.

The captain looked torn between allowing his eager daughter to ease her worries, or begging her to stop fussing.

"I'm fine, Gwen, really, good as new."

She kept arranging the pillows—so tenderly, it made Peter's heart ache.

"Are you sure? Can I bring you anything?"

He put a hand on her wrist. "No, thanks, honey, really."

She patted the hand. "Okay, but if you want something, just bellow, promise?" She paused. "Um… did Peter call on the landline?"

Stacy appeared delighted to have the subject shift away from his health—but Spider-Man's gut twisted. "No. Why? Were you expecting him?"

"I did think…ah, he's not the only boy in the world."

Exactly. There's handsome Flash Thompson, for instance.

"Then why do your eyes glow whenever you mention him?"

She gently slapped her father's shoulder. "Could you stop being a detective for a minute? I'm just worried he's still angry about his run-in with Flash yesterday."

Me? Really? I figured she'd *still be angry with* me.

"Then why don't you call him?"

"Because I'm still angry with him."

There it is. Who wouldn't be?

"I won't pretend to understand that, but as I've said before, my dear, he couldn't make you so angry if you didn't—"

Cutting him off, she whirled to leave. "Sorry, homework's waiting."

The door closed. Stacy waited a few moments, then looked at the window. "She's gone, if you'd care to come in, son."

Gut-knot tightening, Spider-Man sheepishly pulled up the sash and perched on the sill. "How'd you…?"

He seemed bemused. "I've lived here long enough to have a pretty good idea how the shadows outside my own window usually behave."

"I'm sorry I wasn't here last night. Are you okay?"

Stacy sighed. "If you're here about my health, a get-well card would have sufficed. I'd rather not deal with uninvited guests two nights in a row."

"Sorry. Sorry."

"So you said. Anything else?"

"I want to track down the tablet. Is there anything you can tell me about who took it?"

Stacy wrinkled his brow. "Just because I don't think you're as bad as the press makes you out to be, doesn't mean I feel comfortable telling you about an ongoing investigation." He gave off a second sigh. "It was taken by Man Mountain Marko, a Maggia enforcer."

"Man Mountain? So I guess he's big, huh?" Seeing Stacy's stony face, he went on. "Uh, why is the Maggia interested?"

"I don't know, but there's more. Earlier today we

received word from Florida that a Dr. Curt Connors and his family were abducted by known…"

Doc Connors?

Without waiting for Stacy to finish, Spider-Man tumbled backwards into the night, leaving Stacy to call out at his back:

"You know the name? Is there something the police need to know, son?"

Even if I wanted to, I couldn't tell him that Connors is also the Lizard. If I hadn't trapped the doc in a refrigerator car, where the low temps made his primal side go dormant, he'd still be wandering the Everglades, eating small mammals and plotting the rise of reptiles to their "rightful" place at the top of the food chain.

What does the Maggia want with him?

TEN

WHAT have you done with Martha and Billy?" Dr. Curt Connors asked.

Something ached beneath the skin and cauterized muscle of the rounded stub that had once been his right arm. To someone else, it would be a phantom pain, a stray twinge. To him, it was a warning.

The old man who was obviously in charge said nothing, letting the squat one in the gaudy tie—Cicero—answer instead.

"Nothing yet, aside from tying them up a little for their own safety. That boy of yours is a real firecracker."

The thought of his family bound and gagged made the pain shoot across his arm so sharply he stumbled. Part of his brain was already hewing to more primal urges. He felt torn between using his remaining hand to rub the blunted limb, or to reach out and steady himself.

Realizing he wasn't faking, his captors looked at each other.

Cicero took Connors' elbow and steered him to the edge of the desk where he could support himself.

Their aged leader flicked a finger, and Connors heard the sound of pouring liquid.

"War wound acting up?"

These gangsters thought their research told them everything they needed to know about him. They had known enough to find his remote Everglades home, enough to grab his wife and child first, and to threaten their lives to ensure his cooperation.

But they had no idea how dangerous he could be.

The mortar attack that had destroyed Connors' arm had also made him determined to find a way to heal himself, as well as millions of other amputees. He thought he'd found the key in the regenerative abilities of certain lizards. Green anoles, salamanders, geckoes, and chameleons could lose their prehensile tails and regrow them. Why wouldn't the right gene therapy allow humans to do the same? But the experimental serum had transformed him, embedding his brain with ancient predatory instincts that saw other beings purely as a food source.

Maybe next time he should try working with white mice, like everyone else.

Since his capture, a battle had been playing out in his heart and mind. The primal need to save his wife and child struggled against the knowledge that anything he tried could leave them dead. Once the private jet had brought them all to New York, their captors had separated them. No longer being able to see Martha or Billy weakened his reason as much as it fed his rage.

As a result, he found himself caring less and less whether the kidnappers lived or died. The thought that it might be at his own hands brought a sickening sense of relish.

Another sign of the change.

An expensive brandy snifter was set down before him. As they gave him time to drink, he again tried to convince his darker side that, as satisfying as a moment's revenge might be, it could also seal his family's fate.

Even *it*, even the reptile, understood family. For now, it let him maintain control.

"Finished with your drink? Good."

The glass was removed from his hand.

"Listen carefully. You're a veteran, and a doctor. I respect that. So to be clear, you're not here to do anything illegal, okay? You're here to save a life—mine. Do that, nobody gets hurt. Heck, I'll drop you all off anywhere you want—home, Disneyland, whatever—along with a big fat check to use for whatever weird alligator research you like. Eh? That make you feel better?"

Something glinted in the old man's eyes. The reptile found it familiar. Any words this man used, any promises he made, would always hold a distant second to fulfilling his own desires. Complex mammalian communities based on empathy and cooperation were alien to him.

Connors could never trust Silvermane to let his family live. But he *could* trust him to keep them alive until he got what he wanted.

So he nodded.

"Good. Marko, take him to Wesley in the lab."

But the creature was never completely gone. When the giant placed a heavy hand on his shoulder, it stirred. "I want to see my family first."

Marko grabbed Connors by the lapels. The giant's instincts were more recognizably primate in nature.

"You do what Mr. Silvermane, says *when* he says it."

The speed with which the previously motionless Silvermane rose impressed the reptilian part of Connors' mind.

"Didn't you hear anything I just said about respect?"

Silvermane slapped the giant, over and over, until he released the doctor. Eyeing the floor in submission, Marko huffed and touched his reddened cheeks.

"You got no reason to shame me like that, Mr. Silvermane."

Despite his words, the tone was apologetic.

Silvermane stepped back. He was huffing and unsteady himself. His hands groped behind him, reaching for the desk. "No one gives orders except me. Don't ever…"

The coughing that followed brought a pinkish flush to his face that appeared every bit as unhealthy as the gray it had replaced. Silvermane grasped at his chest.

Meanwhile, Cicero looked like a gambler watching his horse pull into the lead. Noticing Connors was watching, he nodded toward his boss and whispered, "You got more reason to hope he makes it than I do."

Understanding, Connors rushed over, reaching

for Silvermane's neck to take his carotid pulse. The mob boss slapped the hand away.

"I'm fine. Just a spell. It's passing." Catching his breath, Silvermane patted the worried Marko. "Easy, kid. We'll speak no more of this."

Cicero took Connors' elbow a second time and pulled him toward an open door. There was a hallway and stairs beyond.

"The lab has a closed-circuit monitor. Every hour you work, you see your family for a minute."

o———————————o

ROBBIE Robertson circled his seated son, pausing occasionally to lean against the bookshelf, window frame, or wall of his office.

"You want to be an activist, great. I'll support you to the bitter end. But the world's stuffed with ignorance, and education's the only solution. Quit school, and you're a soldier unarmed."

A dour Randy kept his hands in his lap. "I get what you're saying. But so many people of color put their trust in the system and get screwed, I don't see how I can fight it *and* let it indoctrinate me at the same time."

"Indoctrinate? You make college sound like a POW camp. I've fought injustice my whole life, with my voice and my work. School didn't stop me—it helped."

Randy twisted his head, struggling for the right words. "How much of a voice do you really have when you're working for that…"

A familiar scream shattered the private bubble.

"ROBERTSON! Where's Robertson?"

Randy threw up his hands. "Speak of the devil."

Hearing the muffled sound of an applauding staff, Robbie relaxed. "Don't worry. It's his first day back. He'll have to make it through a lot of congratulating employees before he gets here. Who knows? It might put him in a better mood."

Without so much as a knock, the door flew open. Jonah stood there in his full glory, bits of confetti clinging to his hair and overcoat.

Robertson sighed. "Or not. Welcome back, Jonah, I—"

"You! There you are, you quisling, you Benedict Arnold!" The hospital rest had apparently done Jameson some good. He brandished the latest edition with the vigor of a much younger man. "The second my back is turned, you make a hero out of Spider-Man!"

Robbie grimaced. "Simmer down, Jonah. I didn't *make* him anything. Those pictures tell the story, and we're supposed to report the truth, right?"

"Wrong! Who taught you journalism?" Jameson crumpled the paper and shook it at Robertson. "It's about the angle, the editorial voice! You know how the *Bugle* feels about that web-slinging weasel. You know how *I* feel about him!"

Randy watched intently as his father responded.

"Jonah, it's your paper. You can write all the editorials you want—on the editorial page. But the news is my department. I call them as I see them."

Jameson's face puffed and twisted. "You think I

can't fire you for this? You think I won't?"

Randy leaned forward in his seat.

Robbie calmly crossed his arms. "You won't have to. If you want reality distorted to suit some paranoid vendetta, I'll quit."

Jameson shuddered. His expression twitched from one extreme to another. "Wait, wait, wait! Hold on a minute! Quit? What are you talking about, quit? Of course it's your news page. I don't know what's gotten into this place. Used to be a man could enjoy blowing his top once in a while. Fine. I accept your apology."

"My what?"

But Jameson was already closing the door on his way out. "I'm too gentle, too sensitive for all of this!"

Once it was clear he wasn't immediately returning, Randy grinned. "Does he *really* think you apologized?"

Robertson waved his hand. "Nah. But he'll never say so. The important thing is that the news this paper prints is as close to the truth as I can make it."

Randy was impressed. "You stood up to him. You were really going to quit."

His father thought about it, then nodded. "I would have, but I also know the man well enough to realize it wouldn't come to that. Sure, he experiences things from a certain perspective, but check out his editorial on white privilege last month. Jameson's no racist—just a blowhard with a very weird grudge against Spider-Man. You want to be an effective force, you have to recognize who the real enemies are."

"Okay, I get it. I'll stay at ESU, if only so I can learn

how to win an argument with someone like Jameson."

Robbie slapped his son's back. "That'll take you all the way through grad school."

———o———————o———

HANGING around outside the window, Spider-Man shifted position before they could spot him.

Guess Randy's taking the "patience" lesson to heart. Wonder if I'll ever be able to do the same.

He made his way along the ledge until he had a view of the open workspace. A grumpy Jameson was surrounded by smiling staff. Whenever it looked like he might scream for everyone to get back to work, Betty Brant and Ned Leeds threw more confetti on him. For a second, Peter thought he caught the publisher trying not to smile.

That man could start an argument in an empty house, but I am glad to see him. Still, a gander at Jameson's sour face isn't why I'm here. I've never tangled with the Maggia before, so I wasted the night looking for their headquarters. Heck, the only member I know by name is Silvermane. But there's nothing like getting the news in advance. Here's hoping it'll give me some ideas.

As the crowd focused on their beloved leader, Spider-Man slid open the window and snatched a printout of the latest edition. Suspended from a flagpole, he flipped through, pausing at a small piece slotted for page two.

So, alleged Maggia attorney Caesar "Big C" Cicero

had Fisk's right-hand man released, huh? That's got to have something to do with the tablet. And look! They mention the fancy address of Cicero's law offices.

He swung from building to building, 30 stories up, heading for the Midtown location a few skyscraper-lined blocks away. This time, once he counted the floors, finding the office was easy—especially when he spotted the attorney grabbing the same coat and hat he'd worn in the *Bugle* photo.

I'm in luck for a change. Another few seconds and I'd have missed him.

Cicero's back to him, Spider-Man couldn't resist flashing his spider-signal on the wall. Cicero whirled. Despite the man's thick brow, his eyes grew large. "Spider-Man!"

Peter opened the casement window and hopped inside. "Glad you noticed so fast. I'm never sure when the batteries in this thing will go dead. You must be the Big C. No offense, but I wish the Maggia would be consistent about the nicknames. If the Big C's ironic, shouldn't it be Molehill Marko?"

"What do you want?"

Usually even the Maggia's street thugs got all defiant when confronted—but Cicero was shaken. Thinking he could use that to his advantage, Spider-Man quickly closed the distance between them. The attorney looked ready to leap out of his coat *and* his skin.

"Just a little conversation. All that web-slinging can make a fellow lonely. How about answering a few questions, like why'd you have Wesley released?"

Cicero straightened, but couldn't stop shaking. "That falls under client-attorney privilege."

Spider-Man moved forward. Cicero backed up, feeling his way along the bookcases. "Seriously, do I look like a court of law? But okay, how about you tell me how the tablet fits in—or, better yet, where the Maggia's HQ is at?"

Caesar managed a sneer. "If I did know, you think I'd be stupid enough to betray the Maggia?"

Spider-Man stared into his beady eyes. "Yes, yes I do."

A small click made him look down. Cicero's finger was on a button hidden beneath one of the shelves. Knowing his spider-sense would have warned him if the threat was imminent, he lifted the attorney off the ground by his fur lapels.

"Why'd you have to go and do that? Now you have to tell me what I want to know even faster!"

Cicero squirmed. "I told you, I'm not blabbing."

Then his spider-sense *did* prickle, nice and harsh. Letting go of the attorney, he turned just as a panel on the opposite wall slid open. It revealed a hidden passage along with the silhouettes of the armed men inside it.

One shouted, "Take cover, Big C. We've got enough muscle to nail him."

Cicero dove, giving them a clearer shot. "Talk is cheap. Do it!"

By the time the first bullets were fired, Spider-Man was bounding off the wall and headed for the attackers. How many were there—four? Five? A bullet shattered the window.

"What's he even doing here?"

"Who cares? We could be the guys who whacked Spider-Man!"

They were eager, but not complete amateurs. Two came forward to flank him while the others stayed back and kept firing. Fingertips securing him to the plasterboard, Spider-Man kicked one advancing mobster into the other.

Before he could take out the trio at the door, they split up. Landing in front of the nearest mobster, he balled up his fist.

"How'd he know we're keeping that Connors dame and her brat here?"

Spider-Man stopped mid-blow. "Wait, what? You have Doc Connors' family *here?*"

Cicero face-palmed. "Idiot! He *didn't* know until you told him!"

No wonder he was so antsy!

Desperate to make up for his mistake, the thug fired haphazardly, spraying the room with bullets. Spider-Man snagged a heavy law book with his webbing and used it to knock the gun away.

Spider-sense tingling, he leapt as a heavy chair cracked the wall beside him. Wrapping his legs around the neck of the bruiser who'd thrown it, Spidey twisted and took him down.

"Pay attention, boys. I think they call that a standing head-scissor!"

More mob-soldiers entered from the passageway, filling the office. Cicero climbed out from under his desk and used them as cover. Holding his fur-lined hat to his head, he sprinted into the secret corridor. A web took down three more gunmen, but by then the hidden panel was closing.

Dammit! I can't let him get away.

Twirling sideways through the air, Spider-Man body-blocked two men, then grabbed another's shooting arm and threw him at the group still on their feet. That bought him enough time to tear open the fake wall and leap into the narrow space beyond.

At the base of a long staircase, a steel door was descending from the ceiling to seal the path. Before it could close, Spider-Man dove down the stairs and managed to get his fingers under the lip. His strength was barely enough to keep the heavy metal from breaking his bones.

Another fine bit of advice from Uncle Ben. Lift with your knees!

Squatting, Spider-Man held on to the door and straightened his legs. Hidden gears groaned. After several grueling seconds, the door's mechanisms snapped, allowing him to raise the door with ease. Beyond, there were more stairs leading down—lots of them, with landings every 15 feet. Remembering how high the office was, he guessed there were 30 stories' worth.

For speed, he took to the wall. His flexible joints allowed him to pull with his clinging hands, push his legs ahead beneath his chest, then pull again, this time with his feet, propelling himself faster and faster downward. A fleeting shadow ahead told him he was catching up to Cicero.

Then a plaintive cry made him stop: "Help! Help us, please!"

"Mrs. Connors?"

Had Cicero let them go to ensure his own escape? Pivoting back, Spider-Man spotted the digital recorder on the previous landing—and realized the trick. The delay had cost seconds, but that was more than enough to change the course of lives. He dropped down from the final landing, where the stairs ended in a small hallway.

Ahead, he heard an engine rev and a garage door clanking open. Not wanting to repeat his mistake with the Kingpin, he tugged a spider-tracer from his belt. Barreling along, he reached a small private garage just as a dark sedan, tires screeching, headed for the street.

Still running, he hurled the tracer.

Before he could see whether it reached his target, his spider-sense flared—but there was no place to go. Multiple bombs erupted in the hall and the garage, their brutal concussive force pushing him four ways at once. Heat and flame followed. He danced as best he could among the raining chunks of concrete until a heavy slab connected, nearly taking him down. He was sure his shoulder was dislocated, a few ribs cracked.

Having narrowly missed being buried, he pushed through the wreckage into a smoky hollow. As far as he could tell, no one else had been caught in the blast.

All that was left of the private garage was a smoldering crater. Wounded, his entire nervous system screaming, he barely noticed the soft tingling beneath the pain, telling him something else had survived the explosion.

Ten feet away, on a bit of undamaged concrete, the small red light on his spider-tracer blinked.

Yep. Lost him.

ELEVEN

WHEN Peter Parker woke, the totality of his heart and mind was consumed by one thing: pain.

Am I strong? Sure. Fast? Better believe it. Drop a half-ton of concrete on me, though, and I'm definitely going to hurt in the morning.

It is morning, isn't it?

Sunlight seeped around the edges of the closed shade, confirming it was daytime. But for all he knew, it could be afternoon already. He had a vague half-memory of Harry saying goodbye on his way out, but that might have been hours ago.

At least he could move, if not quite stand. His joints were stiff as a board.

He tried some stretches, but that only heightened his awareness of the bruises. Thinking a warm shower might soothe him, he crawled into the bathroom. The rush of water against his cuts nearly made him scream.

Agh! Why couldn't my spider-sense warn me about that?

After half an hour he was able to hobble like an old man. At least he was on his feet.

Doc Connors and his family were out there somewhere, but there wasn't a lot Peter could do about it in his current condition, even if he knew where they were.

He was getting better, though, not worse. He looked at the clock: 9:17 a.m. Maybe by nightfall? Meanwhile, since Captain Stacy had told him about the kidnappings, he could be sure the police were on the lookout for the Connors family.

May as well limp over to a class or two. I just hope the professors don't call on me—if they remember who I am.

Walking was a challenge, so he caught a bus. As he shuffled across the plaza, he kept his head down, his shoulders scrunched. Josh and Randy were hanging with friends on the steps of the Physical Sciences building. He pretended he didn't see them, earning a dismissive glare from Kittering.

"What? You too good for us?"

Randy defended him. "Easy, Josh. Just because you say jump doesn't mean everyone has to ask how high."

Kittling chuckled. "Whoa, what did the newbie eat for breakfast? Sticking up for a friend, huh? Good for you."

Peter muttered hello, but kept his eyes focused on the stairs. He was about halfway up when a pair of familiar sneakers stopped in front of him.

"Gwen?"

Cocking her leg to put one foot on a higher step, she started talking, but his enfeebled mind was racing too fast for him to pay attention. He felt like the proverbial deer in the headlights.

When was the last time I saw her? No, when was the last time I saw her as Peter Parker? *Have I even texted her since she told me about the attack on her dad? It's hard enough keeping track when I'm healthy. What if I muddle things, repeat something I heard when I was eavesdropping as Spider-Man?*

"Peter! Did you hear a word I said?"

His mouth dropped open.

Sheesh! No, I didn't! Did she just break up with me? Did she want to go to a movie? Did she say she was engaged to someone else?

He tried to raise his hands in surrender, but it hurt too much. "Gwen, please, I'm so sorry. I'm totally exhausted. I shouldn't even really be out."

She was clearly still annoyed, but she reached out to steady him.

Our relationship. She wants to talk about our relationship. That must be it, right?

"I know we need to talk. Can we do it a little later, when my last class gets out at four?"

She hesitated. "I can't. I'll be busy."

Peter blinked. "Busy?"

"If you must know, I'm running an errand for my father."

"Sorry, I didn't mean…is tomorrow okay? Pick a time."

She nodded. "Lunch."

He was relieved when she walked off, but also a little hurt.

Something's really bothering her.

He limped onward, hoping to make it to the back row of the lecture hall without further incident. He nearly moaned out loud when Harry came running up.

"Roommate! I was hoping to see you!"

He tried to rally. "Hi, Harry."

"'Hi, Harry'? That the best you've got for a friend sporting a new mustache?"

Peter frowned at the vaguely visible facial hair. "Is that new?

It was an honest question. Judging from Harry's reaction, however, this was not the time for honesty.

"Geez," Harry said. "Now I know how MJ feels if I don't notice when she gets her hair done."

He walked off in a huff.

Pausing at the door to the lecture hall, Peter looked around, wondering whether there was anyone left he hadn't offended yet—or, for that matter, whether there was anyone else he *knew*. He didn't even realize he was blocking the way in until someone shouldered by. The slight contact elicited spasms of pain.

Oh, man! Did my parents accidentally offend an evil sorcerer or something?

o———o

WESLEY admired how quickly and completely the Maggia had set up the half-lab, half-library—until it occurred to him they'd probably followed his own notes after hacking his computer.

In any event, the new, state-of-the-art 3D

imaging yielded immediate results. All known forms of writing were two-dimensional, but, as the experts had already discovered, the meaning of the tablet's symbols changed based on regular variations in their carved depth.

On the other hand, while those experts had guessed that the table contained some type of instructions, they'd focused on distinguishing a 'recipe' from the rest of the prose by searching for symbols based on natural ingredients—herbs and so on. Wesley reasoned that the carvers had been far more sophisticated, and the symbols they should be searching for were closer to chemical notation: sodium and chlorine as opposed to salt, a formula as opposed to a recipe. In that case, a biochemist might have an easier time making the distinction. Hence the presence of Dr. Connors.

Indeed, they'd already become the first people to sort a formula from the surrounding prose. Unfortunately, that wasn't the same as *understanding* the formula. Since that initial breakthrough, they'd run into a dozen dead ends.

Wesley was so fascinated, he tended to forget the Maggia's threats. Not Connors. The fate of the man's family weighed so heavily, it acted only as a distraction.

Was it Samuel Johnson who said that when a man knows he is to be hanged, it concentrates the mind wonderfully? Well, he was wrong about my unwilling partner, at least.

To relax, Wesley had taken to flipping a coin and

catching it, something he'd seen George Sanders do in an old movie. Connors, though, kept clenching his fists and throwing a stylus against the wall.

Wesley caught the coin. "You do realize we've made more progress in the last few hours than others have made in centuries?"

Connors grimaced. "Yes, but it's not enough, is it? I couldn't run any tests, so I only have his appearance and that attack to go by—but if his heart's as frail as I suspect, it could kill him any minute. Even if Silvermane means to keep his word, which I doubt, he could die long before we finish."

The information left Wesley feeling torn. Silvermane's death would leave the Maggia in disarray, at least temporarily. On the one hand, it could be just the opportunity Mr. Fisk needed. On the other, it could rob Wesley of both his life and the chance to solve the great mystery.

Connors picked up the stylus and used it to rotate the wall-projected images of the chemical symbols they'd discovered. "Even now that we're just looking at the formula, there are still too many variables. Some could be components, some proportions, some the relationships between ingredients."

When Wesley flipped the coin again, Connors watched it twirl. Eyes wide, the biochemist looked back at the projection. A hooked bar on a symbol marked it as part of the formula. But each symbol also contained a curve in various positions. Connors went from one symbol to the next, tracing the different curves: straight, slanted, and horizontal.

Wesley realized what Connors was thinking before the man spoke.

"The curves appear in *all* the symbols, prose or chemical, in about twenty variations. In the formula, though, there are only three, so they could relate to our variables: ingredient, amount, and relationship. No one noticed before because they were never looking *only* at the formula. I think we've got it!"

○━━━━━━━━━●━━━━━━━━━○

WHEN Cicero and his hostages finally reached the Galby building, he planned to secure them and take a few minutes for himself. The long night hadn't even allowed for a bathroom break. But the instant Silvermane learned they were here, he demanded they all be brought straight to his office. Like a good soldier, Cicero obeyed.

As he stepped out of the crowded elevator, his men shoved the hooded, cuffed mother and child along behind him. Silvermane put his gnarled fists to the desk, pushed himself to standing, and walked over to stare down at Cicero.

"What do you mean by bringing them to our headquarters without informing me?"

Cicero knew that Silvermane was towering over him for show, to accentuate their difference in height and demonstrate that pack-animal superiority. But Cicero was tired and stressed. What should have sounded like a plea came out more like a command.

"Take it easy!"

Recognizing his mistake, he toned himself down. "Mr. Manfredi, Spider-Man showed up at my office. I had to make a judgment call."

The excuse only made things worse. Silvermane pounded the desk. "Spider-Man? He won't stop until he finds them. You've just brought him to our doorstep!"

We wouldn't be in this mess at all if you would just die already, you senile gorilla.

Cicero rubbed his face with his hand and forced himself to adopt a civil tone. "First off, I couldn't call. This is not the kind of thing we could discuss over the phone. Second, last I saw him, the wall-crawler was buried under rubble. Any luck, he's dead; at worst, he's hurting pretty bad. Third, I just spent the entire night and half the morning driving around Jersey and Connecticut to make sure no one tailed us. I don't see what else I could have done."

At some point Silvermane had stopped listening. His nostrils flared. "You stink."

Cicero couldn't take anymore. "Sorry, but they ain't got showers in the sedan!"

The silence that followed was so complete he could almost hear Silvermane's lips twitch as they curved into a thin smile. "If I needed an excuse to gut your treacherous hide, you just gave it to me. Marko, take this miserable—"

But the man mountain had a hand to his earpiece. "Mr. Silvermane, it's the lab. They've made some kind of progress."

When Silvermane's mouth dropped open, Marko flinched. "Sorry. You said I should I tell you first thing, no matter what you were doing. You said I should interrupt—"

"No, Marko. I'm not angry. I'm thrilled." Shaky on his feet, he waved the giant over to use him as a support. "We must go there at once."

On the way out, Silvermane paused to glare at Cicero. Between the wildly confident look in the mob boss's eyes and his wide, skull-like grin, Cicero briefly worried that the rock really did hold some weird, powerful secret.

Once they were out of sight, he pushed the thought away. *Ah, he's delusional.*

A whimper from Martha Connors reminded him that *someone* in the Maggia should act sane. He turned to his men, who were still hanging back near the private elevator, and gestured at the hostages.

"Find some room to keep them in."

When they hesitated, he screamed. "Do I have to check with the boss on that, too? They're here, okay? We have to keep them somewhere! Do it!"

AT FIRST, Connors thought the lights in the hall outside the lab had gone out. But it was Marko, his large form blocking the doorway. The giant eyed them warily, but stayed mute as he helped Silvermane into the room. The Maggia leader looked even closer to death than when Connors had last seen him.

At the same time, his gray face had a strange new shine—a look of, for lack of a more age-appropriate term, childish eagerness.

"Do you have it?"

Connors hoped Wesley would answer, but the man had quietly shifted to the rear of the lab. Did he trust Connors, as a doctor, to better explain the danger? Or was he avoiding Silvermane's attention at all costs?

Seeing no choice, Connors exhaled. "We've isolated a formula for some sort of elixir. But we have no idea what its intended purpose is, let alone whether it would work. The next stage would be to start some tests, then in a few weeks…"

Silvermane waved a crooked, shaky finger in the air. "What's the tablet say about it?"

With a slight pang of guilt, Connors nodded at his partner. By now, they'd both guessed the reason for the aged mobster's interest in the elixir.

"The prose is not my area of expertise. Wesley?"

Before answering, Wesley cast him an admiring glance, as if to say, *Touché!*

"We haven't had time to complete even a rough translation of the full text, but an accurate answer would require years of research. Aside from the variations in meaning, which are problematic in any translation, there seems to be an entire cosmology buried in the layers of the writing—literally."

Silvermane placed his thumb against his cupped fingers, creating a mocking hand-puppet. "Blah blah

blah! Just tell me if it says something like this."

He tilted his head back, closed his eyes as if entering some sort of trance, and sang:

> *"They tell us that we're born to die*
> *But there's no sense in that—say I.*
> *Those of us who know the truth,*
> *Will drink, drink, the nectar of youth."*

Finished, his impatient essence returned from wherever it had gone.

Confused, Wesley looked to Connors.

Silvermane came forward. "Is it anything like that? Either of you. Is it?"

When neither answered, Marko crossed his arms. "Mr. Silvermane asked a question."

Finally Wesley said, "Yes and no. There are some similarities, but—"

Silvermane's childlike delight returned. "Ha! Get to work. Create that nectar for me—now!"

Connors spoke up. "I can't. I have no idea what these chemicals will do to your body. If it kills you, my family dies. Am I wrong?"

When Silvermane bobbed his head, it didn't seem quite attached to his body. "The hard part's done. I could hire any one of a thousand chemists to follow a formula. But I'm in a hurry, so I'll make your decision easier. Either you create that nectar immediately, or they die *now*. Starting with your son. And, to be clear, you'd better hope it works."

As Marko helped his boss to the door, Connors felt the creature stirring in the back of his mind.

"Silvermane!"

The old man turned back. Connors pointed at Wesley. The thing inside him didn't trust partners—or anyone else, for that matter.

"I have a family at stake. He doesn't. I don't want him here."

Silvermane's eyes slid back and forth between the two, then settled on Connors. "Okay."

o———————————o

WHEN class was over, the rush of jostling elbows and shoulders reminded Peter how much his body still ached. The worst of the pain had subsided enough for him to plod along the jam-packed hall without looking severely disabled. But outside, a late-afternoon chill managed to invade the stiffness remaining in his limbs, even through his clothes.

Web-slinging was still out of the question.

A limbering walk helped, but it was clear from the sharpness in his chest that he had one or two cracked ribs. Fortunately, they only hurt when he stretched a certain way or inhaled too deeply. He was thinking of heading to a clinic to have his side bandaged, but the sight of the Coffee Bean conjured more emotional concerns.

Just as well Gwen's busy today. I'm not up to a serious conversation.

As he passed the window, the sight of a cozy

couple at one of the tables made him sigh.

I still feel like a jerk for the way I blew up at Flash. Did I ever apologize for that?

The waitress was obscuring his view, but he caught a glimpse of platinum blonde hair. Thinking it was a trick of the light, he almost kept walking. But something made him stop and draw closer to the glass.

Wait a minute...

The waitress still concealed their faces, but not the male's crisp dress uniform.

Flash? With Gwen? It's isn't possible.

He pressed closer.

It just isn't!

When the woman lifted her head to thank the waitress, Peter couldn't deny it any longer. It *was* Gwen. She and Flash were alone together, leaning across a small table to look into each other's eyes. He couldn't make out what they were saying, but what did it matter? She'd lied to him.

He turned away and stormed along the sidewalk, not caring where he was going.

So that's how it is, huh?

Time passed. The sounds and sights of the city faded: the bustle of the streets, the passing cars.

I was an idiot to think a girl like Gwen could ever...

The cement at his feet was a blur. He didn't even notice as it darkened with the fading day.

But I thought...she and I...

He hit something, or something hit him. It didn't matter. It gave easily enough.

"Watch where you're going, runt!"

The words felt so far off, they might as well have come from a stereo or TV playing somewhere inside one of the apartments above.

I wouldn't have believed it in a million years.

"He ain't listening! Maybe he needs to have his ears cleaned out."

When the two bruisers came up from behind, Peter's spider-sense tingled, but barely. He swatted at them with the back of his left arm.

"Get out of my way."

The fleshy crunch as they slammed into a brick wall snapped him out of it. The wounded men, barely conscious, helped each other to their feet and ran.

No! Didn't JJJ teach me that lesson? If I'd hit them any harder…

It had all happened so fast, he doubted his attackers would remember much, let alone admit how easily they'd been tossed. Had anyone else seen? Where was he, anyway?

He looked around. Somehow he'd managed to wander onto a dark sidewalk on the Lower East Side. The street was one of the few still abandoned to crack dealers.

It's almost as if I was asking for trouble. No wonder Gwen prefers Flash over a nutjob like me.

Understanding didn't make it hurt any less. And when his cell rang, the betrayal felt as fresh as when he'd first seen it, hours ago.

He picked up, then wished he hadn't. "Yeah?"

"Peter? It's Gwen."

"I know."

"Okay…" She sounded confused by his tone. "You were in pretty bad shape this morning. I wanted to see if you were feeling any better."

"Well, I'm not."

A long pause. "That's it? If something's bugging you, I've got a right to know what it is."

Her voice was tinged with that familiar mix of pain and concern—but for the first time, he no longer believed it was real. "Sure, Gwen, you've got your rights. I hope you enjoy sharing them with Flash Thompson, because it won't be at my expense anymore."

He hung up.

After spending some time with his head in hands, he eyed the street and decided that whatever aches his body still had, it was time for some action.

TWELVE

SPIDER-MAN hurtled between buildings, cracked ribs and all. Pushing the range of his web-line to its limit, he rose to the heavens, plunged back toward the Earth, and then careened higher still. Yes, he feared for the Connors family, but whenever his hurt body threatened to fail him, it was the image of Gwen and Flash that pushed him onward.

Did it matter what gave him the energy? His uncle would have said it did—that indulging anger could only cloud his judgment, get in the way at the wrong time. But Peter couldn't help what he was feeling, and this wasn't the time for a mental-health day. If he vented enough, he hoped the pain would wear out faster and clear his mind.

Who am I kidding? Can I even remember the last time my mind felt clear? Wait, yes I can. It was when I got that check from Robbie. Wow. How long did it take for me to screw things up by attacking Flash? Half a day? Or was Gwen already seeing him?

It was Friday night. He might be heartbroken, but all sorts of New Yorkers were out celebrating—

and some of them would be looking for more than a smoothie. With the police in three states focused on the Kingpin, the odds were that any drug runners or distributors still operating on the streets would be Maggia. All he had to do was find one and break them.

He really felt like breaking something.

As he hunted for an informer, a few false alarms led him to interrupt some private, but perfectly legal, conversations. An hour later, a top-down Porsche packed with upper-crust teens screaming about "hardy partying" looked like a better bet. The driver, oblivious to Spider-Man's presence above and behind them, turned down a quiet side street and tried to hush his rowdy friends. They kept chortling as he pulled up in front of a dingy walk-up and flashed his headlights.

As the web-slinger watched from a fire escape, a scraggily figure on the stoop flicked a cigarette lighter in response.

I bet he's not selling exam answers.

A smaller figure scrabbled out from the trash at the man's feet—a boy, his raggedy clothes too thin for the weather. When the driver handed the kid a roll of bills, Spider-Man landed on the hood of the Porsche and stomped his feet.

"Don't you have homework or something?"

Two of the teens chortled. One held up a phone.

"What the…?" Spider-Man began. "You think we're going to pose for a selfie? Do I *have* to explain?"

The driver, understanding better than his friends, said, "Sorry, sir!" and hit the gas.

Spider-Man leapt up, letting the Porsche peel out beneath him. The boy with the roll of bills was halfway down the block. But Peter wasn't interested in catching *him*. Zipping along the grime-slick building bricks, he grabbed the fleeing dealer by the nape of his jacket and dangled him in the air.

Favoring his hurt ribs, Spider-Man turned his catch around, bringing them nose to nose.

The dealer was roughly Peter's age, his jacket and clothes far warmer than the boy's. "You use children to peddle your poison? What was that kid, eight?"

The answer came easily. "He's hiding from social services while his mom's in rehab. If you think about it, I'm doing him a favor. It's not like I adopted him."

"You miserable…"

Holding on tight, Spider-Man crept backwards up the wall, towing his captive along with him. As the ground receded, the crook kept looking down. Whenever he turned away or closed his eyes, Spider-Man nodded at the ground so he'd look again.

Four stories, five, six…at seven, he asked:

"Where's Maggia headquarters?"

The dealer grimaced. "No way. Web me up for the cops to find, I'll be out in a week."

Spider-Man shook him—just enough to make the seams in his jacket start to tear. The dealer scoffed. "I'm not falling for it. You're no Punisher. You're the *friendly* neighborhood Spider-Man."

Peter shook him a little more. This time, the tearing lowered his body a few inches. "Not when

I'm dealing with murderous scum."

The man squirmed, making his jacket rip all the more. In seconds, he was dangling by threads.

"Fine! It's the Galby building! Right across town. You tell anyone it was me, I'm worse than dead."

"What do I care? I didn't adopt you." Peter gave him a little shove—just enough to drop him into a trash bin thick with kitchen garbage.

The dealer shouted up at him. "Freaking bully! You don't know how good you got it with that mask covering your face."

"Hey, you and I are *not* the same. You're the bad guy,"

He scuttled down, webbed up the thug, and left him for the police to find. Gagged, the dealer couldn't speak, but the terror in his eyes made Peter pause. Okay, yes, he was being a bully, sort of. And sure, maybe he'd enjoyed it a little, but only because the guy deserved it, right? Why not let the lowlife spend some time looking over his shoulder for a hitman?

He scowled at himself. "Don't worry, I'm not in the habit of giving up anyone to crooks, even if they are other crooks. Besides, I couldn't if I wanted to. I don't know who you are, either."

⊶━━━━━━━━━━⊷

THE KINGPIN had assured Vanessa that the beach house was safe. It was bought and maintained by a holding company, so it couldn't possibly be traced back to them. The security system was the best money could buy, the men outside his most trusted.

But every night when he lay in their huge bed, he seemed gripped by the same nightmare. Though the bruises from his battle with Spider-Man had healed, the scars clearly remained. His expressions alternated between terror and rage, his arms and legs flailing hard and fast. At those times, Vanessa had to scramble to get out of his way, for her own safety.

Usually she woke him and tried to calm him. Tonight, though, she let him thrash about, hoping she might come to some decision about him, about *them*. He had lied to her about Richard, torn open her heart, severed the bond of their trust. She watched him breathe, thinking idly of what might happen if his breathing stopped. The very idea made her hate herself. *He'd* lost Richard, too, and when he said he was trying protect her, she believed him. Still, she couldn't help wondering what other horrid truths he might be "protecting" her from.

She slipped on a robe and stepped out on the bedroom balcony—as much to escape his pained moans as to watch the ocean. The sky was clear, the night almost warm. Having been kept up every night by Wilson's kicks and flails, her nerves were frayed. The experience, though, *had* accustomed her to sudden surprises. So when she saw the figure standing in the shadows a few yards away, staring at her, she barely gasped at all.

"Come here," it whispered.

She wanted to scream, to let Wilson know his

nightmares were real. But something held her back, and she let herself be led away, where her husband could not hear.

○———————○

FOR HOURS, Silvio Manfredi watched his captured chemist work. He needed a nap, but feared something more than sleep was waiting—that if he closed his eyes for an instant, he'd never open them again. His failing body felt distant, as if he weren't crumpled in the extra chair Marko had brought to the lab. Instead, he felt halfway around the world, in a place he'd never been, sitting cross-legged on a rocky throne. Below, along a green slope, younger male primates picked their teeth with blades of grass, waiting for him to die.

The clink of a glass stirring rod made him flick his eyes upward. Dr. Connors faced him, a beaker in hand. The liquid in it was so clear it looked like water—except for the sparkling silvery mist hovering over its surface like steam over a warm bath.

Or was his eyesight failing, too?

He reached for it, but it was farther than he thought. "Bring it closer. Give it to me."

"It could kill you."

The fear in the man's voice was of no interest. "So? You're a doctor, you must've figured out by now that I'm dead anyway."

Marko's bark was so deep he felt it in his bones. "Mr. Silvermane, don't. We don't know what those chemicals are. What if it's a trick? What if he poisons you?"

The stupid, loyal dog. Better to keep it happy a little longer, in case he still needed its protection. "No, Marko. I might have expected that from Wesley, but Dr. Connors has his family at stake. We can trust his fear for them."

The beaker was still out of reach. Silvermane forced himself to his feet. He wrapped his fingers around the glass and tugged, but the doctor did not let go.

"Don't test me," Silvermane said. "To get what I want, I'd eat my own children."

"I believe you," Connors said, relinquishing his grip.

Silvermane tilted his head and downed the nectar. It went down like tepid water. Exhaling, he thought he saw that diamond fog emerge from his mouth like vapor in winter. There was a wet sensation at the base of his gut, the same feeling he always had when he was parched and took a drink. But the feeling didn't stop in his stomach. It kept going down, all the way to his feet, then back up into his head.

Manfredi felt himself straighten, as if he were growing taller. Then, all of a sudden, he was outside his body, floating in the lab, watching his hands grasp the sides of his head. He didn't feel any pain, but he heard himself scream, saw himself fall.

Marko cried out: "You killed him! You thought it would save you, did you?"

Connors shouted back: "Don't push me! You

don't know what you're dealing with!"

Then they were gone. Silvio Manfredi was back on that verdant slope. Every male gorilla below him lifted its head, each thinking its time had arrived at last.

But it hadn't. Not yet.

THIRTEEN

HOWLING, the man mountain turned on a pale and rattled Curt Connors. "You killed him! You killed the boss! And now *you're* gonna die!"

A single stride put his long arms in reach of their target. Trying to avoid them, Connors lurched back and tripped. Before he could hit the ground, Marko caught his lab coat and held him. Suspended above the tiled floor, Connors thrashed. His panicked eyes danced wildly. All at once, he grew rigid.

"Let go of me—while you still can…"

Not understanding or caring what he meant, Marko pulled back, ready to smash the scientist's head into the tiles.

A harsh voice cried out, "Stop!"

As if responding to a Pavlovian bell, Marko obeyed instantly. The voice was familiar—but too deep, too full-throated.

"Mr. Silvermane?"

Marko shook his head, then gasped at what he saw.

A 50-year-old man stood in the center of the lab.

He was wearing the same tailored clothes as the boss, but his hair wasn't white. It was gray, and his wrinkles had nearly disappeared.

"It's some kind of trick! You...you can't be him."

Marko tried to look behind the man, to the spot on the floor where Mr. Silvermane's body should have been.

"Look at me, Marko! Study my face. It's the same, only younger. Listen to me! Isn't this the voice of your master? This is the tablet's secret: eternal youth. With it, I'll run this town for another 60 years!"

Marko felt hypnotized. He was only vaguely aware of Connors scrambling along the floor toward the door.

"You tell me what happened to Mr. Silvermane, Doc, or I'll take you apart!"

Ignoring them both, the man in Silvio Manfredi's clothes stretched his arms, his muscles pressing against the fabric of the shirt. "Sixty years? Ha! With that nectar, I'll be around forever!"

○━━━━━━━━━━○

FRESHLY showered and dressed, Caesar Cicero rushed from his quarters to find the source of the ungodly shrieks. He hoped it was Silvermane. He hoped Silvermane was dying, or, with any luck, already dead. Halfway to the lab, he nearly banged into the fleeing Connors. The doctor shoved him aside without a word and kept going.

"What the...?"

Cicero thought of following, but he'd never been

much of a runner. His men were with the family, anyway, so the doc wouldn't get far.

Besides, if that nutty formula poisoned Manfredi, then Connors did me a huge favor.

He trotted up to the lab, stopping short at the open door.

Holy...!

Someone who could've been Silvermane's kid was in the science-geek paradise, wearing Silvio's outfit. He was barking orders at Man Mountain as if he *was* Silvermane. The resemblance was crazy—so perfect that Cicero must've gasped without realizing it, because whoever the hell it was turned his way.

"Come in, Caesar! Been waiting for you, just like you've been waiting for me to die!"

Poser or not, the man's eyes burned with Manfredi's predatory sheen.

Marko stepped up to explain. "He got younger, Big C, on accounta the tablet!"

Despite the shock, Cicero's mind went to work, calculating his best move. *Okay, so I don't know for sure what the hell happened here—but, bottom line, do I care? If that is Silvermane, he's going to kill me. If it's not, Marko should be killing him. Get them to turn on each other, and I kill two birds without even throwing a stone.*

"Marko, you stupid lug, it's a trick! That can't be Silvermane. He must be a plant, in league with the cops! They're trying to trap us, make us tip our hand."

"That's what I thought, but he said—"

"And you believed him? It's not like he's going to

confess! Get him, before it's too late!"

Marko's brow twisted so hard, it hurt just to see. He'd have to decide one way or another fast, if only to ease the tension. And he did.

"Don't worry, Big C. I'll take care of him!"

Looking proud that he hadn't been fooled, Marko pivoted and punched.

Yes! Just one shot should do it!

But the fist didn't connect. Instead of ducking, whoever-it-was pushed past Man Mountain's long arms and clocked Marko in the jaw.

"You brainless mongrel! I beat my way to the top of the Maggia decades before you were born. You think you're going to stop me now?"

The arrogant self-aggrandizing was so familiar, it made Cicero's eye twitch. Maybe this *was* Silvermane. Silvermane on steroids.

Marko tried the same move again, only to walk his jaw into another blow.

"Ha! You're a good dog, Marko, but you don't know many tricks."

Man Mountain paused. His eyes widened.

"The way you use your fists…it's like the stories they used to tell."

Marko went limp, letting his attacker grab his head and lift it so they were face to face. "Speak! Tell me you know who I am."

"Yeah. It's gotta be you, only younger. I see it in your eyes. It was the stuff you drank…and it's *still* doing it. Your hair, it ain't gray no more. You look younger than me!"

What?

It was true. The salt and pepper was gone, leaving a lustrous brown. As Cicero watched, Silvermane's hair thickened, and more wrinkles vanished. His muscles grew lithe, losing some of their bulk, the shirt and jacket loosening around him. Silvermane—and yes, somehow it was Silvermane—changed from a man in his 50s to one in his 40s.

Any hope Cicero had of turning Marko against his boss was gone. Even the best attorney in the world couldn't have convinced Marko that what he saw and heard wasn't true.

Neither of them was paying attention to him. Cicero backed toward the exit and sprinted down the hall, pressing his short legs to the max. The last thing he heard from the lab was Marko saying, "It's like magic. Like watching a clock move backwards."

As it turned out, Cicero was a pretty good runner after all.

o———o

SPIDER-MAN didn't have to check the address. Even from blocks away, the 14-story Galby building, with its tan brick façade and clock-tower top, looked as if it had materialized right out of the roaring '20s, back in the days of the mob.

And those tall narrow windows, bless 'em, make it easy to see inside.

He'd planned to start at the top and work his way down, but along the way a fancy lab behind some frosted glass caught his eye—mostly because of the two figures within.

The extra-large Frankenstein type looks like a man mountain to me! As far as the other one, the Bugle *photo was black and white, but I'll be damned if he doesn't look like Silvermane.*

Spider-Man burst in through the window. As soon as he landed between them, his bruised body reminded him how unhappy it was.

Ow. Gotta make this fast, focus on what's important, even if it means leaving the tablet behind for now.

"All right, kiddies. I'm here for Dr. Connors and his family. So if you'll just tell me where…?"

He blinked at his first clear view of the man he'd *thought* was Silvermane.

"Wait," Spider-Man said. "Whoa. What?"

This guy's way too young. Is this some lower-echelon captain?

The man crossed his arms. "Time to prove your loyalty, Marko. Sic him!"

Either that, or Marko's trainer.

"I was hoping you'd ask, Mr. Silvermane."

The aptly nicknamed Man Mountain stomped toward the hero.

Spider-Man was waiting. "Silvermane? He looks Crypt-Keeper-old in the photos. Do cameras really age you that much?"

Marko looked stronger than the Kingpin, but he wasn't nearly as fast. A simple straddle jump took Peter out of reach with time to spare. Missing, Man

Mountain's leaden fist shattered the console of what looked like a *very* expensive 3D-scanning system.

Guess what they say about big ships turning slowly is true. Broken ribs or not, this part should be easy.

Taking to the ceiling, Spider-Man grabbed Marko's wide collar and pulled him into the air.

This is making my bruises hurt like hell, but no reason to tell him that.

Spider-Man let go. The man mountain let out a yelp. The drop was only 10 feet, but Marko's broad back hit the tiles hard, his legs smashing into a beaker-filled table. Long before he could recover, Spider-Man was on him, fist raised for a knockout blow. But a triumphant, rough-throated shout made them both turn toward the man in the suit.

"I'm still getting younger, more powerful! I feel like I'm in my 20s!"

Spider-Man had to look twice before realizing it was the same man. His clothes were looser, his face that of someone in their prime. Obvious as the conclusion might be, it wasn't easy to accept.

"That…that *is* Silvermane?" Spider-Man asked.

Marko nodded. "It was the drink they made from that tablet."

Spider-Man's fist was still poised for the punch. He slammed it into Marko, and the large body went limp. "Thanks."

Silvermane tossed off his jacket and loosened his tie, as if he were getting ready for a street brawl. "Not even you can oppose me now."

"If you say so, Peter Pan. But as much as I'd like to oppose you, I've got places to be, hostages to rescue." He bounded for the door. "If you want to wait a bit, I'll be happy to come back and oppose you in a few…"

His spider-sense pulled him back. A beaker smashed into the spot where he would have landed. Splashing acid bubbled through the paint and seared his costume, burning bits of skin on his already pained back. Writhing, he dropped to the floor.

The Maggia leader rolled up his sleeves. "I'm going to make an example of you. Once words hits the streets that I beat Spider-Man, all of New York will fall in line."

Is it the pain, or is his voice getting higher? Younger?

His spider-sense warned him again, but the agony made him sluggish. He felt Silvermane grab his head, then shove a knee into his chin. The force sent him sprawling backwards.

Ow. Okay, sure, he's pretty strong—but he's still human. Once I shake off this excruciating pain, I can—

Again his spider-sense fired, and again, he wasn't fast enough. Silvermane slammed both fists into Spider-Man's broken ribs. Peter felt the hard knuckles press the bones inward toward his lungs, then thought he heard the ribs crack again as Silvermane withdrew. His whole form flared in anguish.

He somehow sensed my weak spot. Did something about the way I moved give it away?

No longer quite so confident, Spider-Man rolled

sideways, protecting his ribs. The young Manfredi stepped forward and kicked the burns on his back.

"I've got decades of experience," Manfredi said. "A thousand brawls to draw on. And I always bring guns to a knife fight!"

Dizzy, finding it hard to move or think, Spider-Man folded into a fetal ball. Silvermane knelt at his back and pounded his knuckles into the burns.

"What are *you?* Just some smart-ass kid? Some freak?"

Spider-Man tried to rally—but one look into Manfredi's eyes, brimming over with sadistic pleasure, and he froze. The driving rage Peter had carried since seeing Gwen with Thompson fled, taking its heated energy along with it.

All that remained was an old, overwhelming sense of helplessness.

He closed his eyes. Images of high-school bullies, the gloating Flash and his cronies, swirled in his mind. As the mobster continued to pummel him, the sharp sting of his blows mixed with a deep, inky pool of remembered shame. It felt all-encompassing, undefeatable, bottomless.

He'd been through this many times before: tussling in schoolyards, being attacked by Jameson, combating super villains far stronger than Manfredi— and sometimes, it seemed, fighting the whole of the world. It had all hurt, inside and out.

Then he realized: It had also never stopped him. *And I'm not some pitiful school kid anymore.*

The inner dialogue of constant judgment paused, leaving him with only the present moment—the feel of the floor beneath him, the thudding fists at his back. The pain was only physical; the memories, only ghosts.

He lay still and waited, gathering his strength.

Silvermane's blows seemed to grow softer.

"Why don't you give up and die?"

Opening his eyes, Peter saw that the Maggia chief looked like a teenager now. Though fit, his muscles weren't as fully developed as they'd been even a few minutes ago. He'd reached a point where his youth left him weaker, not stronger.

More than that, his punches were no longer focused on Spider-Man's wounds.

He's frustrated. The younger he gets, the more impatient he is, too.

When the time was right, Spider-Man straightened and slammed his shoulders into Silvermane. Manfredi flew back. He rose half the distance to the ceiling, then came crashing down.

The mobster lay on his back, eyes open, motionless save for a slight shivering in his limbs. He looked even younger now—so much so that, for a scant second, Silvermane reminded Peter of himself before he was Spider-Man. But there was a difference, a predatory gleam in his eyes that banished the thought of any similarity.

Peter wasn't a bully. And Silvermane wasn't a kid.

He glared at Maggia leader. "Where's the Connors family?"

There was no response. Despite his open eyes, Silvio Manfredi seemed unconscious.

Cradling his rib, Spider-Man headed into a surprisingly empty hallway.

For that matter, where's the rest of the Maggia?

The first few rooms he checked were vacant. In one, he found a landline and used it to place an anonymous call to the police.

Gunfire pops sent him bolting up the stairs and into a wide-open area that looked like a set from *Scarface*, complete with gaudy chandelier. At the far end, Maggia soldiers jostled for position, aiming down a corridor.

"The next one won't be a warning shot, Connors! No one's getting into that room until we hear from Silvermane. You've got to the count of three to get back here. One…"

A gooey bit of web slapped the man's mouth closed. Another web snatched his gun.

The others, 10 in all, whirled to see Spider-Man suspended from the chandelier. Despite his aches, he was pretty sure he could take them, but not easily—and in the struggle, a stray bullet could strike Dr. Connors.

If he *was* still Dr. Connors.

"Listen up!" Spider-Man called. "You gave the doc a chance, so let me return the favor. Your creepy boss is upstairs sleeping like a…well, let's just say he's out cold. I'm not sure if he's going to jail or reform school, but the police are on their way, and the exit's behind me. Run for it, and maybe I'll be too focused on freeing your captives to pay much attention. Start shooting, and—well, how many of you want a new attempted murder charge added to your rap street?"

Two raised their weapons to fire, but when his webs snagged them before they could squeeze off a shot, the rest raced for the door.

Spider-Man was headed for the corridor when he spotted Caesar Cicero crawling out from behind the enormous desk, trying to join the stampede. Using a web to snag his ankle, Spider-Man tugged. Cicero's leg flew out from under him. He landed flat on his face, inches from the door.

"Sorry, this offer does not apply to management."

"Let me go! I gotta get out of here. I'll make it worth your while."

"Nah. I don't see what could be worth more than watching you squirm, given all the lives you helped the Maggia ruin."

He left Cicero and kept moving. In a room at the corridor's end, he found them: Dr. Connors sitting on the floor, his single arm wrapped around Martha and Billy. All four of theirs were wrapped around him.

"Doc, are you…okay? Got things, you know, under control?"

Connors looked up, nodded briefly, and then went back to hugging his family. Their sobs soon mixed with muffled sirens.

Feeling a bit as if he were intruding on the reunion, Spider-Man took a few steps back. "So… that'll be the police. You should be fine until they get up here, but if you like, I can hang around…"

An anguished, high-pitched wail rose. It sounded like some sort of small animal was being tortured on the floor below.

Then he realized it was human.

Silvermane?

Spider-Man sprinted back through the office. Cicero was gone, one polished shoe and silk sock still held fast by the web. Spidey figured he'd run off with the others until he found the Maggia attorney in the lower hallway. He was limping toward the lab, wincing at the cold floor against his bare foot.

"Senile *idiota!* You and that rock have destroyed us! If that elixir hasn't killed you, I'll put a bullet—"

His threat was cut short when what appeared to be Silvio Manfredi's suit, crumpled into a disheveled mass, flew out of the lab and knocked an astonished Cicero out of the way. Huffing and puffing, the bundle threw itself into the nearest empty room, slammed the door, and locked it.

Dumbfounded, Cicero leaned into the wall and slid to the ground. As Spider-Man webbed up his ankles and shoulders, he asked, "Is there any other way out of there?"

Cicero numbly shook his head.

Spider-Man grabbed the knob and twisted. The lock broke; the door creaked open.

Somewhere within, a childlike voice warned, "Stay back! I'll kill you! I'll tear out your heart with my freaking fingernails!"

City light stretched in from the windows, but not far enough to eliminate every shadow. In the darkest corner of the room, Silvermane's clothes lay in a bundle, quivering. As Spider-Man cautiously approached, the over-the-top threats gave way to infantile wailing.

An baby's pink, oversized head peeked from the folds of the finely tailored suit. As Peter watched, Silvermane shrank, growing smaller and smaller, newer and newer. But with every step back along life's path, his eyes retained that terrible gleam.

It's like part of him refuses to change, no matter how old—or young—he gets.

It might have been a trick of the scant light skimming a diamond cufflink, but even when Silvio Manfredi finally disappeared, the gleam remained.

So, in a way, he got what he wanted.

FOURTEEN

THE FURNISHINGS in the Long Island beach manor were adequate, the ocean view breathtaking. The open floor plan gave even a large man plenty of room to pace.

But it wasn't home.

Without Hell's Kitchen to remind Wilson Fisk how far he'd risen, he felt like a king in exile. Until today. He was never hopeless, but for the first time since they'd gone into hiding, the news was good—so good that despite their strained relations, he was eager to share it with Vanessa.

She stood in the center of a long row of windows, looking dully at the water. He strode back and forth behind her, occasionally clenching his fists in triumph.

"Some details are missing, others subject to rumor, but the most important facts are crystal clear. Silvermane is gone, presumed dead. The Maggia's lauded attorney is awaiting trial. Our enemies have defeated themselves! Perhaps I should locate Wesley. No doubt he already has ideas on who the traitor is."

Hoping she'd respond, he paused. She had the

sliding glass door open a crack; the salt-tinged breeze swept her gown. She looked regal, as always. A queen. His queen. But a sad and mourning queen.

"Do you understand, my love? We can go home."

She said nothing.

"I know I've been difficult, fighting phantoms, dreaming of being trapped in jail while you were in danger. You saw how I thrashed in my sleep. You know how strong I am—I only asked you to stay in a separate bed for your protection. But that's over now."

She pulled open the door farther. A briny gust hit his face. The distant winter was already in the air. "It's not that, Wilson. It's never been that."

He grimaced. "You rescued me from the street. You refused to abandon me completely, but your heart remains out of reach. Are we to stay in this purgatory, then? Together, but apart? I knew how hard you'd take Richard's death. I realize now that my fruitless lies only deepened that pain. But so long as you refuse to speak of it, to show it to me, that depth remains unfathomable."

He reached out, daring to touch her shoulder. She trembled so fiercely that he expected her to be in tears when she turned.

But she was laughing.

"Vanessa, are you all right? Should I get you one of your pills?"

She pushed his hand away.

He held his ground. "Tell me what you're feeling! I'd prefer that you raged at me, beat me. Whatever it is, let it out. If not to free us both, then at least to free yourself."

She shook her head. "I still love you too much to do that, but I'm not going to protect you from the truth anymore, either."

"The truth? What truth?"

Ever alert to threats, his eyes caught an odd movement on the beach. The sand on what appeared to be a dune shivered as if hit by a strong wind. As the vibrations continued, an ebon vehicle shed its camouflage.

A hooded man stepped out.

The Kingpin stiffened. "Who is that? How did he get past our security?"

Vanessa's hand on his chest kept him briefly still. "I invited him. It was time you heard him out."

His eyes shot between his wife's face and the approaching figure. "Invited him? Invited who? Is that the traitor? The Schemer?"

The hope that had filled him with purpose fled.

"Vanessa, have you betrayed me? Waited all this time to drive the knife into my heart yourself? All you had to do was ask. I would have died for you willingly."

She petted his cheek, as she always did when trying to calm him. "No, no. No matter what you've done, my love, I could not betray you. You have betrayed yourself."

"What are you saying? What do you mean?"

The figure reached the porch. In seconds, he'd be at the door. Vanessa tried to keep herself between them, but Fisk thrust her aside.

"I will not let him in our home!" Heedless of the doorframe's narrow width, he charged at the intruder on the other side. His shoulders tore the doors from the guide rail as if they were air.

The roar of the surf was loud. The Kingpin raised his voice to make certain he was heard. "You and I have accounts to settle."

The Schemer nodded. "We do."

Without another word, Fisk punched the intruder. The Schemer folded in on himself, his hood covering even more of his face.

Vanessa screamed.

The Kingpin growled. "Your muscle is the sort achieved in a gym, but you're clearly no fighter. A second blow is all it will take to kill you. But I don't intend to let your secrets die with you."

Fisk slapped the Schemer with the back of his hand, letting his ring scratch the skin along the man's cheek. He yanked him closer. "Talk! How did you learn so much about me?"

"I'll tell you."

He slapped him again. "Why did you challenge my leadership?"

"I'll tell you."

And again. *"What is there between you and my wife?"*

"Wilson!" Vanessa cried. "Hear him out."

"I'll tell you everything. And then you can kill me if you like."

He pushed the Schemer toward the glass wall,

standing close enough to ensure he couldn't run. "Make it fast."

The hooded figure panted, keeping his head down. "Some sons might fear living in the shadow of a powerful father, but I only wanted to be more like him—until I learned how bloody his shadow was. I was so disgusted, so ashamed, I planned to throw myself off the highest cliff I could find. But I lived through my suicide attempt. I even lived through an avalanche."

Fisk threw him up against the glass. "An avalanche? Do you think I'm a fool? You read about Richard in my stolen files!"

"No. If you were only a fool, I wouldn't still wish I were dead. As it was, the only way to live with myself was to try to turn my shame into a fury like your own. I dedicated myself to one goal—destroying what had once comforted me: your damned, bloody shadow. Your arrogance made that easy. The only surprise was how hard it was for my own mother to recognize me, how hard it still is for you to recognize your son."

Fisk back-handed him once more. "Liar! You're just some Maggia lackey, not fit to mention my son's name!"

The Schemer collapsed. Before Fisk could strike him again, Vanessa knelt by him, caressing their enemy's torn cheek the same way she'd caressed her husband moments ago.

After casting a warning glance at Wilson Fisk, she lowered the Schemer's hood. The face was bruised, twisted into a whimpering rage, the ginger hair freckled with sand—but the sun clearly showed the features of Richard Fisk.

"It *is* him, Wilson," Vanessa said. "He approached me days ago. I had it confirmed. So I suppose we've committed the same sin against each other. You couldn't bear to tell me he was dead. I couldn't bear to tell you he was alive."

Staring at his son, Fisk fell back into a patio chair. "You hate me."

Richard wiped blood from his lip. "No. I love you, even though I wish with every fiber of my being that you were not my father."

"You hate me," Fisk repeated once more. Then he fell silent. The horrid sensation from his nightmares consumed him, but this time, distant though his body felt, he was not asleep.

He heard voices. His wife, his son.

"Is he dead?"

"He's not moving!"

They sounded afraid, panicked. Briefly, Wilson Fisk considered doing something about it. But then, all at once, he no longer felt any need to protect them.

He no longer felt anything at all.

"Richard, call a doctor!"

The voices of those he loved faded. Soon, even the steady sound of the surf was gone.

○─────────────○

THE DINGY window of Peter's Parker's bedroom filtered the late-morning sun. Flipping through the

Bugle while lying in bed, rather than hanging from a flagpole, felt very different. Kind of nice, actually. While that corner of his heart reserved for Gwen still hurt, the repose did wonders for the rest of his pains.

Wasn't it only a little while ago the bad guys would just go to jail? Now the Kingpin's in some kind of weird coma, and Silvermane, well…don't really want to think about that. Sure, some new foe will turn up eventually. But with Connors and his family back home, the city's biggest crime organizations in meltdown, and the tablet in some kind of super-secret police custody, a hard-working costumed do-gooder such as myself can actually afford to put his feet up.

A hearty banging at the apartment door carried through to Peter's bedroom.

Or not.

He lifted his head, listening while Harry answered. "He's in his room. Pete?"

Determined to maintain the rare sense of peace, he called back. "No, I'm not! Whoever it is, tell them I'm busy!"

"Not too busy for what I have to tell you."

Recognizing the voice, but wishing he was somehow mistaken, he dropped the paper and sprang from bed. He reached the living room just as Flash Thompson entered.

Part of Peter was embarrassed by how quickly his temper rose, but he couldn't help himself. "You've got some nerve showing your face here."

"At ease, Junior. I just want to talk to you."

Thompson's hat was in his hand, too, no doubt because the military had taught him it was the polite thing to do. Shame they hadn't taught him to stay away from someone else's girl.

Peter came at him. "Talk? The only talking you're going to do is with my fist!"

This time I'm going to hit him. Not hard enough to put him in the hospital—just enough so he'll remember it.

Harry intervened. "Pete, c'mon! Simmer down."

"Oh, let him go. It's about time puny Parker showed some backbone."

Harry again tried to get in front of Flash. "Look, he just wants to explain about…"

But Peter was already lunging. "Nope. He's not talking his way out of this one."

As his right arm pulled back, his left slammed the soldier into the wall, and held him in place for the punch.

Peter paused, but only to make his reasons clear. "I saw you with Gwen when she said she was too busy for me. I'll show you exactly how much backbone I've got."

Flash held up his hands. "Look, bookworm, you want to tussle after I say my piece, fine. But I promised a certain blonde I'd do my best to make sure you heard me out. Okay?"

Flash didn't seem afraid, but he didn't look arrogant, either. Still not trusting him enough to let go, Peter narrowed his eyes.

"So what're you going to do, ask me to step aside?"

Thompson nearly laughed. "No! Geez, you're the

smartest guy I know. How can you be so stupid? She was only talking to me because she was worried about you."

"Huh?"

He nodded. "Yeah. Not that I was thrilled about it, but she thought I might have an inside track on your gloomy 'tude and disappearing act."

Peter scrunched his face. "You? She wanted to talk to *you* about *me?*"

"I know, right?"

Still dubious, Peter relaxed his grip a little. "Why not someone I get along with, like Harry or MJ? Or a complete stranger for that matter?"

"That's what *I* asked, but Gwendolyn pointed out that the rest of the gang's only known you two years. You and I go back to middle school. She figured that might give me some extra insight, like maybe you'd been different and I'd seen you change. Best I could do was confirm you were always the same scrawny, sullen nerd."

Flash tried to tug Peter's hand away from the jacket of his uniform. It stayed in place, rigid as steel, until Peter let go. Surprised, Thompson adjusted his clothes, a slight, reluctant admiration in his eyes.

"Fine, maybe a little *less* scrawny. Maybe."

Peter's brain churned, trying to make the new information fit with what he'd seen. "There isn't anything between you?"

Flash looked him in the eye. "Didn't you hear the *no* part? Not that I never tried, but we entered the friend zone ages ago. You don't have to worry about her, except for the fact that she must be crazy to be so into you."

Peter looked down, around, then back at Flash. "Uh…thanks?"

Thompson awkwardly patted his shoulder. "You're welcome. Let's not make it a regular thing, okay?"

Visibly relieved, Harry rubbed his hands and headed for the kitchen. "Now that we're all buddies, anyone for espresso?"

Thompson pulled up a chair. "Don't make it too strong. The bookworm here could use less caffeine."

"Excuse me, guys, I have a call to make."

Flash rolled his eyes. "No kidding."

Peter raced into his room, closing the door as Flash said, "Hey, Osborn, is that mustache new?"

Gwen picked up on the first ring. "Peter? Do I know a Peter?"

"Flash is here, Gwendy. I know you sent him."

"No, no, you must be mistaken. The only Peter I know seems to have deleted me from his contacts."

"I deserve that! I'm sorry. And I feel like a complete idiot. How soon can I see you to apologize in person?"

She paused, but not for long. "Well, I've always been partial to complete idiots. How about now? I'm at what's left of the Exhibition Hall. There's a lecture starting in half an hour, but I'm yours till then."

"You don't have to ask twice."

Hanging up, he headed for the door. Harry was

working his espresso machine, while Flash sat at the table, hands clasped.

"No time for java?"

"Let him go, Harry. Honestly, I like it when Parker disappears."

ESU was only 10 blocks away, but an eager Peter ducked into an alley, switched to Spider-Man, swung over, and changed back—all in less than five minutes. He ran across the plaza toward the still-damaged hall, now half-covered in scaffolding.

Fighting to keep his gait at a normal human speed was tough, especially when he saw Gwen leaning against one the faux columns. As the students streamed in for the lecture, she came forward.

A few steps below, Peter took her hand and almost felt like proposing.

Gwen was more pleased than surprised. "How did you get here so fast?"

Glancing at the crowd, he tugged her off to the side. "Let's go somewhere we can talk privately."

Thanks to the scaffolding, the area behind the columns was even quieter than usual. He took her hands and looked into her eyes for a full minute.

She looked as if she might blush, but didn't turn away. "Why are you looking at me that way?"

"Maybe I finally realized how much I miss you when you're not around. Or maybe I don't feel like talking after all."

The first kiss seemed to last forever. The second kiss was even longer. As for the third and fourth...

well, at some point he had to let her go to class.

"Pick you up in an hour, or should I just wait here all moony until it's over?"

"Your choice, boo. Your choice. As long as you're here when I come out."

"I will be, I swear." He crossed his finger over his heart. "Hope to die."

"See that you don't, Mr. Parker. I have too many plans for you."

She winked and went inside. He wasn't sure how long he stared at the closed door, but it didn't really matter.

We do have a future together. What do you know?

Suddenly, he didn't have a worry in the world.

I guess growing up's not so bad. Given what happened to Silvermane, it sure as hell beats the alternative.

"Knowledge is knowing that a tomato is a fruit. Wisdom is not putting it in a fruit salad."
— MILES KINGTON, BRITISH JOURNALIST, MUSICIAN, AND BROADCASTER

PART TWO:
ADULTHOOD

TWO YEARS LATER...

FIFTEEN

ROUGHLY three million people were buried in the Queens cemetery, more than actually lived in the borough. Here—in the endless field of headstones and crosses, obelisks and mausoleums—all were equal: athletes, entertainers, police, military, criminals, politicians, writers, and more.

But to Peter Parker, some were more special than others.

Uncle Ben was buried here. The guilt Peter carried over his death was so old, the memory so worn, that he imagined Ben himself would say, "Enough! How could you have known?"

Peter's answer—*I should have*—was still the same, though.

Now he stood before Captain Stacy's headstone. The police captain had died saving a child from falling wreckage, a boy he'd never seen before. Remembering that sacrifice made Peter's guilt feel petty.

At least until he looked at the grave he'd come to visit: Gwen's.

Then, petty or not, the remorse competed with the pain.

I should have. I should have known.

But he hadn't. He'd been so busy saving the world, so wrapped up in his own worries, that he'd never even noticed the obvious, like Harry's new mustache—let alone how many pills his roommate was taking, or how quickly that habit became a full-blown addiction.

Sure, Peter was the one who raced Harry to the hospital when he OD'd, but after that? He'd assumed Harry had learned his lesson. Then he got the call from Gwen telling him Harry had overdosed and experienced a psychotic break. When he was shocked, she called him naïve.

Funny, Gwen's last words to me were about Harry. "All his life he's had whatever he wanted. What could have happened to him to make him so…so desperate?"

Peter remembered the glazed look in Norman Osborn's eyes when he blamed Peter for his son's decline. Guilt aside, it meant the only villain who knew Spider-Man's identity might recover his memory.

I should have known.

But again, he hadn't known Osborn would revert to the Green Goblin, kidnap Gwen, and take her to the top of the Brooklyn Bridge. Knowing she was Peter's girlfriend, he waited for Spider-Man to arrive, and then…kicked her off.

Captain Stacy's death was a reminder that there were things no one could control. But the image of

Gwen, twisting and tumbling through the air, kept playing in his mind.

Of course, he jumped after her. He'd have leapt into hell for her. But even Spider-Man couldn't defy gravity. So he tried a long shot, snagging her ankle with a web before she could hit one of the concrete pylons. He carried her to what he thought was safety—and, for a little while, less than a minute, he thought she was fine.

But she wasn't. She was already dead.

When the numbness wore off and the tears flowed more freely, the questions began to plague him. If he'd twisted one way and not the other—if he'd been faster—could he have saved her? What if he'd stayed with her all day? If he'd been a better friend to Harry? If he'd never been Spider-Man at all? If he'd done this and not done that?

If I'd known.

"Enough, already! How could you have known?"

But I should have.

Thinking about it had nearly driven him mad. Finally he'd had to accept the truth that *yes*, with 20-20 hindsight, there *were* dozens of things, large and small, that he could have done—but it was too late. He didn't know whether facing that would make him more mature, but the effort definitely made him feel older.

The spring night was pleasant, the sky clear and welcoming. But rather than swing back to the Village, he took the subway to give himself more time alone and Harry some space. He wanted to be a better friend in case his roommate slipped again, and he definitely didn't want his own glum mood to add to Harry's problems. So before entering their apartment, Peter exhaled and took a moment to put on a good face.

The space was dark, save for a small lamp on the crowded kitchen table. Harry sat half in shadow, hunched over the pile of business papers he'd been forced to deal with since his father's death.

Pete waved. "Hey, roomie."

He didn't even look up. "Peter."

Peter tossed his jacket on the hanger. "Want to hang out, grab a pizza?"

"Not tonight."

Harry scooped up the contracts, walked into his room, and shut the door.

The rebuff wasn't a surprise. Peter's efforts to approach Harry were stuck in yet another web of lies and irony. Unaware of Norman's crazed alter ego, Harry blamed Spider-Man for his father's murder. Peter had encouraged the fiction that he worked with the wall-crawler to get photos, so Harry was angry with Peter by association.

For once Peter was certain this was a case where telling the truth would only make things worse. Not that part of him *hadn't* wanted to kill the Goblin, but circumstance had robbed him of the choice. Desperate and beaten, Osborn had sent his remote-controlled glider careering at Spider-Man's back, hoping to eviscerate him. Peter's spider-sense threw him into a last-second leap—and the jet-propelled device hit the Goblin's chest instead.

Peter still remembered the exact sound the glider made against the concrete when it, and Norman Osborn, fell.

He left his own door open in case Harry came back out and decided he wanted to talk. Despite everything that had changed, Peter's room looked pretty much the same as the day he'd moved in. So much of his life just bumbled on, as if by momentum.

He was a staff photographer at the *Bugle* now, but still struggled to pay his bills. He was still trying to graduate ESU, but his college career might be grinding to a halt. There were only so many classes even the brightest student could miss. After he'd failed Advanced Experimental Physics twice due to multiple absences and late work, the deadline-obsessed Prof. Blanton had given him his last, last, last chance.

Honestly, it would've been hard for Peter to care about school at all if not for Aunt May. Though they seldom spoke of their grief, he knew Gwen's death had hit her nearly as hard as it had him. She'd accepted Gwen as a daughter, thought of her as the future mother of her grandchildren. Now, with Gwen gone, Peter felt even more obligated to graduate, fulfill his potential, and make his only living relative proud.

No matter how many lives Spider-Man saved, if he broke that sweet, loving woman's heart, he'd never be able to look himself in the mirror again.

That meant cracking the books, which he did until sleep overtook him. Tonight at least, his slumber was peaceful, dark, deep, and thoughtless.

At some point a ringtone woke him. A heavy textbook sat half on his face, a folded page stuck to his lip. Trying not to lower the resale value of the pricey tome, he peeled it away carefully and answered his phone.

"Peter Parker?"

Not knowing the voice, he assumed the obvious.

"Whatever you're selling, I'm not..."

"May Parker's nephew?"

He sat up. A glance at the clock told him it was midnight, too late for a telemarketer. "Yes?"

"This is Dr. Amelia Fent. Your aunt's been admitted to Presbyterian Hospital following an incident. She was—"

"An incident? What kind of incident?"

"She was unusually disoriented, so her friend Anna brought her in. I just got the results of her blood work, and her liver function isn't where we'd like it to be. Given her history..."

The doctor was calm and clear, but the more she spoke, the less he understood.

"History? What history? Where's Dr. Bromwell, her regular doctor?"

"He's on his way in. She's in stable condition for now..."

"For now?"

"She's in no immediate danger. But it would probably be best if you came in. Dr. Bromwell can give you the details when you arrive."

o———o

IN THE largest private room of the new ward built by her donations, Vanessa Fisk watched her husband's chest rise and fall. Like most everything, the ventilator had been built for lesser men. Already the pressure had needed to be raised three times to fill his lungs with enough oxygen. It was a steady movement, but calm—so unlike the quick, sharp panting she was used to. The fire that at times made him part animal was gone.

The doctors said if she talked to him, he might hear her, but she couldn't bring herself to utter a word. Even holding his hand only brought the pained sensation that despite the evidence of the body in the bed, Wilson Fisk wasn't here at all.

If you were alive, I could love you. If you were dead, I could mourn you.

Most days, the antidepressants helped. At times she found herself humming as she wandered their Long Island beach house alone. But whenever she visited here, she felt as though the same abyss that had consumed Wilson would reach out and claim her, as well.

The newest "expert" to examine him was younger than the last. While polite and professional, his callow eyes held little compassion, as if he were trying to solve a crossword puzzle rather than restore a life. Perhaps it was just as well. Vanessa had hired him for his skills, not his heart.

"It's unusual to require a ventilator even in the worst cases of catatonia, but his breathing had slowed to such a dangerous point, we had no choice."

"Two years, and not one doctor has the slightest idea how to help him."

"I admit, I'm at a loss, too. Brain trauma would explain a coma, but there's no indication that occurred. Mental disorders can cause catatonia, but he hasn't responded to benzodiazepine, or any other psychoactive medications. I tried L-Dopa, in case the tests failed to detect encephalitis lethargica, but nothing's helped. The only thing left is electro-convulsive therapy."

She winced at the thought. "I understand the shocks are administered with greater control than in the past. But do you have any sense of whether it might work?"

"Honestly, no. I have no idea. At this stage, I would argue that it couldn't hurt."

She wanted to give him a withering look, but lacked the energy. "One could say the same of chicken soup."

"You've said he had a serious emotional shock, but you've never explained what it was."

"Would it help? It's a private family matter."

"Maybe. I've run out of things to try."

"You know what the papers say about my husband? You understand why I schedule these consultations so late after hours?"

He nodded.

"What if I told you that knowing what happened to him might put certain people in danger?"

His sudden fear was palpable. "In that case, maybe it's best you don't tell me."

The doctor was thinking of himself, but she was thinking of her son. Consumed with remorse over what he'd done to his father, Richard had fled the country. Though it meant she'd lost him as well, that was probably for the best. There were those out there still loyal, if not to the Kingpin, then to the organization he'd left in ruins. Some venal newcomer wanting to make a name for themselves wouldn't hesitate to track down Richard and harm him.

"I can tell you that I was there, that I saw the heart ripped from a great man whose love was the only thing fiercer than his anger—so fierce it terrified him. In a single moment, it was ripped away. It was as if he simply lost the will to live."

The expert shrugged. "Mrs. Fisk, I wish I could tell you more, but that metaphor is as good a diagnosis as any I can offer. Do you want to consider shock therapy?"

She put her hand on the rising chest, hoping the feel of his heartbeat might convince her that her husband was still somehow present. It did not.

"I'll think about it."

"Of course. Take your time. He's, uh, not going anywhere."

This time she did raise her head to glare at him—but the loud, intrusive squeak of sneakers turned her toward the door.

A young man was running down the private hall, his handsome face pale with worry. She didn't think him a threat, but lacking her husband's instincts in such matters, she wasn't sure. A security guard immediately appeared to reassure her.

"Sorry, Mrs. Fisk, that guy must have taken a wrong turn. We'll have him removed."

"Be gentle about it. He probably has his own bad news to deal with."

AFTER speaking with the gray-haired, mustachioed Dr. Bromwell in the lobby, Peter was in such a daze he'd wandered down two wrong halls before finding his aunt. The second bed in the gray semi-private room was empty, but the nurse cautioned she might be getting a roommate at any time.

Aunt May was in the bed near the radiator and window. The mattress was propped up so she lay at an angle. The blankets tucked in around her were perfectly smooth, as if she hadn't moved since arriving.

Bromwell had warned that her high bilirubin had changed her appearance, but until Peter stepped closer, he had no idea how much. The buzzing fluorescents made everyone look a little green, but the yellow tinge to his aunt's skin was so unreal, she looked like an image on a television with a skewed color balance.

Swallowing, he sat by her side and placed his palm on her thin shoulder. At his touch, her eyelids opened, and he saw that the yellow had spread to her eyes. He choked back a sob. Fortunately, her gaze wandered dreamily; by the time she fully woke and recognized him, he'd managed to compose himself.

"Peter!"

"Liver disease? Aunt May, why didn't you tell me?"

She pursed her lips the same way she would if he'd uncovered a more benign secret, like the time she'd sold some of her jewelry to buy him a new microscope.

"The silly doctors told me this was years away. After all you've been through, I just didn't have the heart."

Twisting her lips into a wispy smile, she grabbed his hand and patted it. Her fingertips felt bony and cold. He clasped them and rubbed them until they were warm.

"If I don't know what's going on, how can I help you?"

She rolled her eyes. "Young man, I've said the same to you for years. Half the time I have no idea what you're feeling."

"Sorry, Aunt May, I…"

She pinched his cheek. "Hush. We've been through that. If you ever want to know the best way to help me, the answer is to help yourself. Be happy and productive."

"But Aunt May…"

Neither of them noticed Dr. Bromwell at the door until he spoke. "Peter, a word?"

"Sure." He turned back to his aunt. "Stay right there, okay? None of those acrobatics, now."

She raised her eyebrows. "And here I was looking forward to starting that body-sculpting class."

Peter chuckled, hoping it didn't sound forced. "Look who's telling jokes for a change. That's a good sign, right, Doc?"

"It certainly is." Dr. Bromwell didn't laugh, but

he nodded pleasantly. "Outside, please."

In a scene he'd seen in a dozen sappy movies and soap operas, Peter slumped against the hallway wall. The doctor stood up straight, bending his neck closer as he whispered.

"Her liver function has been declining for years. She'll need a transplant if it gets any worse. The procedure is common, but at her age any invasive surgery carries greater risk. Because of that, she'll be far down the donor waiting list. On the other hand, if a family member volunteered, we could perform the transplant as soon as she's strong enough—perhaps as early as next week. I know she's not a blood relative, but your medical records indicate you're likely compatible. If you're willing, there are some tests I'd like to perform. We could start in the morning."

Peter was nodding the whole time. "Of course, of course."

But as the doctor described the biopsy, a terrible reality dawned on him. *My blood's radioactive—my DNA has been altered. A transplant from me could kill her!*

Mouth half-open, the nodding stopped and he found himself shaking his head. "No, no, sorry, I'm gonna…I'm going to have think about this."

If Bromwell was surprised, he was experienced enough not to show it. "Of course. You've already had a shock today, and it's a big decision. Take some time, study the information in this packet. But be aware her liver function will most likely continue to fail. We are on the clock."

The doctor kept talking, but Peter's mind was

reeling. At some point he mumbled his thanks and stumbled to the waiting room to stare numbly at the pamphlet describing the procedure. No more than a second later, Anna Watson stormed in, her eyes red and wide.

Wielding a bouquet of flowers like a cudgel, she slammed them into his shoulder. Fresh petals flew everywhere.

"You have to *think* about it?"

He raised his hand to block the second blow, but Anna's real weapon was the horrified pain in her voice, and it cut deep. "I heard everything, you selfish coward! You're just going to let her die? That woman's done everything for you, your whole life, and you're going to let her die?"

And, of course, he couldn't explain.

SIXTEEN

AS SOON as he left the hospital, Peter found the nearest hiding spot and switched into his red-and-blues.

Aunt May's dying—and there's nothing I can do.

He took to the building tops, soared above the streets, raced through urban nooks and mazes only he could find. But even New York couldn't supply the distraction he needed. If anything, the city bore the same old stink as his life.

Nothing ever changes, except that it gets worse.

No matter how high or how fast he moved, it all felt like a worthless routine.

What else can I do—sit around and wait? Where else can I go? Back home to hope Harry feels sorry enough for me to have a conversation? Ahhh...I may as well try to take some Spider-Man pics.

He'd turned in so few to the *Bugle* lately that JJJ was threatening to fire him. Without that lousy salary, he couldn't afford the lousy books to pass his lousy class. And then...

Then what? If I can't even protect Aunt May, what difference does it make what I do?

He dropped down onto a townhouse roof near ESU, and resisted the temptation to kick the brick chimney to pieces. He looked out and around, hoping the stillness would somehow reach inside and calm him.

What is it, like 3 a.m.?

He swooped by Captain Stacy's old precinct house. When a new building had been constructed a few blocks away, this one had been converted into an annex to store old files and evidence. No one cared about the place anymore. The brick walls sported bits of graffiti; some windows were cracked. While a few security lights still glowed in the halls of the upper floors, most were broken.

But there was another light, weak and flickering, visible beyond the low basement windows. And it was moving. Hopping down for a closer look, he saw that one of the windows wasn't just cracked. It had been smashed.

Randy said some students think the place is haunted. It's probably some freshman ghost-hunting on a dare, but a break-in is a break-in.

Angling through the broken window, he entered quietly. The entire floor was packed with shelves and filing cabinets. The only remnants of the building's previous purpose were a few concrete walls with the cell doors removed. Without their iron bars, they formed a sort of open maze; he could see the flickering light moving along the far wall.

Kind of a mini-version of that warehouse at the end of Raiders.

Spider-Man set up his camera in a high corner. He hoped the wide angle would provide a decent view of the ad hoc labyrinth. As he clicked it on, he heard a satisfied, "Ah!"

Sounds like whoever it is found whatever it was they wanted.

The flickering light went out. Fortunately, the camera's infrared could capture the vandal's face even in the dark.

Guess they'll be leaving soon, which gives me an idea for a better photo-op.

Sealing the broken window with webbing, he angled the camera toward the only other way out: the basement door. Then he blocked the exit and waited. Sure enough, a slight figure appeared beneath the window. Peter couldn't make out his features—it was just a shadow emerging from shadow.

The figure climbed to the windowsill. Finding his way out sealed, the crook grunted, looked around, and hopped back down.

Okay, come to poppa.

The figure reemerged dead ahead—just as Spider-Man had planned. They saw each other at the same time, illuminated by the headlights of a passing car.

That's no college student—it's a kid!

A surprisingly young-sounding voice muttered some surprisingly adult words.

"Dude," Spider-Man replied. "You kiss your mother with that mouth?"

His webs shot out, but the boy dove into

the labyrinth. After a few more scraping sounds, everything went silent.

"I know you think you can play hide-and-seek in there, pal, but this is the only way out, and I'm feeling pretty patient." A full five minutes passed before he added, "I'm not going to turn you in. Just put whatever it is you've got back, and we can call it a night. Okay?"

After another five minutes, Spider-Man realized he *wasn't* feeling all that patient.

Thinking his spider-signal might spook the boy, he flashed his insignia along the aisles formed by the shelves. Nothing budged. On the other hand, the footprints it revealed in dust told him where the boy was hiding. Clicking off the light, he crept among the tall shelves.

A couple of more steps and I can…

A low rustling turned him around.

Aw! The little brat doubled back behind me!

His spider-sense told him the attack was coming, but not how fast and hard it would be. He spun, hands out, and faced a wave of falling evidence racks. With no time to leap away—nowhere to go in the mess of boxes and metal framed-shelves—he was buried in seconds.

But not for long. He flexed his arms, clearing enough of the files for him to spot the boy at the exit. A cardboard box cradled under one arm, he was trying to pry open the door with a crowbar.

Spider-Man tried to move, but his ankle was pinned between a collapsed shelf's scissored supports.

He could yank himself free, but the sharp steel would do some damage, leaving him with a limp he'd rather not have to deal with or explain.

With two *thwips,* he fired dual webs from his wrist-shooters. One missed, hitting the debris. The other sailed through and caught the box the boy was holding. An easy tug wrenched it away from him, resulting in another flurry of decidedly adult language.

Spider-Man caught the box, then turned to prying apart the steel wrapped around his ankle. The thief hesitated an instant, then tore open the door and bolted into the night.

In the seconds it took Peter to free himself and follow, the kid had vanished along one of a dozen possible paths. Taking to the roof, Spider-Man scanned the streets and sidewalks, but they were empty. The thief was gone.

The web-slinger turned to the box, marked "evidence." The seal was already broken, so he opened it, revealing a familiar stone tablet.

This thing again? *No way.*

He thought about it a moment. *Hey, it's not my responsibility. Easy enough to leave it dangling for the police to find. Right?*

SEVENTEEN

THE NEXT morning, back in his room, Peter sat at his desk staring at the tablet, asking himself over and over:

Why didn't I just leave it there? What's wrong with me?

In part it was because of the signature on the form he'd found in the evidence box. George Stacy's confident pen strokes were their own sort of relic, conjuring memories of the captain's wise, steady hand.

The thing that had really sealed Peter's decision, though, was the images his camera had captured. There were six shots of the boy's face. None were perfect, but a few were clear enough to see a vague resemblance to a certain Silvio Manfredi.

Is it his grandson? A relative? Or worse, is Silvermane somehow back?

Peter flipped over the stone, hefted the weight, and returned it to the box. He slipped it under his bed.

At this rate, I should probably keep the damn thing and have it made into a lamp.

Truthfully, though? It was a welcome distraction. He still had time before class, and hospital visiting hours weren't until midafternoon. The latest update from Dr. Bromwell said that Aunt May's levels were stable, but again with that ominous "for now." At least he had some time to figure out what to say about the transplant.

Maybe I should tell Bromwell the truth about me, if only so he starts looking for other ways to help her. Is there some sort of client-attorney privilege with doctors? If nothing else, I sure could use some advice.

Speaking of attorneys, I know the perfect place to start investigating the break-in. It's been awhile, but I still remember the way to Caesar Cicero's office.

He made the switch to Spider-Man and headed for Midtown. He scaled the building's 30 stories, looked in through a window, and frowned. Several walls inside the venerable skyscraper had been knocked down, giving the new Maggia leader's personal office a full quarter of the floor.

Looks like he's still feeling his oats. Which only makes the delightful fellow that much easier to find.

Indeed, no fewer than 12 windows gave the clinging hero a view of the squat man seated behind the largest desk he'd ever seen.

Talk about compensating! You could land an airplane on that thing.

Cicero was the picture of satisfaction, his feet up and shoes off. He flexed his toes, staring happily out at the billowing clouds and blue sky above the city. His wide face wore a relaxed smile, as if the world were a joke and someone had just slipped him the punchline.

The smile remained undisturbed until Spider-

Man wrenched open the window and hopped inside.

"Glad you didn't replace these classic push-out casements with something I couldn't open. Otherwise I'd have had to smash my way in."

Cicero scrambled forward, reaching for an alarm button—or a concealed weapon. Then he seemed to think better of it. He flopped back into his seat, *tsked,* and sighed.

"There's also a nice new front door, which you could have, you know, used."

"And miss that beautiful mix of fear and guilt on your face? No way."

"Peh. You like it so much, take a picture. For that matter, take my keys and get the whole place on video." Straightening his spine, he unhooked a keyring from his pants and tossed it on the carpeted floor between them.

Spider-Man pointed at the keys. "Is the one for the secret corridor labelled this time?"

"I've got nothing to hide from you, or anyone else."

"Really? Pinky square?"

Cicero slashed his stubby finger across his shirt, making his power tie flutter. "Cross my heart and hope *you* die. These days, the businesses I run are completely legit."

"Riiiiight. The kinder, gentler Maggia I've been reading about in *Gangster Today.* All on the up and up—on paper, anyway."

"You're the lawyer now?" Cicero's thick broad lips

reclaimed their grin. "Of course, 'on paper.' How do they say it? The age of the physical object is over." He waved a hand in the air. "It's all in the ether. We make more money moving money around than we ever did, excuse me, ever *would* have, from any illegal trade—if we had ever done such things, which, of course, we did not."

Unimpressed, Spider-Man sat on the desk. "Things like kidnapping? I always wondered how you got out of that."

"Want to chat about the old days? Fine, let's chat."

Cicero stood, turned his back on the web-slinger, and poured some scotch from a crystal decanter on the bar behind his desk. "Sorry I'm not offering you any, but it's the good stuff, and—well, you ain't worth it."

He took a swig and smacked his lips.

"Where were we? Right. Kidnapping. As per the depositions, yeah, I was present in certain named locations along with those unfortunate victims. On the other hand, during the actual commission of any crimes perpetrated upon them, said victims were hooded and, *ergo ipso facto,* unable to distinguish between those responsible and mere bystanders like myself. As I said under oath, I was en route to report their captivity to the authorities when I was assaulted and illegally detained by a certain web-crawler. He, as it turned out, was unavailable to testify, rendering his side of the story moot."

Cicero smacked his lips again. "And maybe, just maybe, someone with my resources managed to pin the remaining charges on the Kingpin's pal, Wesley. He'll probably weasel out of it when the case goes to trial in another six months. So before I add trespassing and intimidation charges to the long list of beefs the cops have with you, why don't you stop with the self-righteous BS and tell me what the hell you want?"

"Have it your way." Spider-Man pinged a paperclip on the desk into the snifter in Cicero's hand.

As it shattered, the lawyer jumped back from the broken glass and spilling liquid. "Did you have to?"

"Yeah, kinda. But to answer your first question, there was an attempted theft last night."

Cicero pantomimed fainting, raising the back of his hand to his forehead. "Ooh. An attempted theft in New York City! Mercy, how shocking! I already told you, we don't do that stuff no more."

He reached down to the floor, scooped up his key ring, and jangled it in front of Peter. "See for yourself."

Without touching any part of the attorney, Spider-Man kicked the ring from his hand. The keys flew across the office, end over end, and landed in the pocket of the fur-lined overcoat hanging in the corner.

Cicero stared the wall-crawler in the costumed whites of his eyes. "I'm telling the truth. If it's illegal, I don't know about it. I even let Marko go. Believe me, it was tough. That dumb giant was so loyal, it hurt—but he just didn't fit in with the new corporate culture, y'know?" He narrowed his eyes. "What'd they try to take? Must've been big to bring you out from the cobwebs. Gold bullion? Some experimental death-ray that turns hamsters into monster trucks?"

"Somebody tried to steal the tablet."

Cicero looked as if he'd swallowed vinegar. "The tablet? Why?"

Huh. Maybe he doesn't know anything.

"I was hoping you'd tell me."

He cleared his throat. "Wish I could. I never believed in curses until I ran into that hunk of stone. Kingpin wanted it; he's in a coma. It nearly brought down the Maggia, and you saw how it worked out for Silvermane. Knowing that, why would I—scratch that, why would *anyone*—want something that turns you into…into nothing?! As a poison? There's a thousand easier ways to kill a guy. If I ever heard someone was after it, I'd be the first to call the cops."

On the one hand, Cicero sounded sincere. On the other hand, that was his job, and he was good at it. Peter had brought the photos of the thief. He thought about showing them to Cicero, but held back.

If the Maggia is behind this, I don't want them to know about any evidence I have. If not, I don't want to give them any reason to get involved.

He tried a different tack. "Did Silvermane have any family?"

Cicero laughed. "If he did, they'd sure as hell be hiding from me."

THE WAREHOUSE had been scheduled for demolition for years, but not everything dies as it should. The owners had planned to put up a new high-rise on the lot, but their funding had collapsed along with the fortunes of their largest investor, Wilson Fisk. Now the building stood neglected, occasionally shedding hunks of rusted steel and shards of glass like rotting teeth or thinning hair. So much of the structure was already gone that whatever nature the city allowed would soon claim all of it, without the need for a wrecking ball or human will.

Those few people desolate or desperate enough to ignore the hazard signs were kept away by the constant creaking that threatened a final collapse. In fact, every form of life stayed away, rats and roaches included—except the boy.

The always-angry boy.

While he couldn't be sure whether he'd been here before, he somehow felt he belonged. He'd found the half-collapsed stairs that led to the basement easily enough. There, the concrete walls and foundation remained as solid and silent as a tomb—or better yet, a memorial, a shrine he could build for himself.

For his anger.

No, not a shrine, a palace—a *memory* palace, like in that book he'd found, *Rhetorica ad Herennium*. It was written by Cicero, a name he associated with treachery. But this was some other Cicero, a Roman. The book said to pick a place in your head, a place you know, and fill it up with the stuff you want to remember. Then, whenever you needed to remember something, you could find it where you left it.

But when he got here, the boy could barely remember anything on his own. So he decided to one-up the Roman smart-ass by making his palace *real*—and filling it up with memories he could actually touch. And so here it was, lit by stolen candles and stolen flashlights, furnished with stolen chairs and a stolen bed. The only thing he hadn't stolen was the cinderblocks. There were plenty already lying around, so he used them to build the stepped platform at the center of his place. The platform that led to his throne.

He didn't know why everything had to be stolen. Maybe because nothing was really his, but stealing made everything his. Stealing felt important, so he went with it, tearing pages out of library newspapers and books when he could, using stolen credit cards for the printouts when he had to. Old things felt important, too, like the 1928 Thompson submachine gun he'd swiped from the antique gun shop. Old things made him feel safer, as if he were less likely to lose them because they'd been around for so long.

That didn't make sense, exactly, but again, he went with it.

He knelt before the cinderblock throne—not to bow before a great power, just to make it easier to reach the pictures he had of the *really* old thing. The tablet. That wasn't his yet, but he wanted it most of all. After all his work finding it, the guy in the costume, Spider-Man, had stopped him. Touching the image, though, let him imagine he was touching the stone.

Sometimes he imagined so hard, he thought he

might actually remember his past.

When he was done with that, he pulled out the only thing he thought maybe he hadn't stolen, the only thing that might really be his. Gently, he brushed away the bits of concrete and wetness from the cover of the flip-over notebook, rolled the rubber band off, and found a particular page. Reading the words, he tried to sing.

"Drink, drink."

It was wrong. His voice was wrong. The melody was wrong.

He tried again, raising his tone on the first word, lowering it for the second.

"Drink, drink."

Still not right. He knew the words—he'd memorized them from the notebook—but the notebook didn't have the melody, and he couldn't read music even if it did.

So he *had* to remember it.

He tried starting low, then let his voice fish around for anything that sounded familiar.

"Drink, drink!"

No! That wasn't it at all!

The answer had to be somewhere—if not in the palace he'd made, then locked inside himself. Locks didn't scare him. He had a pretty strong feeling he could pick any he came across.

But first, he had to find the right door.

EIGHTEEN

WELL after 1 a.m., Detective Darryl Tanner was still buried in papers. He was so absorbed in his work that his partner, Miles Langston, had to rap twice against the door frame to make him look up.

"Done with my filing, so I thought I'd say goodnight. Or good morning." Seeing the stacks of paper, Miles gave a low whistle. "What'd you do to get on Connolly's bad side?"

They'd been working together for a few years now. Darryl had always been sort of jealous of that whistle. He wondered how Miles got it so deep and loud. Darryl could never whistle.

"Nothing. I asked for it. Need the overtime. Things are tight back home."

Tight was an understatement, but there were reasons he kept the specifics of his financial problems private. When the Kingpin had vanished, Darryl's take-home had dropped by half. These days, the Maggia gave him a little something, but not enough to keep him from having to raid his daughter's college fund to pay the mortgage.

Miles was single and seemed carefree, but he nodded sympathetically. "I hear that. Want me to put on another pot for you before I head out?"

"Nah. I'm almost done, but I thought I'd run up the clock a bit, you know."

Miles wagged his finger. "I didn't hear that. Say hi to the family."

Freaking kid thinks he's funny.

Darryl gave him a weak wave. "Will do."

He watched Miles walk down the hall and enter the elevator. He kept watching until the little light above indicated his partner had reached the lobby.

Satisfied he was alone, he turned back to his work. It had taken the boys on site at the old annex half a day to clean up the mess from the break-in. Most of that time was spent picking things up and matching them with their boxes. It was Darryl's job to match what they found with the old paper logs. Half the time the files weren't in the same format as the log. The rest of the time he couldn't read the handwriting.

He checked things over twice more. He was right. There was only one box missing, placed there under the authority of the late Captain George Stacy.

Putting aside the master list, Darryl flipped through the physical carbons, found the matching number, and tugged the sheet free. Though the description was vague, he knew what it meant. He folded the paper and put it in his pocket. Then he went back to the master and logged in the only empty box, so the rest of the world would think it was still there, safe and sound.

He read the news until nearly 2 a.m. Then he got up and headed to the chief detective's office.

Darryl had no idea why Connolly always worked so late, and he never felt like asking.

At her door he cleared his throat. "Chief?"

She gave him a tired smile. "Got that report for me, Darryl?"

"Yes, ma'am, I do."

"And?"

"Six different kinds of forms, three databases, and everything's accounted for. Guess we owe the integrity of our evidence annex to Spider-Man."

She rolled her eyes as he handed over the lists. "Unless he was the one doing the breaking and entering." She scanned them. "This is good work— glad I had an old pro on it. Take an extra hour on the time sheet, but no more."

"Thanks, boss."

Rather than head home, he walked a few blocks and then pulled out the burner he used for special calls. His contact picked up on the first ring.

"I think I've got something. That old tablet the Maggia stole a couple years ago? All this time it's been in the evidence annex—at least until yesterday. Someone lifted it. Judging from the webbing on the scene, Spider-Man either has it himself or has an idea who does. I figure knowing it's back on the streets is worth something."

The voice on the other end laughed. "You

figured wrong. Cicero doesn't want anything to do with that thing."

"What, it spooks him? I know it's supposed to be magic, but—"

"Spooked? No. More like he doesn't want anything around that reminds him of Silvermane. You've been with us a while, so I'll tell you, but you didn't hear it from me. Gossip upstairs is that the wall-crawler paid a visit today. After that, the Big C needed a four-hour massage just to take a nap. My advice? Forget about it."

The line went dead. He stared at the phone.

Damn. All that work for an extra $200? If I'd told the chief a priceless artifact had gone missing, I could have been up for a bonus. Now there won't even be a case file on the theft.

The only other number in the burner's contact list caught his eye. It was old, probably useless, but thinking about that college fund, he gave it a try.

After three rings, a woman answered. "Hello? Who is this? How did you get this number?"

He'd only seen her once or twice, but that sad singsong voice was tough to forget.

"Mrs. Fisk? Darryl Tanner. I don't know if you remember me."

"Detective Tanner. Of course, from our holiday party three years ago. This is…a surprise. It's very late. Is something wrong?"

"Nothing wrong. I was just working on a case that reminded me of your husband. It's about something I know he wanted very badly."

At least she was listening. If he played it right, the information could be worth something, after all.

○─────────○

IF WESLEY weren't in prison, he would have answered that call; instead it had gone to Vanessa Fisk. She wasn't sure what she'd hoped to hear, what pale ghost she'd imagined might speak to her. She wasn't even sure why she *cared* enough to keep the phone here, let alone answer. But she had, and what she heard stirred her dormant heart.

Having taken to sleeping in the center of the colossal bed she'd shared with Wilson, she had to use her legs to pull herself across the width before reaching the edge. For the first time in 16 hours, she put her bare feet to the floor. By rote rather than modesty, she donned an opaque green robe to cover her negligée. She remembered the way her husband had looked at her, and nearly ventured a smile.

But that was back when love had been something other than cruel.

When love was the heart of creation.

She pressed her forehead to the glass and watched the surf. She remembered him warning her to avoid windows, always fearful one of his many enemies would come for her.

There was no reason for anyone to threaten her now. The only thing of value she'd ever held was the Kingpin's heart, and it was forfeit. The two guards downstairs, and the two on the grounds of the beach house, had only been kept on to honor her husband's loyalty to his people.

Why *had* she answered the phone?

When Wilson had been healthy…no, the word *healthy* didn't do him justice. When he'd been the brutish force whose very presence screamed *life,* she'd had no interest in his business dealings. Even now, when personal necessity should have been enough to force her involvement, she only paid enough attention to his moribund empire's intricacies to ensure the continued payment of his medical bills. And in that case, she allowed the lawyers to tell her which papers to sign—she never, ever cared.

Ever since he'd entered that horrid torpor, she'd had little interest in anything. She often startled herself with the number of hours she could spend staring off into nothing.

But the tablet could change everything. There were many things she recalled about Wilson: his moods, his delights, his demons. But she particularly remembered the sparkle in his eyes when he'd first decided that the artifact had to be his.

And among the few things she knew about the underworld, she was aware of the rumors that the stone had somehow made Silvermane young and whole again. She'd also heard rumors about the dread result, and wondered whether that was due to Wesley's interference.

Her head and heart had been empty for so long, the world drained of meaning. Her favorite dishes tasted like ash; paintings that had once taken her breath away were hollow scrawls. Music that had once lifted her soul jangled like a distant cacophony.

But this new thought echoed so strongly, it filled her:

Could the tablet do the same for my love? Could it make Wilson whole again?

If so, there'd be no need for Richard's guilt. With the right words, she could convince the proud beast-father to forgive his only son. She knew she could. And then, they could all be together again.

The possibility—no matter how distant, no matter how slight—kept her from going back to bed. Even if it meant caring again, even if it meant embracing the darker side of her husband's dealings.

Because love was once the heart of creation.

And creation could be a bloody, bloody thing.

NINETEEN

THE FOLLOWING morning, Peter emerged to greet Harry. His thoughts were dominated by his aunt and the tablet, but he was still determined to make an effort.

"Hey, Harry. Got to head to the *Bugle* to drop off some photos, then get to class, but I've got some time. I thought I'd see who was hanging at the Coffee Bean. Want to come with?"

The death-stare Harry gave him stopped him mid-stride. Harry picked up his breakfast plate, still half-full of food, and tossed it into the sink so hard it sounded like the dish cracked. Peter had seen his roommate afraid, arrogant, and irritable when struggling with drugs—but this was different.

"What's up with you?"

Harry pushed past Peter, grabbed his cardigan from the thrift-store coat stand, and stuffed it under his arm. The slamming door shook the wall, rattling the kitschy Big Eye poster MJ had given them as a joke.

"Harry?"

Peter tried to think of anything he might have said or done, or anything he *hadn't* said or done, that might've set Harry off. But he couldn't. They barely spoke anymore.

I could follow him as Spidey, make sure he's clean. But I don't want to start eavesdropping on the poor guy like he's some super villain unless I've got a good reason.

Peter's arrival at the Coffee Bean made the point moot. Harry still looked grim, slouched over a hot cup of java. Mary Jane, Randy, and Flash Thompson— home for good since his tour had ended—sat with him. They didn't look particularly happy, either. In fact, when he tried to pull up a chair to join them, they all gave him the same death-stare.

"What? Did I rob a bank in my sleep or something?"

Harry's face twitched. Flash clenched a fist. Randy turned away.

Mary Jane pursed her lips. Wrapping her hand around her mug, she turned it left and right as she tried to explain.

"Tiger, Aunt Anna told me what happened at the hospital last night. She was very upset."

Had there been more bad news about Aunt May? No, the doctors would have called him. When he furrowed his brow, she spelled it out.

"The transplant. The doctor wanted to test you, but you refused?"

His heart lodged in his throat. "Oh."

Flash looked him in the eyes. "I spent the last two years taking enemy fire for people I didn't even know, and you're afraid to save your aunt's life because…what? You're too much a coward to go under the knife?"

The old accusation didn't hit him as hard as it once had, but the disappointment in all their eyes did.

He felt himself stammering. "It's not that."

"Then what is it?" Randy asked.

Peter opened his mouth. Nothing came out.

The silence stretched until Harry pressed a fingernail hard into the wooden tabletop, trying to scratch out one of the old stains.

"I know what it is," he said. "We all do. Maybe… it's only Peter being Peter, thinking only about Peter, just like Peter always has."

Mary Jane gave him a sharp glance. "Hey, take it easy! His aunt's really sick."

He picked his head up and glared back. "And my father's dead."

Mary Jane sighed. "It's been a rough year for all of us." She looked at Peter. "You know me, I keep it light whenever I can. *You* like to be the silent brooding type. But I think we've all gotten old enough to know you can't always be what you want. Some things you just have to deal with. So please, Petey, why don't you tell us what's going on?"

He tried to conjure some explanation that would at least make some sense, but he couldn't. Or maybe, after all this time, he just didn't have the heart.

So he said, "I can't."

And he left.

Thinking that for once dealing with Jonah

wouldn't be the most painful part of his day, Peter made his way to the *Bugle* offices. Betty was out sick; a polite but befuddled intern was trying to cover the phones in her absence. The intern let him pass without a second glance.

On the way to Jameson's door, Robbie Robertson stepped up and put a sympathetic hand on Peter's shoulder.

"Randy told me what's going on with your aunt. I hope she recovers."

Peter managed a brave smile. "Thanks, Mr. Robertson."

The City Editor tapped his knuckle to his lips as if debating whether to speak his mind. "Pete, before you head in, I want to show you something."

His back to the staff, Robbie slightly lifted his white shirt to reveal a five-inch scar down the center of his abdomen. "Appendectomy, when I was in high school, before laparoscopy. The ER surgeon left some bleeding, so they had to go back in to cauterize it. Was I scared? Sure. But I made it. You can, too."

Not sure what to say, Peter nodded dumbly.

"Did I hear that lazy ingrate who calls himself a photographer come in?"

At least I can count on JJJ to stick to business…

The door flew open. Jameson leveled a pencil at him. "It *is* you!"

Peter held up his camera. "I've got some Spidey pics."

Jonah *tsked.* "Your aunt's lying in the hospital and

you're out gallivanting with that vigilante? I thought you were better than that, kid."

Peter threw up his hands. "Last time I saw you, you were screaming that if I didn't bring in more pictures fast, I'd be fired!"

"Sure, blame the man who provides you with a living." Jameson grabbed the camera and clicked through. "Peh. I *could* splatter these across the front page: Spider-Menace Beaten by Ten-Year-Old. But I won't, and you know why?"

"Because people are sick of you attacking Spider-Man?"

"No! Wait, did that new intern show you our survey results? Well, that's got nothing to do with it! The only reason I'm not using these photos is to teach you a lesson about priorities." He shook his finger in Peter's face. "Family first!"

Between the hospital, class, and the tablet, Peter had expected a long day. He hadn't expected the morning, all on its own, to feel like two weeks.

So when he switched to Spider-Man and took to traveling high above the sidewalks, he didn't kid himself that acrobatics could take his mind off things. It wasn't the usual guilt that plagued him, or the sense that the world had done him wrong.

It wasn't, *Oh, no, everyone hates me!*

It wasn't even, *Aunt May needs me and I can't be there for her!*

It was the sickly realization that she could actually die.

Part of him knew it had to happen eventually. But she was his mother figure, his anchor. He hated to think her feet might get chilly if she didn't have enough blankets, let alone that one day she'd end up beneath the ground in that endless field of stones.

He was still thinking about it when he landed on the rear wall of ESU's Life Sciences building. Long minutes passed before he remembered why he'd come.

I'm so twisted up I can't think straight. No wonder Aunt May didn't want to tell me about her health.

He rapped on the glass. A one-armed man, alone in the classroom, whirled from his blackboard calculations and greeted Spider-Man with a smile. This time, Peter didn't need to look up a hieroglyph expert online. One of the only two people who'd managed to translate the tablet, Dr. Curt Connors, happened to be an ESU adjunct, on track to becoming a full professor.

He cranked open the window and beckoned Spider-Man in. "What can I do for you?"

Spider-Man touched down on the floor and pulled the webbed stone off his back.

"I really hate to tell you this, but…"

After a brief explanation, he showed Connors the photos. "Is it possible Silvermane survived?"

A grim Connors circled the boy's face with his finger. "I see the resemblance, especially in his eyes. But, honestly, I have no idea if it's possible, or what it might mean."

"Did the tablet have any instructions? Like, 'Take two of me and call me in the morning'?"

Connors nodded. "Once Wesley and I separated the chemical formulation from the prose, we focused on the chemistry. With some further study, though, I might be able to learn something. Do you want to leave it with me?"

Spider-Man shook his head. "Doc, you're one of the only people in the world I trust, but as long as I don't know who's after this thing or why, I don't want to let it out of my sight. That's as much for your safety as it is for anyone else's. Can you make a charcoal rubbing of it or something?"

"A rubbing wouldn't work. The meaning of the glyphs varies with their depth." Tapping his chin, he looked around. "I don't have a 3D scanner handy, but I do have some quick-setting silicone that I use to make fossil molds. I hesitate to use it on such a singular artifact, but the stone seems durable, and I suppose we don't have much choice. Can you spare 15 minutes?"

Spider-Man glanced at the clock. There was plenty of time before his Advanced Experimental Physics class. "For an ancient relic? Sure."

He set the tablet on the desk. Connors covered it with lubricant, then poured the liquid silicone and worked it into the carved runes. As Spider-Man watched, his mind drifted back to Aunt May.

He is *one of the only people I can trust. Why not trust him with something else?*

"Doc, you mind if I ask you about something more personal?"

"Are you kidding?" Connors smiled. "You saved my family's life and kept me from spending the rest of mine as a mindless predator. Ask whatever you want."

Peter exhaled. "Okay, then. Someone I love is going to need a liver transplant, and I'm the most available donor. Only, my body and my blood are, well, radioactive, for starters—it's tied in with how I became what I am. I want to help, but I'm afraid that disqualifies me."

Connors nodded in sympathy. "I'm sorry. Have you told the surgeon?"

Peter pointed at his mask.

"Right. Your identity. Of course." The tablet was covered with silicone now. Connors set a small timer and placed it next to the stone. "You probably don't want to hear this, but from what I already know about your physiology, it certainly *does* disqualify you. Modern surgical teams are trained to deal with a lot of things, but radioactive blood isn't one of them."

Spider-Man stiffened. "I…have to do something."

Connors put a hand on his shoulder. "I understand, better than most. It wasn't long ago I was fiddling with the DNA of other creatures because *I* had to do something to help. We know how that worked out. Even if they did go ahead with the transplant, it would be the first of its kind, adding huge layers of risk to an already complicated procedure. I certainly wouldn't risk it, particularly with someone I cared for. I would…try to find another way."

The wall-crawler sighed and lowered his head. "I

was afraid you'd say something like that. Now I just have to figure out how to tell them without telling them. Thanks, Doc."

The room fell silent save for the ticking timer. When it dinged, Connors peeled the rubbery cast from the stone. "How should I contact you if I learn anything?"

"Oh." Spider-Man grabbed a pen and scribbled a number on a pad. "This is Peter Parker's number. He can get a hold of me. He's a student here."

Connors looked at the name. "The fellow who takes photos of you. If you speak to him before I do, you might want to tell him Professor Blanton mentioned his name at a faculty meeting, and not in a good way."

Perfect.

"I'll, uh, do that."

"Wait. Before you go, I think I have an airtight case about the right size for the tablet. It *is* our only relic from a lost civilization."

"Sure. As long as I can carry it."

The slim silver case was a snug fit, but it worked. Spider-Man secured it to his back and left Dr. Connors to his work. Crawling to the front of the building, he glanced across the plaza at the large Art Deco clock tower atop the recently reopened Exhibition Hall. With plenty of time to get to class, his eyes wandered down to the line at the entrance.

Took them long enough to finish the renovations, but at least it looks like the hall's attracting plenty of those potential donors that the dean—

His body flew into a tuck jump. A park bench, of all things, came flying at him. It'd been ripped from the asphalt and thrown. That meant two things: Whatever had thrown it was very strong, and not particularly subtle.

A baritone shouted, "For the love of…! Stay still a second, will ya?"

Spider-Man didn't have to get closer to recognize his attacker.

I'd know that man mountain anywhere!

TWENTY

MICHAEL Marko stood on the sidewalk, shaking his fists. Students, food-cart vendors, and faculty fled in all directions.

"Get down here!"

Got to keep him where he is long enough for everyone to get to safety.

Spider-Man shot a web-line that snagged a lamppost, and used it to zip across the sidewalk. The balls of his feet skimmed Marko's thick black hair.

"Is your memory that short? I mean, you're a perfectly fine bruiser in a pinch, but do you really want to tangle with me again?"

His heels sticking to the lamppost, Spider-Man went into a sideways crouch and leapt to the thickest branch of a nearby oak. Meanwhile, Marko had torn a second bench from its foundation.

"Hey, you put that back!"

But of course Marko threw it. Spider-Man's web snagged the bench in midair, letting him bring it to a landing on the grass below.

By then, Marko was already ripping out a third.

"Stop that! Geez. I heard you tore a couch in half at the Stacys', now it's park benches? You got something against people sitting down?"

"You want me to stop, come down here and face me!"

"Nothing personal, but have you seen your face lately? Besides, how much longer you think you've got before the cops show?"

"Long enough!" He wrenched the third bench free and chucked it. Considering its awkward shape, the projectile flew with surprising accuracy. Spider-Man caught it with both hands, glanced at the copper plaque mounted on the top slat, and wedged it down on the branch beside him.

"Aw! This one's a memorial to Ms. Maddie Blaustein of Long Island!"

When Spider-Man stood up, Marko looked excited, eager to fight. But instead of heading down to meet him on the grass, Spider-Man sat on the treed bench. Seeing how much it irritated Man Mountain, he clasped his hands behind his head and pretended to yawn.

"So, what brings you, Man? Or would you rather I called you Mr. Mountain?"

As far as keeping people safe, so far so good. The plaza's almost empty, the building's sealed, and campus security's blocking off the perimeter.

Unfortunately, a lean, blond, bespectacled student chose that moment to leave his hiding spot in the bushes and run out into the open. "Help! For the love of god, help me!" he screamed.

Nuts.

Spider-Man and Marko saw the student at the same time, but the giant was closer. Marko took off at a run, his long strides moving him farther and faster than Peter remembered. Before Spider-Man could move, Marko had snatched the runner and pinned both his arms to his chest.

"Heeellllp!"

"Right in my freaking ear!" Marko covered the youth's mouth—his entire face, actually—with his large hand. "One more peep and I push your head so far down into your chest, you'll have to undo your fly to sneeze, got me?"

When his captive shakily nodded, Marko turned to Spider-Man. "Gonna come down now?"

"Okay, okay!" He sailed from the tree and crouched on the ground a few yards away. "You move pretty fast, big guy. You working out?"

He nodded. "I got a trainer helping me turn my deficits into advantages."

"Good to know. I've come to the mountain, so what do you want?"

"Can't you guess? The rock, I figure, is in that case on your back. Got a client willing to pay, and I could really use the cash."

Spider-Man titled his head. "The Maggia says they're not interested. Who hired you? Was it Silvermane?"

Marko's eyes went wide. "No! You trying to trick me? He's dead!"

Just hearing his old master's name really rattled him. Marko must be working for someone else.

"No trick, but as long as you're going to get all shook-up like that, it'd be a shame if I didn't take advantage."

A gooey *thwip* covered Marko's eyes with webbing. Blinded, he reached for the sticky mass, releasing the terrified student long enough for Spider-Man to grab him and deposit him a hundred yards away.

As soon as they landed, the student started screaming again. "Help! Help!"

"Take a breath, okay?"

By the time Peter turned back, Marko was gone.

He pulled off my web already? Apparently he's stronger than I remember, too.

A search of the plaza and the streets beyond the Life Sciences building yielded nothing but pedestrians and cars.

How does someone his size hide so fast? Maybe I'm lucky I didn't fight him.

He glanced again at the tower clock.

And now I really do have to change and get to Professor Blanton's class.

o———————————o

MARKO lay low in the rear of the stolen service van, pulling the remains of the gross webbing from his skin.

This stuff's worse than chewing gum!

A wad had even gotten wedged up into his hair.

Word on the street was that it dissolved if you waited long enough, but Marko had never been a patient man. He grabbed it and yanked.

"YEOW!"

He slammed his hand over his mouth and looked through the windshield. He'd reached the van just before the cops started arriving. Now they were all over. He was lucky they hadn't heard.

Head stinging, he looked down at the little bloody clump of hair and scalp in his hand.

What a freaking waste! I don't get it. That first bench should've nailed him, but it was like he saw it coming without seeing it coming.

Marko had thought he was being so smart. Knowing that Spider-Man was present when the tablet was heisted, he'd spent hours scanning the police band. He wondered whether that costumed idiot had any idea how many eyes the cops had on him. From the chatter, it sounded like half the NYPD had a Spidey-sighting pool going.

When he saw the bulge on Spidey's back, he figured he'd hit pay dirt.

But he'd blown it. Hearing Silvermane's name was like seeing the bogeyman come to life.

He can't be back. It was a trick. But…if Mr. Silvermane did come back, would he be angry with me for working with someone else?

Right now, it didn't matter. Spider-Man and the tablet were gone, along with Marko's chance of collecting that sweet piece of change from Vanessa

Fisk—and his big shot at impressing her.

That hurt, and not just because he needed a new job. Yeah, he was strapped for cash. Since Cicero had let him go, the odd freelance enforcement jobs he got were barely enough to keep him in pocket change. But ever since he'd first scoped out the Kingpin for the Maggia, there was something about Vanessa Fisk he found alluring. He even kept some pictures of her tacked up over his bed, trying to add a little class to that dump.

And besides, he really *did* want to squash Spider-Man.

FOR OBVIOUS reasons, Peter didn't carry his cell phone into combat. He also turned it off whenever he left it behind, lest he forget to mute it. Otherwise, a buzz or ringtone might alert a passeby to the bundle of clothing concealed in a web-sack.

With seconds remaining before Advanced Experimental Physics began, Peter turned the phone back on, in case the hospital called. Reaching the lecture hall, he saw the dour Professor Blanton through the little window in the closed door, waving for him to hurry. Peter's hand grabbed the doorknob, but before he could turn it, a string of missed emergency texts made him freeze.

Through the window, Blanton gave him a wary nod. There was no time to explain. Peter mouthed "I'm sorry" and bolted away.

Dr. Bromwell and Dr. Fent, the woman he'd

spoken with on the phone, met him in the lobby of the Presbyterian Center for Liver Disease and Transplantation. Peter's eyes shot between them. Their placid expressions were unreadable.

"What happened? Is she all right?"

Dr. Bromwell replied. "She's fine."

But Dr. Fent added, "For now. Her condition has worsened, so she's been moved to the ICU. To slow down her metabolism, and hopefully stabilize her, we've put her in an induced coma."

Peter gasped. "A coma?"

She nodded. "She's on a steady drip of propanol. She was aware of the need and gave her consent for any treatment we deemed necessary. She wanted to see you before we proceeded, in case, well…we texted and waited as long as we thought safe."

Peter's eyes darted about, focusing on nothing. "My phone…the charge ran out. Can I see her?"

"Of course." Bromwell half-smiled. "Peter, I've known you since you were a child. I'd like to talk to you a minute about the transplant."

"Actually, Doc, I want to talk about that, too, but I'd like to speak to Dr. Fent alone, if that's okay."

"Oh." Bromwell looked taken aback, but acquiesced. "Certainly."

He stepped back to the information desk and began checking his phone.

Dr. Fent looked at Peter expectantly.

He wasn't sure where to start. "Uh, Dr. Bromwell's very close to the family, and, he's great, but he gets a little chatty with my aunt sometimes. There are things about me I'd rather she not know."

She raised an eyebrow. "Your family's not big on sharing about their medical problems, are they?"

Peter tried to offer a wry smile. "Yeah, well, I guess we worry too much about each other. Anyway, I have a…blood condition that Doc Conn…uh, my *other* doctor…says makes me a lousy candidate for a transplant. For her safety, not mine."

"Is your doctor certain? Today even HIV-positive patients are allowed to donate organs."

"It's not AIDS. And yes, we're pretty sure."

Fent looked dubious, but didn't challenge the information. "This condition—do you have it under control?"

"Pretty much. I like to think so, anyway. I'm not contagious, if that's what you're getting at. But this isn't about me. Is there anything else that can be done for my aunt?"

"She's already on the donor list, but I believe Dr. Bromwell explained that her age puts her at a disadvantage. There is an experimental treatment, Obetical, that's shown promise restoring liver function. This hospital is conducting trials—but again, her age makes her a poor candidate. And it hasn't been approved yet, so no insurance will cover it."

"What would it cost without insurance?"

"Over a hundred thousand dollars, I'm afraid."

Peter wasn't sure how long he stood there with his mouth open before he finally said, "Oh."

TWENTY-ONE

COMPARED to the gray semi-private room, the ICU was open and bright, with light-green walls and wide window views. Cushioned seats were scattered among ten beds, accommodating visitors staying only a few minutes as well as family members curled up for a long haul. Peter's eyes cast about nervously until he spotted Aunt May.

The thought that she would like the view of the Hudson brought some relief. Even the steady mechanical hush didn't bother him...until he was close enough to realize it came from a ventilator connected to a flexible blue tube that ran down her throat.

The yellow tinge had faded a bit from her skin. Some pink showed through beneath the nearly invisible peach fuzz on her face. She appeared well cared for, freshly bathed, her gray and white hair neatly combed back. The pattern on her hospital gown was faded, but clean. The off-blue would have matched her eyes, had they been open.

Still holding it together, he pulled up a chair. But when he sat down, suddenly he didn't know whether to scream or sob. Whatever slight wisdom the years had given him, there would always be some things that made him feel like a helpless child.

Great power may bring great responsibility, but it can also be pretty damn useless. I don't have anywhere near the money to save her, but I've got the secret of eternal youth sitting under my bed, something humanity's been after since we got up on two feet—and what good is it? If it wasn't so sad, it'd be funny. Unless…

Suddenly, a thought struck him.

If Silvermane is still alive, maybe that elixir can help Aunt May.

An odd intuition made him look up. Anna Watson was at the entrance, not quite coming in, not quite turning back. Wondering how long she'd been standing there, he rose to offer her his chair.

"Mrs. Watson?"

As if bracing herself for something unpleasant, she inhaled and stepped closer. Noticing the brush she carried in her hand, Peter realized she was the one who'd combed his aunt's hair.

"You've been here all this time?"

"She's my best friend."

"Of course…I'm grateful she has you."

"And you…" she began. Then she literally bit her lip. "No. I promised Mary Jane I wouldn't say anything, so I'll keep my opinions to myself. I think it would be best if I waited outside until you've left."

I hate having her feel that way.

"No, you take the chair, please. I was just leaving."

Her silence was worse than her recriminations.

He slinked out. With little over an hour left in Professor Blanton's three-hour class, he headed back to ESU.

Hoping to avoid attention, Peter tried to sneak in the back of the lecture hall. Of course, the door was locked. He rapped softly on the glass panel until a student seated along the aisle took pity and reached out to turn the handle. As she did, she knocked her textbook to the floor. Blanton immediately stopped speaking. Worse, the hinges squeaked as Peter stepped in, and all eyes turned to him. The door squeaked even louder. A few students tittered sympathetically.

The wiry, balding Blanton, who always looked exasperated, slapped the side of his lectern to get their attention. "Quiet!"

Peter tried to move toward an empty seat, but the professor called to him.

"Don't sit just yet, Mr. Parker. I'd like to know what sort of excuse you have this time."

Even Blanton would have to understand that his aunt's condition was an emergency, but this wasn't the right time or place to explain.

"I realize I owe you an apology, sir, but I'd rather discuss that in private."

After a pregnant pause, Blanton gave him a curt nod. "Very well. Let's get back to the rules for counting significant figures. As I was saying, all zeroes between non-zero digits are significant…"

Maneuvering an obstacle course of backpacks and

folded legs, Peter tried to reach the only open spot quietly. But then the door squeaked open again.

Entering, a harried Doctor Connors zeroed in on Peter. "Sorry for the interruption, John. Do you mind if I borrow Peter Parker for a bit?"

Blanton tossed his hands in the air. "Not at all, Curt. Please, by all means. Keep him."

Abashed, Peter struggled back along the cramped seats. All the while, Connors excitingly waved for him to hurry, while Blanton remained deadly silent.

They all but ran to the Life Sciences building.

"What is it, Doc? Spider-Man told me you were trying to figure something out from that old tablet. Did you?"

"I did. Turns out he was right. Silvermane is alive!"

"But how? I thought the guy vanished into non-existence or something."

"The problem is 'or something.' I was making progress with the inscriptions when it dawned on me that a simple experiment could provide a much faster answer. It'd probably be best if I showed you."

Once they were inside his faculty lab, the door locked behind them, Connors flipped on an electron microscope. "Usually, the specimen has to be specially prepared and held inside a vacuum chamber, but this new microscope, donated by Oscorp, is much more flexible."

As Connor adjusted the device, a monstrous image appeared on a monitor: a gangly winged creature, its exoskeleton translucent ochre, its oversized head consisting almost entirely of two bulbous red eyes.

Peter wasn't sure what he was looking at. "It looks like a refugee from a 1950s monster movie. What's it got to do with the tablet?"

"I'm getting to it. That's *Dolania americana*, a species of mayfly. It's unique in that the females have a normal life expectancy of roughly five minutes. When Silvermane drank that formula, he began getting younger. As that process continued, it accelerated, so that within hours he was an infant. Now, if you consider human life expectancy is roughly 70 years—"

"I get it. With the mayfly, it would all happen in seconds. So you made more formula?"

He removed a small vial from his lab-coat pocket and held it up. It was half-filled with a clear, sparkling liquid. "Frankly, I was surprised it worked at all on an insect. It's as if the chemical composition adapts to its host."

Using a dropper, he placed a small amount on the specimen. On the screen, a single drop appeared as a deluge. The mayfly sloshed in the liquid, but ultimately pulled itself to the surface.

"The life cycle of the mayfly consists of four stages, which for our purposes I'll recite backwards. The last, the adult stage, is called the imago."

As the fly tried to dry itself, its color grew softer and duller, its legs and tail shorter. The wings acquired a bluish tint. "This is the subimago."

The wings folded into the body, which became

long and slender. Small claws appeared at the ends of its six legs. "The nymph."

In less than a second, the body shrank into a tiny oval that settled to the bottom of the specimen container. "And the egg."

As the egg kept shrinking, Connors adjusted the magnification. Some embryonic features remained visible, but as it grew smaller still, the lines between body parts vanished.

"Now we're basically watching individuation in reverse…"

Connors made a final adjustment. The individual cells popped back into one another, until there was only one single cell left.

"…until we're left with the initial zygote, or fertilized egg. From here, you'd think the cell would disintegrate into nothingness, the way we thought Silvermane ended. However…"

After a few moments, the cells began to divide. "…the cycle starts over at the beginning. At first, things proceed at a normal pace, but then the process accelerates until the mayfly reaches the end of its cycle."

Peter watched the egg form. A nymph emerged and become a subimago, then a fully formed imago. Another second later, the fly fell on its back, twitched its legs, and stopped moving.

"Is it dead?"

Connors shrugged. "If not, it's as close to it as anything can get."

But then the legs twitched again, and the imago

righted itself. Over the next half-minute, it went through the cycle backwards again—subimago, nymph, egg, zygote.

Peter frowned. "And it keeps doing that over and over…forever?"

"As far as I can tell."

"But when Silvermane drank that stuff, he lost decades in hours, and that was about two years ago. The boy Spider-Man saw was around 10. Wouldn't he be older…or younger…by now?"

"I can't be sure exactly how it works, or if it's as stable in humans—but judging by the mayfly, the process starts off at a normal rate, then gradually accelerates. It may have taken this long for him to reach age 10."

"That's why he wants the tablet. He must know what's happening to him, and has to suspect where his aging is headed. He's probably hoping the tablet contains some way to stop the cycle. Who wouldn't? It's like a curse."

"Yes. Silvermane as a child is bad enough—and he'll be an adult pretty soon. I thought Spider-Man should know."

"I'll get him the message right away."

"Good. After that, you should probably try to catch the end of that class. Blanton looked pretty angry." Connors clicked a pen open on his knee and scribbled on an ESU memo pad. "I'll give you a note, saying I needed your help saving some lab samples."

"I'm not sure it'll help, but thanks."

Then it struck him. *If there is a way to stop the cycle, the elixir could help Aunt May.*

"Something else?" Connors asked.

Spider-Man told him about the transplant, so that question would be better coming from the web-slinger, not Peter Parker.

"No, the whole thing is just so freaky. Thanks again for the note."

CONNORS waited for Parker to leave before destroying the mayfly specimen. It had already lived four times its normal lifespan. Not knowing how its altered biology might interact with the ecosystem, he couldn't very well release it. The alternative—letting it loop through infinite lifetimes while trapped in the confines of a specimen dish—felt cruel.

He rinsed the container at the lab sink, crushed the tiny body between his fingers, and watched it swirl into the hazardous-waste disposal. From the recesses of his subconscious mind, an odd urge arose—a desire to eat the mayfly.

Lizards were fond of bugs.

It was only the sort of passing thought he had every day, the way an average person might experience a fleeting desire to throttle a driver who cut him off in traffic. The Lizard hadn't posed any real danger of resurfacing since the kidnapping.

It did make Connors sure he'd given Spider-Man the right advice about a transplant. The wall-crawler was fortunate to be able to use his powers for the benefit of others, but the two of them shared that invisible wall that separated them from the rest of their species.

From the corner of his eye, he caught a lithe figure climbing in from the window.

Speak of the devil.

"Spider-Man?" he called.

But the clothes were wrong, the voice too young.

"Silvermane!"

"My nickname, right? Good to have someone call me that again."

Studying him, Connors asked, "You're not sure?"

"I'm sure enough." He looked down at a scrap of paper in his hand. "Dr. Connors, right? The guy who got me here in the first place. It's funny what memories come and go, Doc, but listening in on your chat with that college kid filled in some more blanks. Maybe I forgot my nickname for a second, but I still followed most of that conversation. And smart as you are, you missed some stuff."

The gangly teen grew closer. His entire body was a bit off, as if stretched too quickly by the hormonal changes of puberty. But Connors was more concerned with the thing in his long-fingered hands: an old-fashioned tommy gun. Hit by a body-memory of the gangster's previous threats, Connors fought to stay calm. Silvermane's memory was clearly piecemeal, his very identity muddled. He couldn't have his former connections.

And Billy and Martha were safe, visiting relatives in Florida.

"Do you want to tell me what I missed?" Connors asked.

The question confused the boy, then angered him. "Do I *want* to tell you? No. But you're gonna *want* to listen, like your life depended on it."

When he waved the barrel in Connors' face, the Lizard writhed inside. "First off, it's not so smooth, like that fly you just flushed. Sometimes nothing happens for weeks, or months, then I get this growth spurt that hurts so bad I'm moaning on the ground like a whipped dog. When I get back up, I'm a year older and wiser."

Noticing his reflection in the window, the boy rubbed his cheek. "What do you think I am now? Fourteen? Can't wait to get some decent facial hair. Anyway, when I first came back from that, I don't know, darkness? Next I know there's these fat, fat arms lifting me, up, up, up into this huge face. Not the face of God or nothing, just some cleaning lady. She took me to a hospital, where they poked and prodded me like a pin cushion. I was like a baby. I had no idea who I was, but I knew I had to be someone. It was like the idea of me had never gone away, but it wasn't really *with* me, either. Like you think you know everything about the love of your life, only it turns out they've been a tease all along. I hightailed it out of there as soon as I could, but it wasn't until I taught myself to read that I started piecing it all together."

His acne-pocked brow twisted. He whimpered, as if he were a lost soul, desperate to be understood by someone, by anyone. But when Connors nodded sympathetically, the boy turned the gun on him again. The familiar predatory glow of Silvermane's eyes shone against the black of his pupils. He put his chin down and bobbed his head in a classic gesture of aggression.

Connors realized his mistake. *He's only telling me his symptoms because he expects me to cure him. In the end, like everything else, he'd rather keep his experiences to himself. I know what that's like.*

Silvermane sneered. "Happy as I am to have kicked the Grim Reaper's butt, by the time I hit 30, it's gotta stop—and you've gotta help. Not here, though. Don't want your buddy Spider-Man or that Parker kid sniffing around. Take what you need, but either you come with me or they won't find enough of you to bury."

Connors went into a submissive pose, eyes down. "I'll do what I can, but I'll need equipment. I have a place, not far. No one knows about it, I swear."

For some reason, his captor chuckled. "Guess we all have our secrets, huh? Well then, what are we waiting for? I ain't getting any younger—yet. Let's get going."

While Connors collected his notes and the cast of the tablet, the tommy gun remained trained on him. As he wondered what to do next, a dark thing prodded from the back of his mind:

You should have eaten that bug.

TWENTY-TWO

THEY sloshed through the dank sewers. Connors held the flashlight while Silvermane kept the machine gun pressed into the small of his back. The persistent danger hadn't riled the creature to the point of transformation yet, but Connors was increasingly struggling with its presence. The humidity reminded the Lizard of the Everglade swamps, its home. Unfortunately, it also reminded the creature of the importance of defending its territory.

Reaching the right spot, Connors set the flashlight on a ridge above the muck and felt along the wall for the hidden lever. It was only when he found it that he started questioning *why* he'd been so ready to reveal his lab's location. It made some sense: His equipment and old files were down here, and if the gun were fired, no one else need be involved. But it was equally possible that a more primal motive lurked beneath his selfless veneer.

Everyone thinks Silvermane is dead. No one would miss him.

Putting the thought into words gave it power.

Throttling his enemy seemed *so* reasonable, it made Connors shudder.

If the resurrected gangster noticed, he didn't seem to care. His attention was fixed on the curved wall tugging away from the slime with a moist plop. Full-spectrum lighting spilled into the dismal dark, revealing a clean white space equipped with high-tech apparatus and scores of bubbling bio-tanks populated by rare plants and reptiles.

Silvermane let out a low whistle. "All this on a professor's salary, huh? That university must be choking on change."

The creature twitched as the invader stepped inside its nest.

"Actually," Connors said, "I did a lot of the construction myself, and my research provided some valuable patents that have earned back my salary several times over."

Silvermane quickly located the only comfortable chair and plopped down in it. The creature didn't like that, either. Seeing the look on Connors' face, Silvermane waved the gun, as if a reminder of its presence was somehow necessary.

"I'd advise you not to waste time getting that big brain all steamed. You got work to do."

The acne on Silvermane's face was a little thinner now, his features slightly more adult.

Maybe I could trap him here, contact Spider-Man. Or better yet...leave him until he's a helpless infant again, and take care of him myself.

"Would you mind not aiming that right at me, please?"

Silvermane sniggered and lowered the weapon.

The creature grew quieter, if not docile. Connors placed the rubber cast beneath an overhead lens and projected its image on the wall. "You heard me say I'd only translated the chemical formula—that to get farther, I had to study the prose?"

Silvermane made a face, as if to say maybe he had and maybe he hadn't. "So?"

"I have some hunches, but I'll need a few hours to confirm them."

Fidgety, Silvermane looked around. Noticing a big red Emergency button on one wall, he asked. "What's that for, launching a rocket?"

Connors was afraid he'd have to answer, but before he'd parted his lips, the gangster had moved on. "Got internet down here?"

He not only looks like a teen—in many ways, he is one. He needs distraction.

Connors set him up with a browser at one of the terminals and went to work.

o——————————o

BY THE clock, there were 10 minutes remaining, but when Blanton spotted Peter attempting to tiptoe back in, he abruptly dismissed the class. As the students exited, he stared at Peter, not speaking, not really moving at all. Peter didn't move, either. Only his shoulders sagged lower and lower.

Once the other students were gone, Peter walked up, the scrawled memo from Dr. Connors in his outstretched hand. He felt like a little boy in grade school instead of a brilliant physics student speaking to an erudite instructor.

"I have a note."

Blanton took the sheet and read it. "You had to assist Dr. Connors in preserving some valuable specimens. That makes at least one faculty member at ESU grateful for being able to rely on your presence."

He crumpled the note into a ball and tossed it toward the wastebasket. Neither of them noticed whether it went in.

"Mr. Parker, do you have any idea how many of my classes you've missed this semester?"

Peter shrugged helplessly.

"I sympathize. Neither do I. But it's far, far easier to recall exactly how many times you *have* been here. Three. Three times."

"I'm so sorry, Professor Blanton, but my aunt—"

He held up his hand like a traffic cop. "I don't doubt there are reasons. As physics teaches us, nothing occurs without them. But there comes a point where the very idea that anyone can somehow complete this department's rigorous requirements in absentia is no longer viable."

"I understand. I'll try harder. I swear. I'm happy to do any makeup assignments or extra work—"

Blanton waved his raised palm dismissively. "I've brought your case up with the disciplinary committee. When they convene tomorrow at 3:15, I'll be recommending a year-long academic suspension. That should provide you some time to examine your priorities."

Blanton turned to leave. Stunned, Peter followed him into the hall.

"Sir, please! I'll have to reapply for my scholarship. I'll never get the same level of aid with my current GPA. I won't be able to finish school!"

"Mr. Parker, there are a lot of equally qualified applicants who could use that money, and I can't help but think most of them would actually be *sitting* in that very expensive seat currently reserved for you."

"But—"

Blanton snapped. "For pity's sake, man! Save your breath. You're going to need it for the review committee. *If* you manage to attend."

o————————o

FOR ABOUT 15 minutes, Silvermane's eyes twitched between Connors at work and the borrowed computer. Then he settled down, enraptured by whatever he'd found. That made it easier for the biochemist to focus on the task at hand.

Sooner than expected, Connors had gone as far as his limited linguistics background could take him. Rather than announce that fact, he took the opportunity to study his abductor. While the scientist within him sought a fuller understanding of the elixir's effects, the creature hunted for a sign of weakness.

Manfredi seemed to understand the computer well enough. But unlike a modern youth, whose fingers might fly across a keyboard, Silvermane hunted and pecked with one hand.

Curious, Connors crept closer, barely aware of how silently he moved. On the screen were a series of articles and photos from the *Bugle*, the *Times*, CNN, and more. Some were as recent as a year old; others went back to World War II. All shared the same subject: Silvio Manfredi, from his birth in Corleone, Sicily, through his career as a racketeer, his bloody rise in the Maggia, and his disappearance.

He's trying to rediscover his own history. Not having that connection must make someone so egocentric feel... vulnerable. But, like any animal, that only makes him more dangerous.

The tommy gun was on the table. Silvermane's free hand covered the fore-grip as if it were a computer mouse. Still certain that he hadn't been noticed, Connors turned his attention from the screen to the youth. It'd been over an hour, but the acne wasn't quite clear yet, and Silvermane didn't appear much older.

I should eat him now while he's still tender.

Either Connors' shock at his own thought gave away his presence, or Silvermane had known he was there all along. Without moving his eyes from the screen, the gangster leisurely raised the gun and tucked the long barrel under Connors' chin.

"Got something for me yet?"

Knock it away. He won't expect it. Protect the nest.

Connors fought to bury the urge. "Yes. You know how the legends believe it contained the formula for a fountain of youth?"

Silvermane indicated his own face. "And the legends were true. Duh."

"No, they weren't. Not exactly. From what I can gather, the ancients who created the tablet had loftier goals in mind. Their belief system is similar enough to Hindu and other Eastern religions to make me think it may have been an antecedent. Basically, they believed the soul not only reincarnates, it has to experience multiple incarnations in order to perfect itself. The elixir's goal is to speed that process, to take a soul through as many lifetimes as necessary to remove its impurities and achieve what they considered life's ultimate state: a transcendent, omniscient, omnipotent form."

Silvermane's scrunched-up face reminded Connors of a high-school student trying to grasp calculus. "Omnipotent, like a god? I like the sound of that. But why is my memory all jiggedy? Don't I have to remember stuff, if I'm supposed to learn?"

Connors struggled to put it in simple terms. "I'm no philosopher, but to their way of thinking, the self and all its attachments are an illusion. Ideally, the ego has to be *lost* to reach perfection."

"An illusion? You mean like 'Merrily, merrily, life's but a dream'?"

"Sort of. More like the self is made up of desire, and desire is the dream. Nirvana is understanding that everything is already as it should be, and nothing need be changed. In that supreme state, all desire—including any desire to wield power—is gone." He pointed to the screen. "From what I've read, these efforts to cling to your history could keep you trapped in the cycle forever."

Disappointment and resentment mixed with the confusion on the teen's face. It made him look older, more like the Silvio Manfredi that Connors recalled with dread.

"What, so to get what I want I have to stop wanting it? That don't make no sense. It's a lousy cheat. A lie. There's got to be a way to stop it, a cure."

As a teacher, Connors knew that simply telling Silvermane he was wrong would only create more resistance. But he'd always been better at research than dealing with students.

"You're not thinking about it correctly."

The reaction was more extreme than expected. Silvermane hopped off his stool. Swinging the gun barrel, jutting his head forward, he spat as he spoke. "I'm not what? You think it's smart to tell me how I should be thinking?"

The scientist backed up, trying to keep Manfredi from invading the creature's personal space. "Please. I'm not telling you what to do. I'm only trying to explain their way of thinking. They didn't see what you're going through as a curse or disease. They saw it as a cure, *the* cure for all the pains of our impermanent lives."

"Nah. Nah. Nah! That's like saying death's a cure

for life. I've cured more than enough people that way to know it ain't for me. Those ancients were freaking crazy."

If it had been an academic argument, that might've been the end of it. But for an ego that already took disagreement as disobedience, there was so much more at stake. Silvermane turned his head left and right, as if trying to physically dislodge Connor's explanation.

I can almost see the wheels turning. If the facts don't give him what he wants, then the facts must be wrong.

Sure enough, inner conviction seemed to force the confusion from Silvermane's face. "You must've missed something, or that hunk of rubber ain't got the whole story. There's got to be more on that tablet. I got to get it back." He advanced on Connors. "And you're not going anywhere until I do."

Backed into a wall, there was nowhere for the scientist, or the creature, to go. Silvermane was so close, so threatening, that before Connors could censor it, the thing inside him answered.

"There *is* nothing else, you fool!"

Silvermane cracked the gun into Connor's jaw, smacking his head into the wall. His body sank to the floor.

"Think you're better than me, huh? Think you've outgrown *your* personal attachments?" Silvermane strutted back to the monitor and clicked a browser tab. "Like your wife and kid?"

Pictures of Billy and Martha came up on the screen.

"That's right, Connors, I might be a slow typist,

but I tracked their freaking hotel reservations. I know exactly where they are."

Curt Connors wanted to stay down, but his body began rising just the same. "If you harm them—"

Silvermane came at him again. "If? There's no if about it. But let's get even more personal. How's your leg? Think you've outgrown *that?*"

He kicked Connors just below the knee. Pain roared through Connors' body. If he went prone, acted submissive again, Silvermane might back off—but the Lizard wasn't a pack animal and didn't understand. Refusing to fall, to show any sign of weakness, it remained half-standing, infuriating the mobster all the more.

"How about your head? Still attached to that?"

Again the gun whipped forward. Connors used his single arm to block the blow. The still-human part of him pleaded, "Stop! You don't understand the danger…"

Silvermane's face turned red. "Still won't go down? Fine—you learned to live without one arm, how about I take care of the other? Maybe then you'll STOP GIVING ME ORDERS!"

He grabbed Connors' arm and twisted. Again, the pain roared through his body. This time, something roared back. Connors howled, bucked, and buckled— but not because of the mammal holding his arm.

"Finally! Now tell me how to contact that Parker kid you were talking to. He can lead me to Spider-Man."

Silvermane didn't seem to notice the new limb erupting from Connors' stump. It wasn't until the scales started rippling along Connors' good arm that the fool realized what was happening.

It felt so very good, like shedding a tight dry shell and feeling air against fresh, new skin.

"I'd…be happy to give you…his number," Connors hissed. "In fact, I'll write it down…in your blood!"

Before the reptilian snout could finish growing, the Lizard tried to snap it shut on Silvermane's face. But the youth was too fast. He pulled back, barely in time.

"Holy…"

Only slightly disappointed, the Lizard hissed again. Its spine was now fully extended, ending in the thick tail that provided its powerful form with uncanny balance as well as the equivalent of a fifth limb.

Its prey would not escape again.

"Little mouse, little mouse, so full of its feeble little hungers. Let's see how you fare with mine!"

"Stay away from me!" Manfredi fired, but the spray didn't last long, and the bullets bounced off the creature's thick hide.

"No." It snatched the tommy gun and threw it away. "I won't."

Silvermane scrambled to escape. The Lizard took its time, tilting its head left and then right, first sizing him up, then hunching forward and gliding toward him. The Lizard was surprised that anger still remained on the mammal's face, rather than fear. But at least the food wasn't talking anymore.

Manfredi kept backing away, throwing whatever he could—specimen tanks, computer terminals, chemical vials—in the creature's path.

It'd been so long since the Lizard had hunted, it considered opening the door and letting the prey out, so it could have the pleasure of chasing him through the sewers. But no—this warm-blooded lump of protein had not only threatened the nest, he'd threatened the boy and the woman.

Silvermane had just about run out of things to throw when his eye went to the big red button on the wall.

Recalling the precautions that the fool Connors had prepared, the creature shouted, "No!"

Hearing the panic in the Lizard's voice, Silvermane slammed the button so hard, he cracked the plastic surface in half. In an instant, hissing white clouds streamed down from nozzles hidden in the ceiling. The temperature dropped precipitously.

Silvermane dove beneath a table, but the Lizard was no longer interested in hunting. It tried to raise itself up on its tail to stop the freezing gas. Its claws reached the nozzles, but they were *so cold*—their very touch burned its skin, making it flake a dull gray. In preparing this safeguard against his own transformation, Connors had installed no off-switch. All the Lizard could do was flail and pound the walls as the clouds of liquid nitrogen forced it down to the floor. It curled into a ball as the air grew colder and colder, until it had to close its eyes. As darkness overtook the Lizard-mind, it feared Connors would reassert himself.

But when the creature woke, it was still in its reptile form. There were chains on it, though, clasping its arms and legs. Its tail remained free, but the youth who should have been a meal stood just out of reach, chuckling.

"Wow, people got all *kinds* of secrets, huh? Found those chains in a drawer here, and there were hooks in the wall, so I figured they were meant for times like this."

The boy looked a little older, a little stronger—but not nearly strong enough. "Connors may have wanted to protect his warm-blooded associates, but the Lizard has no such compunctions," the Lizard hissed. "Peter Parker's number is on Connors' phone. It's right here, in the pocket of his lab coat. Why don't you reach in to get it?"

"And lose a finger? No thanks, I think I'll just look it up. How many Peter Parkers attending ESU could there be? Meantime, you can stay put. From what I read about myself, I was a dog lover. Never had a lizard before, but we'll see how it goes."

Seeing himself reflected in the glass of one of the few unbroken terrariums, Manfredi slicked back his hair and adjusted his jacket.

"Speaking of dogs, I think it's time I reintroduced myself to some of my old associates. Starting with…" He struggled to recall the name. "Molehill? Nah. Mountain? That's it. Man Mountain Marko. I bet that dog misses his master."

TWENTY-THREE

LOVELY as the Brooklyn Bridge looked with the early morning sun glinting through its web of steel cables, it held painful memories. As Spider-Man sat on the base of the Manhattan-side tower foundation, he wondered why on Earth he'd chosen this spot.

I used to come here with my scooter, just to think. I miss that scooter.

I miss Gwen.

He used his web-shooters to fashion an air sack, the sort he'd seen diving bell spiders on documentaries use to stay underwater for long periods. He rolled his mask halfway up, covered his nose and mouth with the air sack, and dove. He swam deeper and deeper, keeping an eye on the cement foundation to guide him through the murky darkness.

The cold didn't bother him as much as the oily feeling of the river water; he'd probably never get the grime out of his costume. Luckily, the air sack held, all the way down to the riverbed. He removed the protective case from his back and lodged it in the mud at the massive pillar's southwest corner. Lastly, he rolled a heavy stone atop it to secure it against the current.

I'd like to see someone find it down here.

He pushed against the muddy bottom. Unsettled muck swirled around him. As he swam back up, he corrected himself. *Actually, no. I wouldn't like to see anyone try to find it. I'm hoping no one even looks. But if Silvermane is after it, I can't have him somehow tracing it back to Peter Parker's apartment. My identity, and the safety of my friends, are the last things I need to be worrying about now.*

When his head pierced the surface, he pulled off the web sack and took a breath of what he'd hoped would be fresh air. The smell was appalling. The water, if you could call it that, felt like a gross second skin.

Great. I'm going to need a shower—or two—before I show up for my disciplinary hearing.

At least he'd thought far enough ahead to leave a heavy-duty garbage bag on his roof. But even after he peeled off the costume and sealed the bag, he reeked. He climbed through the window in his underpants, dropped the bag, ran for the bathroom, and soaked himself for as long as he could.

His hair was the biggest problem. When he started lathering, the shampoo bottle was nearly full. By the time he was done, it was empty, and he still had a certain odor about him.

Maybe I'll just leave the tablet down there forever.

It was early enough that the building's laundry room was empty. He sat there as his uniform sloshed through two cycles, using the time to read up on academic suspensions in the ESU handbook.

Everything he read only depressed him more. He'd hoped he was wrong about having to reapply for the scholarship, but he wasn't. Peter had always been grateful to receive the aid, but when he saw the number of applicants and the total budget, he realized exactly how much more grateful he should've been. Oscorp had a new scholarship that would be perfect for him, but somehow he didn't think Harry was in the mood to put in a good word.

Maybe he'll come around by the time my suspension's over...in a year.

After two washings, he was out of quarters, detergent, and time. A few greasy black blotches remained, but most of the red-and-blue suit was clean.

It's not like I'm up for best-dressed wall-crawler this year, anyway.

Donning his best shirt and tie, he combed his hair, hoping it didn't smell as bad as he thought it did. He gave himself a last long look in the bathroom mirror. He didn't have the heart to give the poor schlemiel looking back a dressing-down for letting things get so bad—or the energy to give him a pep talk, either.

A call to the hospital confirmed there was no change. Anna Watson was still sitting with Aunt May. He felt terrible for not being there.

Maybe I do need the time off. A normal person dealing with half this stuff would. If they find a donor, I could be around more to help with her recovery, dote on her for a change.

If...

For once in his life, Peter arrived 10 minutes early. Knowing the faculty would discuss the specifics of his case before inviting him in, he expected the door to be closed—but it was open, the attendees already filing out.

He ran up to the first familiar face, his adviser. "Professor Warren! I know I'm not late. What's going on?"

Warren, who'd always been incredibly patient with him, patted Peter on the shoulder. "It's your lucky day, Mr. Parker. Professor Blanton withdrew his request."

Peter immediately looked the gift horse in the mouth. "Really? Why? He was so adamant."

"Why not ask him yourself?" It was only when Warren nodded down the hall that Peter noticed Professor Blanton hurrying away. The slouch in the normally straight-backed man had made him tough to spot.

It was almost as if he were trying to hide.

"Professor Blanton?" Peter swore the man sped up at the sound of his voice. "Professor!"

Blanton stopped and forced a smile to his face. "Mr. Parker. Peter."

"Don't want to hold you up, sir. I only wanted to thank you, and tell you I won't let you down." He knew he should let it go at that, but Blanton seemed oddly nervous. "Uh...I do have to admit I'm curious about why you decided to give me the extension."

He coughed. "Well…I…I, uh…I heard about your aunt. That's it. You should've mentioned her illness in the first place."

Makes sense, but why is he looking around like he's afraid we're being watched?

"I didn't really have a chance, sir."

"Of course! I wasn't accusing you of anything. Take your time with the deadlines, as much as you need. No. Scratch that. Take as much time as you'd *like*."

"Are you feeling okay, professor?"

"Why wouldn't I be? Now, I really have to be going. If that's all right with you?"

All right with me?

"Yeah."

"Great. See you in class, then. Or…whenever."

Blanton rushed off, nearly at a full run. Peter rubbed his hair and sniffed his fingers. *Does the East River have some kind of hallucinogen in it? Because this sure doesn't feel like reality.*

His day suddenly free. Peter decided to head to the Coffee Bean and study over some caffeine. But as soon as he was off-campus, his spider-sense tingled, alerting him to a large figure emerging from an alley to block his path.

"Marko?"

The giant looked pleased that Peter knew his name. "Read about me, huh? Good for you, kid. Then you also know this'll go a lot easier if you don't put up a fuss." He aimed his thumb back at the alley. "Got someone important who wants a word."

"With me? Why?"

"He'll tell you all about it."

Unable to fight back without revealing his identity, Peter allowed himself to be steered into the alley.

As the muscleman's broad chest and shoulders blocked the sunlight, a man stepped from the shadows. He was Peter's age, maybe a little younger. He wore a drab threadbare jacket over a white collarless shirt, topped by a gray cap. It was the sort of humble outfit a European immigrant from long ago might wear. But the smug look on his face sent a shiver down Peter's spine.

Silvermane! When I fought Marko at ESU, he looked surprised his old boss could still be around—but I guess they are *working together. Didn't think the big lug could lie that well.*

Manfredi looked past Peter, up at Man Mountain. "Why don't you take off? I don't want make our friend here any more nervous than he needs to be. I'll call you when I need you again."

Marko grunted and withdrew, restoring some afternoon sunlight to the alley.

Eyeing Manfredi's tommy gun, Peter held up his hands, pretending to be afraid. "Who are you? What's this about?"

Silvermane offered an ice-cold smile. "That academic-review thing turn out okay for you?"

Peter blinked. Blanton's nervousness was starting to make sense.

"Was that you? Did you *threaten* my professor? Why?"

"Oh, let's call it a gift. All I want is a little something in return. You give it to me, you never have to see me again. You don't, well, let's just say I'm not the kind of guy you want as an enemy."

"What is it you want?"

"No big deal, really. Just some help getting hold of Spider-Man."

Peter tried to suppress a smile. *Boy, did you come to the right place.*

o———————o

WITH Silvermane busy, Marko felt safe climbing into the rear of the oversized SUV parked down the street. He felt even better when he realized how well the seat fit him, and how close he was sitting to Vanessa Fisk.

As he pulled the door closed, he felt her eyes scan his large body. Not in shock, or repulsion, the way some did, but with a kind of admiration and sadness.

"The car was customized for my husband. I trust you find it comfortable, Michael?"

And she calls me Michael.

"Yes, ma'am. Very comfortable. Thank you."

Spying on Silvermane was the biggest risk Marko had ever taken. Silvio Manfredi had given him his first big break with the Maggia. Since then, he'd thought nothing could ever make him betray that man—in life or in death. But once he'd gotten over the shock of seeing the boss again, it was like visiting a house you used to live in when you were a kid: Everything was the same, but it all looked smaller, less threatening.

Of course, Silvermane really *was* smaller. Marko believed him when he said he'd be growing again because of some freaky curse, but it still wasn't likely that Mr. Manfredi would be running the Maggia again anytime soon.

And Vanessa Fisk was worth the gamble. He studied her, wondering whether emerald was the right word for the color of her eyes, or what her porcelain skin might feel like against the backs of his fingers. With a start, he realized she was waiting for him to report.

"Sorry. It's like I told you: He wants the tablet back so he can stop going from being a baby to an old man over and over. He figured out Spider-Man has it and thinks that college kid can lead him to the wall-crawler."

"Michael, are you the only one he's told all this?"

"Far as I know."

She held his gaze. "I want you to think about this carefully before you answer. If I move against Mr. Manfredi to get the tablet, do you think he's in a position to be dangerous?"

The answer was pretty obvious. "Mr. Silvermane's always dangerous, but not like before. It's not like he's going to try to take back the Maggia until he's ready. And if he ever does come after you…"

I'll protect you from him. I'll protect you with my life.

"Yes, Michael?"

"You can count on me."

She put her hand atop his. "Thank you. I appreciate that more than you realize. For now, I want you to stay near him, let me know everything he's up to. Can you do that for me?"

He stared at her hand. It was so small, so fragile, so pretty. "Sure."

"Excellent. Now, if you'll excuse me, it's time I made some plans of my own."

And so sad. So very, very sad.

TWENTY-FOUR

GETTING away from Silvermane was easy enough. All Peter had to do was agree to tell Spidey to show up at the same alley at midnight. Things got a little weird when the gangster pinched his cheek, as if Peter were his grandkid—but that was a small price to pay. Now the tricky part was making sure he hadn't been followed. Then he could change into costume.

After all, why show up later for some trap if I can nab him now?

He trotted a few blocks away, weaving among the afternoon pedestrians. Satisfied he was alone, he kicked off his shoes, scrambled to the top of a fire escape, and jumped to an ESU dormitory roof.

Peter Parkour, that's me. Shame I can't ever say that one out loud.

He checked the street below to make sure no one was following, then put on his uniform. Despite the water stains, it was perfectly dry. In fact, it had that nice clean-laundry smell.

Doubt that'll last.

Vaulting from roof to roof, he retraced his path.

The higher perspective let him keep an eye out for Silvermane. Of course he didn't expect the gangster to stay in the same alley, so he started making wider and wider circles around it.

After a whole lot of nothing, he snagged a higher building and scanned a wider area. A few blocks away, he spotted that old-style hat; it looked like a bottle cap moving through the twists and turns between buildings. A few swings later, Silvermane was only a hundred yards ahead.

Once I find a steady perch, I'll web up his feet and leave him dangling.

But the fire escape he landed on squeaked beneath his weight—and Silvermane looked up. Peter shot twin webs toward him, but Silvermane grabbed an empty garbage can and blocked them. With a grunt, Manfredi hurled the can at Spider-Man and ran.

He was faster than he'd been at the annex.

Swatting the can aside, Spider-Man called to him. "Where are you going? I thought *you* were looking for *me!*"

He scuttled along the walls of the space between buildings. Silvermane was really booking, dodging obstacles with a creepy, confident ease. Ducking around a rusty dumpster propped up on cinderblocks, he took out a phone and started talking.

"You kids these days with your devices!" Spider-Man said. "Anyone ever tell you it's rude to make calls when someone's trying to have an actual in-person conversation?"

By the time Silvermane finished the call, Spider-Man was dangling upside down in front of him.

"So, what walks on four legs in the morning, two in the afternoon, and three at night?" Spider-Man asked. "You! Get it?"

"How'd you find me so fast?"

"Let's just say it's a good thing I saw a documentary on Ellis Island in grade school, or I'd never have recognized that off-the-boat look you're sporting."

Silvermane didn't seem to recognize the reference, but that didn't stop him from swinging the blackjack in his hand. Spider-Man easily pulled his head back to evade it.

"Boy, are *you* old-school. I haven't seen one of those things since...y'know? I don't think I've *ever* seen one of those things."

Manfredi whirled back the way he'd come.

"Come on, Silvio! You *know* I'm going to catch up!"

Silvermane darted around, searching for a viable escape route. Seeing none, he hit the filthy asphalt like a baseball player sliding into home, and skidded beneath the only cover available: the dumpster.

"Gross." Spider-Man dropped to the ground. "Not to mention, how is that going to help you?"

"Come and get me."

"Okay. Fine."

The moment Peter lifted the dumpster above his head, the crazed Silvermane swung an old piece of rebar at his kneecap. Spider-Man cried out, and the dumpster nearly slipped from his grasp. Silvermane's eyes widened as he realized his mistake—the hunk of metal was about to come down right on top of him. Gritting his teeth, Spider-Man regained his grip and tossed the dumpster to the side. Manfredi didn't wait for his recovery; this time the bar missed Spider-Man's kneecap, slamming into his shin instead.

"Ow!"

Silvermane scrambled to his feet and dashed off again. "I can't go on like this! I can't!"

His leg bruised, but not broken, Spider-Man hopped after him. "Turn yourself in and maybe they can find you some kind of help."

"Ha! I've been around the block too many times to buy that line."

At the sidewalk, Silvermane paused as if expecting something. Spider-Man was on him in an instant, pinning him to the ground.

"Time to pack it in, old man...I mean young... uh, maybe just *man*."

Manfredi glared at him. The boiling hatred in his eyes was so intense, it took Peter aback.

It's like he's angry with everything—me, himself, life, the world. Whatever's behind that is way above my pay grade. I'll web him up and let the prison psychologist deal with it.

Fingers nearly on his web-shooters, his spider-sense exploded. On the street, a municipal bus sideswiped a parked car, flipping it toward them. Unable to avoid the car, Spider-Man slammed his shoulder against its passenger side, shifting the momentum enough to bring it down sideways against a laundry storefront.

Down the block, a huge man leapt from the moving bus, rolling when he landed on the street.

Marko!

The bus sped toward a packed intersection. Peter could see the unconscious driver slumped over the wheel, and the terrified passengers trying to wake him. Forced to leave Silvermane, he bolted down the street and swung atop the bus.

As a physics student, he knew he couldn't simply stop 18 tons in motion. Even if he managed to web it to something solid enough, momentum would only tear part of bus free.

But there had to be some way to keep it from crashing.

Hoping to at least change the bus' direction, he shot a web down to the right-front wheel and anchored it to a fire hydrant. The bus pulled a bit to the right, but was still heading for the intersection. The hydrant cracked and gushed water, about to tear free.

But the sudden turn also made the bus' left wheel lift slightly off the asphalt. So he webbed that up, hooked the other end of the line over a lamppost, and pulled. The lamppost bent, his shoulders felt ready to break, but he managed to lift the bus enough to tilt it over. Leaping from the tumbling bus, he laid down a layer of webbing on the street to cushion the landing as best he could.

Even sideways, the bus slid several yards before

stopping. He tore open the door. The passengers were rattled and bruised, but alive.

Phew! Marko's more a head-on kind of guy, not smart or cruel enough for this kind of move. He must have been following Manfredi's orders.

Of course, both crooks were nowhere in sight. In fact, a gray cap and jacket were waiting near the overturned car where Spider-Man had left Silvermane.

Guess he was listening to my fashion advice.

TWENTY-FIVE

AFTER changing back to his civvies, Peter took a walk to ponder his next move.

Silvermane's not the same guy I tangled with last time. He's still smart, but he's flailing around, making stupid moves. Reminds me of myself in younger days, except for that psycho-killer thing he's got going.

He stopped outside the Coffee Bean, surprised to find it empty. The door was locked, the chairs already stacked on the table. A sign explained: Closed Indefinitely.

Wow. Speaking of lost youth. I guess everything has to grow and change—or die. Except Silvermane. He gets to do it all over and over again. Not that I'd trade places—but there are a lot of things I'd love go back and undo.

He touched the glass, thinking about all the times he'd spent at the college dive—good and bad—and the choices he could have made. His mind drifted farther and farther back, until he remembered his uncle's kindly face and imagined his fatherly presence at his back once more.

"Keep your mind on the present, Peter. It's really all anyone ever has."

In the coffeehouse glass, Uncle Ben's visage melded with Peter's. He realized his own face was looking a bit older lately—old enough that he could see the family resemblance Aunt May was always talking about. He knew from photos that Ben and Richard Parker, his long-dead father, had looked very much alike. The thought that he was part of that connection warmed him.

Family makes the difference. Norman Osborn had a soft spot for his son. Even the Lizard always wants to protect Martha and Billy. I doubt Silvio Manfredi will ever have that, no matter how many lives he leads. Was he born that way, or did he get damaged somewhere along the line?

His phone vibrated with a text. He hoped it might be Mary Jane, or Harry, or even Flash, commiserating over the loss of their watering hole. But it was from the hospital, and the five words were cryptic at best:

Your aunt has a visitor.

It wasn't the usual sort of phrasing the patient ward used. His first thought—Silvermane—sent him running for a secluded spot to change.

Dammit! What if he's coming after Spider-Man through Peter Parker's relatives now?

He speed-dialed the nurse's station, then held the phone between his chin and neck as he swung uptown. It was difficult to make himself heard, but the nervous man who answered confirmed that someone was with Aunt May, someone who refused to come to the phone.

And it wasn't Anna Watson.

When Peter arrived, it was all he could do to keep from climbing up the side of the hospital. But he knew that once he was up there, he wouldn't be able to get in without smashing through the window. Aside from jeopardizing his identity, a move like that would likely create *more* danger to his aunt and the other patients. Besides, it didn't sound as if she was under attack.

So he switched back into his regular clothes. Rather than endure the slow torture of an elevator ride, he bounded up the stairs, jumping the landings. Thankfully there was no one else in the stairwell. He slowed only slightly when he opened the door and stormed toward the ICU.

He ignored the nurses. His eyes shot toward a tall, thin figure whose long coat resembled an opera cape, hovering by his Aunt May's bed.

Whoever that is, she isn't a threat, or my spider-sense would be tingling.

Hearing his hurried steps, the figure turned and extended a thin, long-fingered hand. "Mr. Parker?"

He took it. A dozen questions burned on his lips.

"My name is Vanessa Fisk. I am Wilson Fisk's wife."

He snatched back his hand. "Listen, I don't care what—"

"Please. I understand you were threatened earlier today, and how upsetting that must have been, but I assure you that's not my way." She took half a step closer and lowered her voice. "Though, to be clear, I do also want the tablet. Are you aware of my husband's condition?"

"The papers say he's in some kind of coma, but not much else."

"For two years now, the best doctors have failed to help him. That tablet is my last hope to make him whole again. I'd like you to speak to Spider-Man on my behalf."

Peter blinked, then shook his head in disbelief. "Lady, I understand your grief, but Spider-Man would never help a crook like the Kingpin."

Pursing her lips, she glanced down, revealing a deep sorrow in her eyes. "Perhaps, but our money also built this hospital wing, which has saved many lives. Likewise, I could use our fortune to ensure that the tablet's secrets were made available for the benefit of all. Power and money hold no allure for me. I like to think I've already learned what Wilson has yet to discover: that everything in life fades, except what we leave behind."

"What do you mean? What *do* we leave behind?"

She glanced at the comatose Aunt May. "Family. Richard, our son, holds himself responsible for what happened to his father. He's attempted suicide before, and now I don't even know how to contact him. It's my hope that if my husband is restored, Richard will be able to forgive himself and return. He is our future. My family would be whole. From there, who knows what other changes we might make?"

Peter tried to sound sympathetic. "I understand loss—and believe me, I know how guilt can gnaw at someone. But Wilson Fisk has left a pretty long trail of bodies—"

She cut him off, but somehow made even that seem gracious. "Excuse me—I am, as you journalists like to say, burying the lede. If you speak to Spider-Man and he agrees to give me the tablet, I will pay for the experimental drug to treat your aunt."

Peter was stunned.

"You'd be saving her life. But I…I don't know that Spider-Man would put that above right and wrong."

"You may be correct, but I did some checking. I don't know if he considers you a friend, but your lives are clearly intertwined. This is no veiled threat, I assure you. I'm only hoping the gesture might help change his mind, help him better understand that my motives aren't so vile. I hope at least he'll be willing to meet with me."

Giving her the tablet would save Aunt May.

But…I can't help criminals, can I?

"I…I'll pass the message along."

TWENTY-SIX

PETER stood in Brooklyn Bridge Park, the offer swirling in his head like the little vortices of water that formed around the concrete pylons.

The choice seemed so simple. It wasn't a heat-of-the-moment decision, where life and death came down to skill and speed—like how best to take down a villain in a fight, or which way to go to get someone out of a burning building.

He could give the tablet to Vanessa Fisk and save Aunt May—or not.

He could restore to power one of the worst criminals the city had ever seen for the sake of the woman who'd raised him—or not.

In an odd way, actually having *this* choice clarified some of the other turning points in his life. No matter how much his guilt insisted otherwise, there was no way he could have known that crook would kill Uncle Ben, or that the Goblin would kill Gwen. He couldn't have known, until it was too late.

It wasn't even as if any one choice would have fixed everything. Being a hero sooner would've saved

Uncle Ben, but being a hero had killed Gwen. To think that if only he were good and true enough, everything would work out—was its own sort of arrogance. No matter how great his power, or his responsibility, there were times when the big choices weren't his.

Not this time, though. Aunt May's fate really *was* in his hands.

He looked at the filthy water. The tablet was right down there; all he had to do was dive in and retrieve it.

But he hadn't decided, not yet.

He turned away and headed back toward the Village.

The thing was, there were other decisions he was grateful he hadn't made. For a long time, he'd been angry that the Green Goblin's fate had been taken out of his hands. Now, for the first time, he knew he'd been lucky. Of course he liked to think he wouldn't have killed Norman Osborn. Becoming a murderer would have betrayed everything he believed in, tarnished Gwen's memory. But at the time, he'd been so hurt, so eager to lash out. In the heat of the moment, part of him had asked, why not? Why not cross that line just this once?

Just as, now, he asked himself: Why not hand over the tablet?

This is different. It's not about taking a life—it's about restoring two lives. But it's bad enough that the world has to deal with Silvermane again. Vanessa Fisk might believe the Kingpin can change, but I don't. What if there's a way to control the elixir, to stop that cycle of aging and de-aging? That would leave both of them more powerful—even immortal. They could end up battling each other for control of the city…forever.

Sure, I can tell myself I'll capture Fisk if he tries to resume his criminal ways—but isn't that just an excuse to do the wrong thing? Look how long Caesar Cicero stayed in jail.

At the corner of East Houston and Lafayette, he passed a scruffy man in rags, standing on a plastic milk crate. He wasn't begging, or playing music, or preaching the end of the world. He was just reciting a poem that sounded vaguely familiar:

I grow old…I grow old…
I shall wear the bottoms of my trousers rolled.

Shall I part my hair behind? Do I dare to eat a peach?

Peter tossed a bill in the man's hat and kept walking.

And what if the peach isn't even yours?

He wondered what his uncle would do, but had no idea. And even if he could guess at Ben's advice, this was still his decision. Only the living would have to deal with the results.

A head full of ghosts wouldn't change that.

He was alone on this one.

On the way home, he decided to pass the shuttered Coffee Bean. A solitary figure stood out front, hands in pockets, staring at the darkness inside. Probably some other old regular mourning the past. As Peter neared, he recognized him.

Harry?

Peter stepped quietly beside him. When Harry saw Peter's reflection in the glass, he instantly turned to leave. Pete grabbed his shoulder.

"Wait. Please. If we're going to live together, we should at least be able to talk to each other. Unless you plan on kicking me out?"

Harry grimaced and pushed the hand away. "And have the gang hate me for tossing poor Peter Parker on the streets? No thanks."

They both stood there awkwardly for a few moments, staring through the dark glass.

Peter tried to start a conversation. "You'd think they'd have warned the regulars or something."

Harry frowned. "There were signs up for weeks. Figures you wouldn't notice."

After they stood in silence for awhile, Peter gave it another shot. "Look, I get it. You're furious that I work with the guy you think killed your dad. I *know* he didn't do it. If I thought for a second it was him, of course I'd quit—even if it meant losing the little money I earn."

"You could have worked for my father. He offered you a job."

Sure, before he went nuts…

"Yeah, but I'm barely handling my classes as it is. I wanted to wait until I'd graduated."

Harry looked at him sideways. "Brain like yours? You could've handled it."

Pete narrowed his eyes. "Was that, like, a compliment?"

"Just a fact. I wouldn't read much into it."

"Fine, I won't, but can we try putting all this aside for a little while? A temporary truce? I don't know about you, but I'm going through a lot, and I could sure use a friend."

Staring ahead, Harry exhaled and tapped on the glass. "I can almost make out where Flash scratched his name into our table. Hard to believe so much is changing."

"Got that right. I always thought growing up would bring more freedom, but it feels like all you get is tougher choices."

Harry nodded. "You should see how they look at me whenever I go into the Oscorp executive offices. People think because I'm rich I don't have any problems. But I'm barely out of rehab, and all of a sudden I'm deciding which companies to buy or sell. And my biggest concern? Not who gets fired and loses their homes. Nope—it's whether or not I'm disappointing Dad."

Peter wanted to tell Harry he was the only thing that had ever kept Norman Osborn sane, but that would have meant revealing too much. "I'd say you should focus on what you think is right. But, man, lately I'm realizing the big stuff doesn't always have a right and wrong. Just shades of gray."

"That's it exactly. Some days I'm so fed up, I want to fire everyone, take a handful of pills, and let the world burn."

Peter's brow furrowed. "But you wouldn't, would you?"

"One day at a time. Today, I didn't. Tomorrow?"

"Don't forget, I'm here for you, whenever, however. We all are."

Harry shrugged. "What shade of gray are *you* up against?"

"Not sure how to put this, but if someone you loved was dying and to save them you'd have to do something terrible, would you?"

Harry gave off a little laugh. "Guess we're not too old for truth or dare, huh? You're not talking to the bravest guy in the world, Pete. Too much stress and I crumble like paper. But if someone I loved really needed me? I'd like to think I'd do anything—lie, steal, murder, crawl over a pile of dead bodies, whatever it took—to save them." An odd smirk came to his face, as if his father's features were haunting his own. "In fact, if I ever *prove* Spider-Man had a hand in my father's death? Well…one day at a time. One day at a time."

The look evaporated. "But we're not talking about anything like that, right? And maybe that operation's not as bad as you think. There're lots worse things out there to be afraid of, you know."

He thinks I'm talking about donating my liver. That I'm afraid.

Unable to respond any other way, Peter nodded.

After a final glance at their old table, Harry headed off. "Enjoyed the truce, roommate. Helped set me straight on a few things. I'm heading to Dad's penthouse, so the place is yours tonight. Hope your aunt will be okay."

Peter wasn't sure the peace would last, whether they'd ever be close again. It was just something else to add to the long list of things he didn't know. There was one thing he was certain about: He was drained. He needed a good night's sleep.

But the day's strange encounters weren't over yet. Someone was waiting a few yards shy of the entrance to his apartment building. Seeing Peter, he stepped into the light of a streetlamp. Less than 24 hours had passed, but Silvermane was older now. His clothes were still hopelessly out of fashion, but the suit and vest were a better fit.

When he called out Peter's name, he extended the vowels. "Peetaaaah Paaahkaaah!"

Peter stopped short. "Mr. Silvermane. Look, I did as you asked. I gave Spider-Man your message."

Manfredi nodded. "Yeah, and a few seconds later he shows up and nearly beats the crap out of me. I can handle any five normal guys easy, so when I say Spider-Man's powerful, it means something. I didn't even get to ask him about the tablet. Still, I've gone up against worse, and won. You know how? Finding the weak spot. In this case, that's you, Peetahhh Pahhhkahhh."

"I don't know what you heard about my relationship with him—"

"Ah, I don't believe half of what I hear. But I do believe what I see. That's why I've been following you. Watching you duck into some shadows, seeing Spider-Man come out. Seeing Spider-Man swing over to the hospital, watching you go traipsing in the front entrance. See where this is going?" He made some motions in the air with his hands, as if trying to draw out a response, but Peter was speechless. He grinned. "Ah, you know exactly where I'm headed. I can smell it on you. You know that I know who you are. Do I have to say it out loud?"

Peter's worst fear hung in the air between them. As Silvermane reached into his vest pocket, Peter slipped a web-shooter from his belt to his wrist.

Manfredi pulled out an old-style reporter's notebook and flipped it open. "Let's see who we got here…Harold Osborn, Mary Jane Watson, Eugene 'Flash' Thompson. Heh. Eugene. No wonder he prefers Flash. Randolph Robertson, his dad Joseph. Am I leaving anybody out? Oh, yeah. That old lady you were so eager to get to at the hospital: May Reilly Parker."

Every word made his muscles tighten. Hearing his aunt's name, he snapped.

"Is the picture clear enough for you yet? I get the tablet, or they get—"

Peter was on him in an instant. He slammed Silvermane down against a parked car, one hand against his throat, the other pulling back. One good punch, just one, and his friends and family would be safe. The world would be free of a killer.

Was it only an hour ago he'd been wondering what he'd have done to the Goblin in a moment like this? Now he knew.

His fist flew. At the last second, he drove it into

the parked car, bending the door inward so hard its hinge broke off.

Silvermane used the opportunity to kick Peter in the abdomen. It didn't hurt, but it pushed Peter back long enough for Manfredi to point at him and shout:

"Hey, take it easy! I thought you were smarter than that."

Afraid some bystander might glimpse his face, Peter quickly covered it with a web, sheer enough to see through. Dead eyes drilling into his foe, Silvermane adjusted his jacket. "I took precautions, you idiot. Anything happens to me, sealed envelopes get delivered to all the major media. So go get yourself a drink, or suck on a fly, or whatever it is you have to do to wrap your head around the fact that I've won and there's nothing you can do about. Then you go get that tablet and bring it here in exactly six hours, or the people you know start dying. Got me?"

Peter said nothing.

"Good."

When Silvermane turned and strode off, Peter held himself together long enough to flip a spider-tracer onto the mobster. Then he raced several blocks away, stepped into a vacant lot—and screamed.

He kept screaming, but no one answered.

TWENTY-SEVEN

ONCE Peter's hands stopped shaking from rage, he changed back into the red-and-blue. It wasn't only Aunt May at risk. Everyone he knew was in danger. At the same time, this decision was much clearer:

At least Wilson Fisk has Vanessa to temper him. I can't give that monster the tablet. I have to find another way.

Silvermane had traveled quickly. He was already far enough that Peter needed his receiver to track the tracer's signal. It led him to the garment district, to what was left of the metal walls and steel-girder skeleton of an old warehouse.

Something about the building nagged at Spider-Man, as if it should be familiar. Not so much as a physical thing, but a phantom urge he'd neglected to follow.

Silvermane was close, close enough that Peter no longer needed the receiver. His spider-sense led him though the belly of the rotted beast, right up to a pile of old wood lying on the floor. The tracer was somewhere below. He quietly slid the wood aside until there was a gap big enough for his lithe form to slink through to the stairs below. Stooping low on the steps, he crept down.

Most of the basement was in full darkness, but a collection of flickering candles and fading flashlights cast bizarre shadows against the concrete walls and supports. Peter's other senses weren't superhuman, but they were more sensitive and precise than most. He knew he wouldn't be easily seen unless he did something stupid.

Silvio Manfredi was in the center of the open space, kneeling atop some cinderblocks before a frayed wooden sheet. He was muttering, hands clasped as if in prayer. It was the only time Peter had ever seen the man appear humble.

Okay, I found him. Now what? Catch him, and he'll reveal my identity. Well, he found my weakness, maybe I can find his.

The wooden board, the object of the mobster's attention, was covered with photos, articles, torn pages, and bits of cloth and jewelry, all pasted, tacked, or nailed in place. Even from a distance, the common subject was clear.

It's all about him. Silvermane's life.

As Peter's eyes adjusted to the lack of light, he realized that the walls, all of them, were covered with the same sort of pasted data. As he studied it, he saw there was an order to it, like some sort of crazy, cross-referenced catalogue. One area was arranged by year and decade, another by deed: a list of people he'd murdered—by gun, knife, or fist. Another was a ledger of all he'd stolen—cash, jewelry, gold. A fourth grouping held only photos. A fifth was the other way around, a mass of words: letters, journals, articles. Together, the pieces fit in a weird mosaic that formed abstract patterns depending on how the candlelight played against them.

It's like some kind of shrine…to himself?

Silvermane stopped muttering and raised his voice.

"They tell us that we're born to die…"

Now he's singing? And without a karaoke machine?

His self-assured tenor echoed, filling the darkness. But then it faltered and fell back to mumbling. "Nah. Still not right."

The clothes, the way he's been talking—it's as if he's reliving the last 80 years in scattered bits and pieces. He's not praying—he's trying to remember.

"That's it!"

Silvermane had cried out so loudly that, for a second, Spider-Man worried he'd been seen. But no, the mob boss was only congratulating himself. Excited, he pulled a new digital recorder from his pocket, tore away the packaging, and fumbled with the batteries.

Then he clicked the record button, cleared his throat, and started singing again:

> *They tell us that we're born to die*
> *But there's no sense in that—say I.*
> *Those of us who know the truth,*
> *Will drink, drink, the nectar of youth.*

He raised the recorder as if it were a trophy, then brought it back down to his lips and kept talking. "To my future self—I finally got it, the song. And thanks to this thing, it ain't ever going away again. Once Spider-Man caves and gives me the tablet, all I have to do is figure out how to change that freaking dinosaur reject I left in the sewers back into a scientist."

Dinosaur? Dammit! He means Curt Connors!

Startled, Spider-Man brushed his foot along the floor. Silvermane whirled in response, but by the time his piercing gaze reached the stairs, Peter was already upstairs, springing out of the derelict building.

He must have been talking about the doc's hidden lab. Connors must've been under some pretty intense duress to take him there.

Back in the open air, Spider-Man flung himself upward into the city skies.

If Connors is the Lizard again, his panic switch must have failed. Which means I've got a stop to make first.

The clock was ticking on Silvermane's six-hour deadline. Reaching ESU's Life Sciences building, Spider-Man smashed the smallest window he could find. He squeezed through, then tried to tear open the reinforced supply-cabinet door without completely destroying it. Once inside, he grabbed one of the large liquid-nitrogen cylinders Connors kept on hand.

Wonder how he gets that past the budget committee.

He was out before security could even approach the building. Carrying the bulky tank under one arm, he headed for a certain manhole cover near campus. Most had been welded shut since 9/11 to guard against terrorists, but Connors had fashioned this one to open with a twist.

The sewer was hot and humid. The odor was sharp—but not as bad as the bottom of the East River. Moving along the curved wall, Spider-Man didn't have to worry about remembering the right spot. The heavy thudding and pounding noises behind the slime drew him right to it.

I'm guessing that's not banging pipes.

He pressed his ear to the brick cover concealing the entrance and heard the sound of rattling chains.

The Lizard's contained. Good. But who knows for how long? I'm going to have to deal with that thing sooner or later, and it's not like it'll be any easier later. Besides, Connors may know something helpful about the tablet.

Tightening his grip on the tank, he pressed the lever to open the lab. Inside, the damaged full-spectrum lighting flashed erratically, strobing against the chained beast as if it were an animatronic in a haunted house.

Then again, it was always hard to accept that the man-sized reptile was real.

When the Lizard saw Spider-Man, its thrashing grew more violent. The voice was harsh, sibilant, as if its throat wasn't intended for human speech.

"Ah! It's the thick, juicy spider!"

Whenever the Lizard moved, the bones beneath its leathery green skin made a gross clicking sound, like a comb's teeth raked by fingernails. It swayed, judging the distance between them. Then, without warning, its head shot forward like a striking cobra, lifting the rest of its body into the air behind it. As powerful as the sudden lurch was, the chains held, tugging the Lizard's arms and legs so sharply that the creature fell forward on its chest.

As it scrambled up on two feet, Spider-Man scanned what was left of the lab: overturned tables, shattered specimen tanks, and scattered refuse. "This is why you can't have nice things."

"Peh. You mammals think you're so superior—but without the reptile core, your feeble brain wouldn't exist at all."

Gripping the tank, Peter cautiously circled the beast. "You always did make me dizzy, Lizzie."

I have to lower Connors' body temp just enough to cause the change. The Lizard's thick hide will protect him, but only to a point. Too much cold and I might kill him; too little, and I'll drain the liquid nitrogen tank for nothing.

He edged around the room, looking for a clear line of fire. The Lizard followed his movements, all the while pulling at its bonds. The thing's most dangerous weapon, its tail, was unchained. He had to stay out of its reach, making it tough to find a good spot.

"We're in all of you, you know," the Lizard hissed. "Eager to rule, to feed. If only Connors understood how lucky he is to have such a direct connection to the life force itself."

The four chains seemed firmly anchored in the reinforced wall, but Spider-Man could tell from the hunger twinkling in those vertical pupils that the urge to attack was making the Lizard stronger. Already, he could hear the taut chain links creaking.

"Yeah, I'll have to remind him to write you a thank-you note next time you ruin his life."

The debris made it even tougher to find the right angle. But the longer he waited, the more time the Lizard had to figure out a counter move. One corner of the lab had the fewest obstructions, but it was also farthest from the open door. Seeing no better options, he figured it would have to do.

Before he could open the nozzle, his spider-sense sent him darting up the wall, out of the way of a hurtling table.

"You're off your game, Liz. Missed me by a mile, and I've still got the tank."

The chains rattled. "But I wasn't aiming for you."

As clouds of gas puffed down from the ceiling, Spider-Man saw that the Lizard had struck the red panic button on the wall.

"There's still gas in the system? But that'll hurt you more than it'll hurt me."

"Will it? Guesss again."

White clouds fell along every spot in the room—except where the Lizard stood.

He destroyed the nozzles above him! Smart.

"That apish fool who chained me here cracked the button when he used it. He didn't realize he'd only released half the gas. That's how I was able to stay in control."

Spider-Man couldn't escape the freezing clouds without leaping into the Lizard's clutches, so he twisted between the nozzles, hoping to limit his exposure to the gas. The aerated mist was less concentrated than a direct liquid blast from the tank, but it was cold nonetheless.

Frost formed on his costume. Peter felt the chill down to his bones. The Lizard looked groggy, but still conscious.

"Tell me, Spider-Man, does it burn your warm blood the way it burned mine?"

As the gas supply ran out, the clouds began dissipate. Spider-Man, stiff from the cold, staggered in the wrong direction. The Lizard's unchained prehensile tail flew out. It curled around the cylinder in Spider-Man's hands, and snatched it away.

Before Spider-Man could react, the Lizard wrapped one of the chains around the tank and twisted it, tightening the links. The torque wasn't strong enough to penetrate the cylinder's thick steel. But it was more than enough to snap the chain.

Spider-Man rolled to a safe distance, then half-stood and tried to rub the warmth back into his arms. "Brrr! Nice move, Lizzie, but you're out of gas, and you've still got three chains left. You really think you can stop me from getting that tank back?"

"Like any captured beast, I haven't had much to do other than think about escape. Tell me, warm-blood, do you remember what happens when you grab a lizard's tail?"

The Lizard braced its legs, free hand and tail

against the reinforced wall. Then it pulled, stretching its trapped arm taut. With a sickening crack of bone, the limb tore free from the torso. Surprisingly bloodless, the still-chained arm dangled, slapping against the wall.

"Oh, man! I did *not* need to see that!"

The missing limb began to grow back, a nascent stump forming on the Lizard's shoulder. But the creature didn't wait for it to finish. It used the tank to spray liquid nitrogen on one of the chains fastened to its legs. The frigid liquid made it howl in agony, but it held on long enough for the chain to grow brittle. Then it twisted the chain around the cylinder and pulled. The tank shuddered and threatened to crack open—but the frozen chain snapped instead.

Now only one chain remained.

Spider-Man fired both web-shooters, briefly restraining the Lizard's free leg and arms. But the creature's claws tore through the webbing. Peter tried to get closer, scrambling along the wall, then the ceiling. But when he reached out for the tank, the Lizard's tail swatted the him away.

If he gets free…

Spider-Man redoubled his efforts, covering the tail with a long, thick stream of webbing. But that only allowed the Lizard to focus on the final chain.

Now wary of the pain caused by the liquid nitrogen, the creature again tried to use the cylinder alone to torque the chain. But the pressurized cylinder was already badly weakened. Both it and the chain moaned and began to bend—and it was anyone's guess which would give first.

If the tank cracks, it'll explode. The lab will be drenched in over a hundred liters of liquid nitro! But if he snaps that chain, he'll be free—and I can't risk him escaping on top of everything else. At this point, I haven't got a lot of choices.

Looking for anything he might use to stop the Lizard, his eyes settled on the hard metal base of a Bunsen burner lying on the floor.

"Sorry, Doc! This is gonna hurt, but that thick hide will protect you!"

Still twisting the tank, the Lizard turned toward Spider-Man. "What do you—"

Using his last bit of web fluid, Peter snatched the metal base and hurled it directly at the weak spot on the damaged tank. As his desperate shot sailed true, he flipped up the overturned table to shield himself.

The tank ruptured. The terrific blast hurled the table flat into Spider-Man, sending him flying out of the lab door and into the far sewer wall. When he hit, the frozen table shattered against his body like a sheet of glass. The few drops of liquid nitro that hit his arm sent a pain sizzling through him that was worse than any acid.

But most of the released liquid nitro rained down within the lab. Inhuman though the Lizard's anguished howl was, it made Peter wince.

No longer under pressure, the nitrogen quickly reverted to gas, pouring from the lab into the sewer and forming a chilling fog. Grabbing his pained arm, Peter rose to his feet and tried to get close enough to peer inside.

"Dr. Connors?"

Through the haze, he saw a bestial figure. Body shaking, eyes shrinking, the Lizard stumbled out and made a grab for him. His spider-sense warned the attack was coming, but the pain and disorientation from the blast kept him from reacting in time.

The heavy claw grabbed him by the chest, cut through the fabric and into the skin. But the yellow eyes were blinking rapidly, the dread snout receding.

"Connors will never be free of me! Part of me will *always* lie within him, waiting! Part of me…issssss…"

The claw let go. The transformation was complete.

For a while, they both sat in the filth of the sewer floor, panting, checking themselves for wounds.

Connors spoke first. "Looks like I owe you again."

"Uhh…don't mention it."

"I've got some salve in the lab for those freeze burns." Propping himself up on his one arm, he looked back inside the lab. The nitrogen gas, poisonous when concentrated, had been cleared by the air-filtration system, leaving a clear view of the damage. "If I can find it."

As they sifted through the debris, Spider-Man described Silvermane's hideout.

Connors located the ointment and tossed it to the web-slinger. "It makes sense. The elixir is working to evolve him beyond any need for personal history. Of course someone like Silvermane, who's only ever lived and fought for himself, is fighting it tooth and nail. It's as if he somehow keeps generating more ego, while the elixir keeps working at eliminating it."

"So without all those reminders, he'll forget everything again?"

Like, say, my secret identity?

Connors shrugged.

"When does his brain get washed?" Spider-Man asked. "At the end of a cycle?"

"I don't really know. As a scientist, I know that before the brain forms, or once it's too old to function, memory isn't possible. If Manfredi tries to hold on, who knows what he'll remember, or what he'll forget?"

Peter squeezed the ointment onto his fingers and rubbed it into the burns. At first, the skin and muscle stung all the more, but then a soothing sensation ran from the wounds through the whole of his arm.

"Is Silvermane right? Is there a way to stop it?"

"Not from what I was able to read. But the more I try to understand exactly how the elixir works, the more I feel like McCoy from *Star Trek*. I'm a scientist, not a linguist or…a magician." Spotting a piece of silicone on the floor, he picked up the remains of the cast he'd made from the tablet. "And it's not as if I'll be doing any further research with this. Which is probably for the best." He eyed the wall-crawler. "The aging *should* accelerate even more at some point. He'll get more and more desperate, more and more dangerous, right up until the cycle starts again. Why don't you just give him the tablet? It won't help him."

Spider-Man bobbed his head, weighing the possible outcomes. "No offense, Doc, but what if you're wrong?"

Besides, it's more complicated than that. If I give it to Silvermane, Vanessa Fisk won't help Aunt May.

He stood to leave. "I'd love to help clean up, but I've got some decisions to make. And a wacky self-centered mobster to deal with."

"Understood." Connors looked around. "I suppose I could consider my safety precautions a partial success. But clearly, I'm going to need stronger chains."

ALTHOUGH Peter Parker was trying to accept change as a part of life, the return journey to the depths of the East River was no different than the first time. The smell he encountered on breaching the surface was exactly the same. The feeling of being caught between a rock and a hard place, literally, was the same. For that matter, the pivot point of his current misery, the tablet, hadn't changed at all for thousands of years.

He scaled the bridge pylon, perched on the corner, and stared at the relic, thinking about its worth. So much depended on who you asked.

Those crazy ancients thought it was a way to bring humanity to its ultimate form. Silvermane thinks it's a way to stay the same. Vanessa Fisk hopes it can make things the way they used to be for her family.

Me, I'm still thinking paperweight. Or lamp.

Looking up, he realized how close he was to the spot where Gwen had died. Her face floated before him, with Uncle Ben and Captain Stacy not far behind. They still had no advice to offer; the dread decision was still his. But he felt their faith that he would do the best he could.

In a way, I understand Silvermane's desperation. Not because I've got some big reason to stay Peter Parker for all eternity—hell, half the time I'd rather be anyone else. But I never want to forget the people I've loved.

There would always be things he couldn't change. But just knowing Uncle Ben, Captain Stacy and Gwen—loving them, living with them—had changed *him*. They helped give him the strength to keep from lashing out, the patience to step back a little.

He only hoped he had changed enough.

TWENTY-EIGHT

THE GAUDY gold frame was chipped in spots, revealing cheap, blackened wood beneath, but the mirror still served its purpose. Silvermane studied himself, clicked on the recorder, and began to describe what he saw for his future self.

"Fifties. I figure I'm in my 50s now. Got lines around my eyes, those…what do they call 'em? Crow's feet. Otherwise no new wrinkles, but the ones I had look deeper. Hair's getting some salt in the pepper. Funny, though—I'm not feeling any weaker physically. If anything, I feel stronger."

To prove it, he hefted one of the cinderblocks and threw it. It crashed against the far wall. "Stronger than ever. At least as far as I can remember. So, that's my body, but there's that other thing going on, something you'll to have to fight in case I don't beat it this time round. Hey, should I even call you *you?* You're really me! Whatever—you know what I mean. You're my future."

He glared at the reflection and felt briefly jealous of the Silvermane to come, the one who still had his whole life ahead of him.

"Anyway, as healthy as I feel, inside all these bits and pieces are getting peeled away. It's not like my brain's going—I'm still sharp—but it's memories, moments, words that keep slip-sliding away. Which ones go, which stay? It's a crapshoot. Worst part is I can't even say what's gone, 'cause how do you remember what it is you can't remember? All I can do is walk the whole memory palace every 10 minutes or so, to see if anything looks new."

As he spoke, he traveled among the relics, the souvenirs and the stories, aiming a light here and there, studying anything unfamiliar.

"First time I was arrested I was 12. I'd taken a broken bottle to Micky Caleeso. His fat face always looked like hamburger anyway. Then in school, sixth grade, the teacher was…she was…"

It was like a crumbling wall. The mortar couldn't hold the pieces together, and the bricks kept coming loose. Once enough were gone, the whole thing would tumble down.

He'd even forgotten the song again. He fumbled for the right recording, found it and played it back, but had a hard time believing the voice was really his. It was like that talking alligator had said: The elixir was eating away at his identity. Somehow that was supposed to *perfect* him.

He pounded at his own gut. "It's not perfect! It's not! I won't let you, I won't let you…"

But the elixir didn't have legs he could break, a face he could smash, or a heart he could tear out.

He was already scared, but an unexpected shush of wood against concrete filled him with the kind of gut-deep fear he thought only small children could feel. Grabbing his tommy gun, he flipped on the flashlight taped to the barrel and wheeled toward the stairs.

"Who are you? The feds? How'd you find me?"

Two intruders froze in the beam. One was a thin dame, dressed to the nines. The other, right behind her, was either a freaking monster or a door that had grown limbs and a head.

Manfredi howled. "Quit haunting the stairs like a couple of…a couple of…" The word was gone. "Get in the light, or I make with the rat-a-tat-tat."

The woman didn't move, but the man stepped in front of her. The giant's name, at least, came to him.

"Marko? I didn't call you. And hey, no one knows about this place, not even you. You tailed me, you stupid dog!"

Marko put out his hands, palms up, as if to make it clear he wasn't a threat. "No, Mr. Silvermane. I never seen this place before, I swear. We didn't know you'd be here!"

Silvermane wasn't buying. It didn't make sense. Marko *was* here, and that meant he was a threat. "Liar! Think I'm stupid? That I don't remember?"

Surprised by his own speed, the former Maggia leader sprinted to the stairs. It was like one of those dreams about flying. He practically sailed across the distance. As soon as he was close enough, he backhanded the dog. "I remember plenty!"

There was a lot of power behind that slap, more than he intended. "I remember that! Do you?"

But Marko didn't move. He looked to the dame, like she could help him somehow.

Annoyed, Silvermane grabbed Marko's chin and twisted his face back. "No, you look at me and you keep looking! I could rot until I'm just a set of eyeballs and still remember how to treat a traitor!"

Marko's face flushed with shame. "But I didn't—"

When Silvermane slapped him again, Marko twisted and fell to his knees. The sound echoed through the basement.

"That's what you get!"

The woman gasped and tried to run, but Silvermane grabbed her bony wrist. "You stay and watch! This is my dog! Mine! I stole him fair and square."

The initial shock faded from her wan face. She looked like…she *pitied* him. "You're not making any sense."

Silvermane shivered, terrified she might be right—but he couldn't, wouldn't show it. He let go and pushed her. She fell on the steps. Who was she? Was she his date? Had he gotten too rough again?

He pulled out a wad of bills and tossed a 50 at her. It turned in the air and landed on the folds of her fancy cloak. "Beat it, toots. Get yourself a cab. I'll call you later."

"Stop it."

"Who said that?"

It was Marko. The tone was defiant, but his eyes

were still down. Silvermane loomed over the giant, putting his hands on his hips.

"What're you going to do to make me? Cry?"

Silvermane pulled back to hit him again—but this time, Marko's long arm reached out.

"No! Not in front of her!"

The giant paw caught Silvermane's elbow, but when Manfredi exerted some pressure, Marko's entire body skidded backward.

He was getting crazy strong. Was the alligator, Connors, right about that, too? The more he lost of himself, the more powerful he became?

Marko looked up into his eyes. "I swear, boss, I didn't know you'd be here!"

"Bull! Then what're you doing here with…"

He knew the woman. He *knew* he knew her. He strained, as if his brain were like any another muscle. If he pushed hard enough, he could force the big empty spot inside to give way.

And for a time, it did.

The words came rushing back, reassembling Manfredi's place in the world. "Vanessa Fisk! The Kingpin's moll! You brought her here?"

"I'm only doing security for her! Some freelance on the side!"

He raised the tommy gun to Marko's temple. "Liar. The only question is, do I kill you first, or the widow, so you get to watch it happen?"

A deep, hollow crack echoed above. It was so loud, Silvermane wasn't sure whether it had come from the world or from his own mind. A section of the ceiling crumbled. Plaster and wood fell in clumps, leaving behind a little hole. A lithe figure leapt through, twirled like a gymnast, and touched down beside the cinderblock throne.

"Nailed the landing! Hi, folks. Should I have been in the Olympics or what?"

"You look like a court jester in that getup. Get away from my chair!"

The jester raised his hands. "Easy, grandpa. You should know, Marko's not lying. I invited them here."

"Says you, but that still leaves the question of how *you* found…"

Silvermane's face scrunched up, tightening like a wizened gourd ready to crack as he tried to remember something specific about this clown, something lurking right at the edge of his brain. Ah. That was it. Holding the gun in one hand, he used the other to slap at his sides, at his back. He felt along his body with his palm and fingers, as if trying to scratch an itch just out of reach.

"Boss, you okay?"

"Shut up. I'm working here!"

The Fisk woman called to the jester. "Spider-Man! What's the meaning of this? I did as you asked—"

But the costumed idiot held up a hand to silence her. "You're going to have to be a little patient, Mrs. Fisk. Trust me."

Silvermane found it, a small bulge on the edge of his jacket. He ripped the spider-tracer free, tossed it to the floor, and crushed it beneath his heel.

"Wall-crawler, right? No, it's Spider-Man! Still thinking like a stupid kid, huh? Do you realize what happens next? You realize what I do to you?"

Silvermane could swear he saw a brow furrow beneath the webbed mask.

"Are you asking me or telling me?" Spider-Man asked.

"The names, idiot! I know the name of every…"

"Okay! I already heard the offer I can't refuse, godfather. You wanted *this,* right?"

He crawled up the wall and along the ceiling to a spot above Silvermane's head, then yanked a silver case from his back and pulled out a flat stone. There was writing on it. Silvermane knew what it was. He'd have remembered even if Vanessa Fisk hadn't blurted out:

"The tablet!"

Its color was dull, the details obscured in the scant light, but his attention was glued to it as if it were a diamond. It was the thing he wanted, the thing he needed most. The last stone for his palace.

Silvio Manfredi might have kept right on gawking at it, but Vanessa Fisk whispered, "My husband's last hope."

And the treacherous dog answered, "You want me to get it for you, Mrs. Fisk, just say the word."

Silvermane wheeled on them. "No! It's mine!"

A single punch to the chest sent Man Mountain flying across the basement. He crashed headfirst into the cinderblocks that formed the throne.

Spider-Man started. "Whoa. Someone's been eating their Wheaties. How—"

Manfredi cracked his knuckles. "It's the elixir, Bugsy, making me stronger. And that's just a taste. Why don't you make this easy on yourself and hand it over?"

Spider-Man dangled the tablet in front of Silvermane. "Salivate all you want, but this thing is not going to help you. I mean, it's not like you can even read it, right?"

Vanessa Fisk ran—not for the stone, but toward the fallen Marko. Seeing her concern seemed to make it easier for the dog to shake off the punch.

It didn't matter to Silvermane. Nothing else mattered. Just the stone. It was so close! Silvermane almost had his hands on it, but Spider-Man snatched the web away at the last instant and held the stone in his hand.

"Hand it over."

Spider-Man inched along the ceiling toward the staircase hollow that led up to the warehouse proper. "Listen to me. You're stuck, pal. You're going to spend all eternity growing up, then growing…down. I guess. Sort of like Peter Pan on steroids—only butt-ugly, and with no Wendy to tell you stories."

"You're wrong. Everyone's still trying to fool me. They think I'm weak, too old, on the way out, but no one fools…no one fools…"

Marko's ears perked. "Boss, did you just…forget your name?"

Manfredi's head turned from the tablet above him to Marko, then back to the tablet. He gritted his teeth and crouched.

"I don't need a name. I know exactly who I am."

Then he jumped, faster and higher than he ever had, even as a boy, high enough to wrap his hands around the stone.

○———————————○

GO ON!" Spider-Man yelled, waving at Marko and Vanessa Fisk. "Move it!"

Spider-Man had wanted to use the relic to lead Silvermane out of the basement, but the crazed mob boss had somehow made a 10-foot freestanding jump. Peter still held the tablet in his hand, but Silvermane was hanging off of it.

So much for Plan A! Time to improvise.

He shot a web beyond the stairs, far, far up into the warehouse floors. Sailing through the gaps in the upper floors, it stuck fast to one of the roof's remaining cross-supports. Straining, he lifted himself, carrying the stone and the crook up with him.

As he pulled them fifty, then a hundred feet up, the unsteady corrugated sheets making up the colossal roof creaked. Silvermane twisted, trying to free the tablet from the wall-crawler's grip. Either he hadn't noticed the height, or he didn't care.

"Let go!" Silvermane said. Wrinkles swam across his face.

He's aging as I watch!

"No, you let go!"

The gangster's hair whitened, but his eyes shone like black coals.

Shifting his grip so he could cling to the tablet with one hand, Manfredi reached for Spider-Man with the other. His spider-sense tingled. Before he knew what was happening, Silvermane dug his sharp, bony fingers into Peter's bicep.

"Yeow!"

His strength is insane! How is it possible?

Spider-Man let go of the web, allowing them both to fall. Spinning in midair, he managed to wrest the stone from Silvermane. Hoping to both trap and protect the gangster, he spread out a sticky net beneath his tumbling foe.

Spider-Man landed on his feet. Silvermane hit the net—and immediately tore free.

My webs have the tensile strength of steel. No normal man can do that, let alone a guy who looks like he's pushing 70!

But something more than age was changing Silvermane's features. He didn't glow, exactly, or crackle with the Power Cosmic. But while the warehouse was dark with night, Silvermane looked as if he stood in the noonday sun.

"You thought you'd wait me out, hoped I'd grow too weak and feeble to fight you!"

Yep. That was the idea.

Silvermane forced his fingers into a rusted gap between two of the metal sheets that made up one of the walls. "But I'm only getting stronger!"

The more he evolves, though, the more his identity should slip away. But what do I do about it? Stand around with my web in my hand hoping he reaches a higher spiritual plane and starts singing Kumbaya—or try to take him down before he kills me?

The building rattled as Silvermane pulled one of the metal sheets free and threw it. It sliced through the air, toward the web-slinger, threatening to cut him in half. As it flew, Spider-Man hopped up on it, crawled along the surface, then hopped off, landing back where he'd started.

So much for standing around.

Silvermane charged. Peter leaped to the wall and rushed out of reach.

Maybe if I keep him distracted long enough?

He waved the tablet. "Looks like you've got all the power you can handle. What do you need this old rock for?"

The light suffusing Silvermane grew brighter until the highlights of his wrinkles matched his snowy white his hair. "To finish my palace. To be…to be…"

Spider-Man cocked his head. "Or not to be? Just trying to help."

"To be myself! I'm *Silvio Manfredi!* I was born in Corleone, Sicily. My mother died protecting me from bullets, and my grandmother hated me for it! I never owned a thing I didn't take for myself. I never knew anything, never had anything, never *was* anything that didn't…hurt."

The more he spoke, the more the glow subsided.

Spider-Man frowned. "Trust me, I'm not the one to be talking here. But if that's all you think you are, why don't you just…let it go?"

"Because I don't want to!"

Manfredi raced off. At first, Spider-Man thought he was headed for the streets, but he stopped short at the tall outer wall. There, two 20-foot girders ran up the structure's height, forming one of the remaining supports for the building's central I-beam. Silverman grabbed the lower girder and pulled. It didn't come completely free, but the whole side of the warehouse tilted toward the wall-crawler.

"Easy! You'll bring the place down!"

"Don't tell me what to do, Bugsy!"

Out of breath, Silvermane looked up. Skyscraper lights shone through the gaps in the roof. Beyond them were swaths of sky and the few stars bold enough to poke though the city's electric haze. Manfredi gave off a little laugh, redoubled his grip, braced his feet, and pulled on the girder again.

"I may be losing some of that power, but I'm still strong enough to use this to swat you!"

Manfredi was half-right. He was strong enough to tear the lower girder away from its weld-points, but not strong enough to use it as a weapon or keep it from tumbling.

Spider-Man didn't need any help from his spider-sense to know that if he didn't do something fast, the warehouse would collapse. Barely aware he'd let go of the tablet, Peter ran toward the falling girder.

Catching it with both hands, he barely managed to keep the steel edge from cracking his skull.

Now, the hard part: getting it back in place.

Every muscle in his arms, legs, and back felt as if they were tearing but, slowly, he tried to push it back upright. Above, the higher girder that supported the central I-beam began to buckle. Only a few rusted rivets kept it in place against the wall. The remaining supports screeched. The warehouse, neglected for so long, rained stray wood and metal.

In a game of inches, Spider-Man pushed the heavy steel higher. The footpads of his uniform ripped as they pressed against the concrete floor, but at last, he wedged the top of the lower girder back in below its brother.

It wasn't enough. The I-beam listed at an angle. The weight of the entire warehouse pressed down against the lower girder. It slid back toward Spider-Man, but somehow he found the strength to push yet again and force it back toward the wall.

The warehouse was no longer in danger of collapsing, but only as long as he didn't move.

Sweat beaded along his body, on his forehead, some absorbed by the fabric of his mask, some dripping into his eyes.

"It's mine!"

The croaking voice reminded him he'd lost track of Silvermane. Still glowing, but wizened, balding and stooped, he stood atop a pile of debris, holding aloft the ancient stone.

He's got the tablet!

"I will never forget! Never let go! I am Silvio Manfredi! Silvio Manfredi!"

He might have gone on shouting his own name over and over, but Vanessa Fisk's voice carried above both the old man's croaks and the building's creaks.

"Silvermane!"

The plaster splotches and dirt covering her coat and face did nothing to diminish her stiff dignity. Marko was at her side, an electronic device in his hands.

"Your prize collection has been soaked with gasoline. An ignitor is connected to the detonator Michael is holding. That was what Spider-Man asked me to come here to do. I assumed it would be in exchange for the tablet."

Vanessa Fisk glanced back and forth between the two—the web-slinger braced against the girder, the aged Manfredi panting as he held the tablet. "But it looks as if ownership has changed hands. That stone is my husband's only hope. As such, I'd be willing to exchange it for the detonator. Once my people have studied it…"

Spider-Man tried to warn her. "Mrs. Fisk, you don't understand. He can't be reasoned with!"

She gave him a world-weary look. "He's still a man, isn't he? In my experience, any man can be reasoned with."

But Manfredi's feral growl didn't sound human. It was barely possible to make out what he was shouting as he raced toward her.

"My palace! My territory! My walls! My sky!"

The dimming light that covered Silvermane grew erratic. It went dark, then flared again. Against the warehouse shadows, he seemed to flash in and out of existence. Fast as Manfredi was, the distance gave Marko time to place himself between the madman and Vanessa Fisk.

Manfredi hit Man Mountain square in the chest. Marko fell. The detonator he held went flying. It bounced along the refuse. At first it threatened to land harmlessly on its side—but then, as it rolled, the button on it clicked not once, but three times.

Bright reds and yellows erupted from the basement, rising like a molten ocean through the hollow of the stairs. Silvermane scrambled over Marko's body and threw himself down the steps, screaming, "No!"

Spider-Man couldn't tell whether Silvermane was still lit by that inner glow, or just the spreading fire.

Marko rose, a grin on his face. He held up the tablet and handed it to Vanessa Fisk.

"Why, thank you, Michael."

"For a classy lady like you, any time."

Still holding the girder, Spider-Man gritted his teeth. *She'll get away with the tablet...but I can't let Silvermane die. Even if he is nuts, even if it means my identity is exposed...*

"Look, I can't hold on anymore! Both of you have to run for it, now!"

They fled, Marko looming over Vanessa Fisk like

a shield. Once they were gone, Spider-Man eyed the distance to the flaming stairs, pivoted, and then let go. As the girder slid behind him, he pushed against it with both feet, executing a kick that sent him flying half the distance to the stairwell.

The girder he'd been holding fell to the side. The wall bent toward him. Touching down, he curled and again kicked into the air. As soon as his outstretched hands hit the floor, he pulled himself forward, bent his legs, and made a final leap into the basement inferno.

Above, it sounded as if the world was ending. Here, all he could see were the flames, writhing and licking, forming and unforming a thousand shapes as they ate away at anything that wasn't stone. Silvio Manfredi stood in the heart of the blaze, that strange inner light still shining as he tried to pull curling, blackening papers from the fire.

Spider-Man struggled to get to him. "We've got to get out of here!"

Hearing him, Silvermane whirled. He looked as old as a person could get, but the look in his eyes was still that of the boy who'd broken into the police annex, just a few days ago.

Shaking his head, Manfredi fled, ashes trailing from the crumbling papers in his hands. The wall-crawler chased the mobster around the maze of Silvermane's palace—until there was another great crash from above.

Warned by his spider-sense, Spider-Man leaped for cover as half the basement ceiling collapsed. Silvermane's legs were pinned beneath a mass of concrete and steel.

Ignoring the danger and his own pain, Spider-Man raced over and pulled at the debris. His spider-sense wailed again, telling him that the horrid moans above meant that the warehouse had yet to finish dying.

As Peter tugged at the old man's form, Silvermane's eyes swam in his head. The fingers of his one free hand wriggled, as if he was trying to remember something he'd heard.

"Hey, Bugsy, what *do* they call it? You know, that animal that walks on four legs in the morning, two in the afternoon, and three at night? What do they call that? It's like some big secret, and I feel like if I just figured it out, I'd be rich forever."

And then he closed his eyes.

The glow was gone. He looked dead. Spider-Man frowned and continued trying to dig him out.

There was another roar from above, echoed by his spider-sense. What was left of the ceiling looked ready to cave in. Before he could free him, Manfredi's eyes opened again, this time glowing only with the same black, boundless hunger they always had.

He croaked his last/first words: "Who are you?"

The remains of the ceiling fell. Spider-Man tried to stand his ground, but his spider-sense, no longer content to warn him, hurled him away. The final tons of wall and roof crashed into the basement, smothering the fire, destroying the charred memory palace, leaving nothing.

○━━━━━━━━○

BLOCKS away, Vanessa Fisk gripped the tablet and watched the warehouse fall in on itself. The remnants of the fire glowed briefly, then faded, leaving behind a huge, black, empty spot like a missing tooth in a giant's maw.

She turned to the human giant at her side. His arm was bleeding, his clothes torn from his efforts to protect her. His head was down in submission, but he kept stealing sideways glances at her.

In a way, he reminded her of Wilson: They shared a powerful, physical presence. But the obvious differences made her ache all the more for her husband.

"Michael, I had no idea how you felt. If I had, I would have told you there is only one man for me."

"I get it. You don't have to say nothing. Matter of fact, I really wish you wouldn't. I should go." He began to walk off.

"Wait, I haven't paid you."

He kept walking. "Nah. I don't want it."

His receding form grew less distinct, fading into the rest of the night-shapes. Vanessa Fisk let out a lonely sigh.

"Yeah, I kinda feel bad for the big lug, too."

She spun. Spider-Man was hanging upside down behind her.

"You survived."

"Near as I can tell." He shrugged in that sheepish way some young men had, before age made them more certain. "Life's but a dream, right?"

"And Silvermane?"

"Buried, or…I don't know. I couldn't find him. Believe me, I tried, but all I could see was fire." He crossed his arms. "It's not like *you* were hard to find. You could have been out of the city by now."

"I decided to give this to you." She handed him the tablet.

He took it. "Don't want to say I told you so, but I was hoping you'd see the light, to coin a phrase."

She nodded. "I didn't think you were lying when you explained how the elixir worked, but I didn't completely understand what Silvermane had become until he dove into the flames. It's not a fate I'd want for anyone, let alone my husband. I'll have to find another way."

"Wish I could wish you luck with that, but, you know."

She did. She did know. But she also hoped she could prove him wrong someday, that the rest of the world could see the same man she knew.

Spider-Man turned his back to her and placed the stone back in its silver case. He was exhausted and hurt, making it easy for her to step into the shadows—and disappear.

TWENTY-NINE

IT WASN'T the first time Peter Parker had stumbled through a morning with his entire body aching, and he held no illusion that it would be the last. He'd left the tablet with S.H.I.E.L.D. and decided he'd rather not know where they were taking it.

After all, Vanessa Fisk was right. The tablet's formula was too risky to use on anyone—including Aunt May.

Whatever notes Silvermane had on me were destroyed with the warehouse. And if he somehow survived, hopefully he won't remember Peter Parker at all.

The relief about his identity lasted only long enough for his worries about Aunt May to flood back. At least he had no classes today; he could spend the day by her side, where he belonged.

And if Anna Watson wants to glare at me the whole time, so be it. It doesn't matter what anyone else thinks. Well, maybe it does, but I'll get used to it.

He did have to make one stop first, and it wasn't to make excuses.

He expected Professor Blanton to be wary. But

when Peter knocked on the frame of his open office door, the man looked like he might throw himself out the window to get away.

"Sorry! Professor, please. I didn't mean to startle you. I just want to speak with you for a second."

Blanton nodded. "Peter, come in. I…have a class in five minutes, but…I'll cancel it if you like. Dear heaven, you're not here to ask me to hold on to drug money…?" His gaze kept darting over Peter's shoulder, as if expecting Silvio Manfredi to turn up.

Peter went wide-eyed. "No! Never! The opposite! I want to tell you that you don't have to worry about making any special concessions for me. I don't want you to. I mean, you know, aside from what you'd normally do for any student."

Blanton raised a single eyebrow. "That sounds… noble, Peter, but what if…certain people…don't share your ethics?"

"That's what I'm trying to say. It's no secret I take photos of Spider-Man. The crooks who threatened you were trying to use me to get to him. Believe me, sir, I had no idea they'd approached you. But Spider-Man assures me it's all over. The bad guys are gone, and I am so, so very sorry that you were ever involved at all."

Blanton didn't completely relax, but at least he no longer looked like he wanted to hide under his desk.

"If you want to fail me, or bring me up for academic suspension again, I completely understand. While I am incredibly grateful for the opportunities

I've been given here, I know I've been a terrible student, and I'm ready to accept the consequences."

Blanton picked up a red pen and rapped it on his desk. "They're gone?"

"Completely. You have my word."

Blanton paused. He glanced down at the paper he'd been correcting and made a big red X through the first response. It seemed to please him; by the time he looked back up, he seemed much more his old self.

Wait. Is that my *paper?*

"Your aunt is sick, Mr. Parker, and I'm not a monster. Besides, the committee would think me insane after I dropped the suspension recommendation the first time. There will be no further proceedings for now, and the extension will remain in place."

"Yes!"

"But it *will* be the last one."

"Understood. Thank you."

Peter backed out quietly. He was halfway down the hall when his phone buzzed.

It was a text from the hospital, asking him to call immediately. Why would they be trying to reach him? Unless…

No. No, no, no.

He felt as if his finger was moving through molasses as he hit the speed-dial. Between each ring, a lifetime passed. Thankfully, he didn't have to go through the nurse's station. Dr. Bromwell himself picked up.

"Good news, Peter. The Obetical is working

perfectly. Her bilirubin levels are already up, and by morning we'll be bringing her out of the coma."

Peter shook his head, not sure he was hearing correctly. "You're saying she's out of danger?"

"Well…yes."

The relief flooded him so quickly he couldn't help but laugh. "That's fantastic, Doc! But I'm confused. Obetical is that experimental treatment, right?"

"Yes, of course. Your aunt signed off on any treatment when she agreed to the induced coma."

"But we can't afford it. Hard to believe the insurance company would change its mind."

"No. Vanessa Fisk paid for it. She left a note for you saying that you'd done your best to live up to your side of some agreement, even if the results weren't what she'd hoped for."

Marko was right. She is a classy lady.

<hr>

THE HISSING respirator filled her ears, the great chest rising and falling before her eyes. Vanessa Fisk sat stiff-backed on a plush chair by her husband's bed, still trying to decide whether he was somehow still here—whether, despite her previous doubts, he *could* hear her. There wasn't any particular moment at which she changed her mind, but eventually she started speaking.

"Wilson…I wanted to die without you. I know we've said that to each other a thousand times, but this was different. The hole you'd left behind was so deep,

I wanted to close my eyes and fall in. The only thing that stopped me was knowing that Richard would blame himself for that, too. So I went on, but I was moving through my days the same way that machine makes you breathe—mechanically, soullessly.

"Then, almost by accident, I was given hope. And even though it was a false hope, it made me face the world again. The more I did, the more I realized you were still there—in the unanswered calls of my heart, the photos of Richard's face, even in the men who remind me of you more by their differences than their similarities. That will never, never be enough to make me happy—but it is enough to make me keep searching for a way to bring you back."

A squeak against the tiles outside made her turn toward the door.

It was just a nurse, pushing a rubber-wheeled cart. It reminded her of a certain worried young man she'd glimpsed running down the hall just a week ago.

She wondered how things would work out for him.

A HALF hour later, a deeply relieved Peter arrived at his aunt's bed in ICU.

The moment she saw him, Anna Watson rose to leave.

"Please, Mrs. Watson, stay," he said. "You're family."

She glared and walked out.

He sat there the rest of the day and through the

night, holding Aunt May's hands, rubbing them to keep them warm, watching the yellow fade from her skin. He thought of the games they'd played with Uncle Ben when he was a child, of the sandwiches she'd made for his lunch. He told himself that even if Doctor Octopus were terrorizing Midtown, or the Rhino were robbing a bank—even if the world were ending, for once someone else would have to deal with it.

There was no more important place for him to be.

Near dawn, Dr. Fent stopped the pentobarbital drip that kept May Parker in the induced coma. When she said his aunt would likely be awake in an hour or two, he decided Anna Watson should be there when her best friend opened her eyes. He called Mary Jane and asked her to convince her to return.

In short order, MJ arrived with Anna—and Harry Osborn and Flash Thompson.

Peter rose to greet them. "Wow, MJ. I knew you could be convincing, but…"

She grinned. "I just knew Flash felt bad about that *coward* crack, and I figured friends should stick together. Besides, they weren't doing anything other than sleeping, right boys?"

Harry grunted.

A yawning Flash mumbled something along the lines of, "Glad your aunt's doing better."

Though clearly relieved, Anna Watson still wouldn't look at him. "No thanks to you."

"Anna Watson!"

The voice came from the bed. It was Aunt May, struggling to raise herself into a seated position.

Grinning, Peter rushed over. "How long have you been awake?"

She smiled and patted his hand. "A little while. It was so peaceful with you here by my side, I didn't have the heart to say anything."

Her smile faded when she turned her blue eyes on the woman behind her nephew. "Anna, I don't care how long we've been friends. If you *ever* want me to speak to you again, you will apologize to my nephew this instant!"

Peter tried to get her to lie back down. "Take it easy! She was just concerned about you. She doesn't owe me an apology for anything!"

She swatted his hands away. "Oh, yes she does! For years I said nothing while those ruffians bullied you at school, because your uncle told me it would only make things worse. But bullies come in all shapes and sizes."

At the word *ruffian,* Flash took a sheepish step back.

"Anna, what you don't know is that it wasn't his fault. *I* made him swear he'd never, ever put himself at risk for me. He was only trying to keep his promise."

Anna Watson pursed her lips. "May, I…I had no idea that's how you felt."

May harrumphed. "Well, next time, think twice before you go opening your mouth about things you know nothing about!"

Mrs. Watson swallowed and faced Peter. "I'm sorry."

Mary Jane leaned over to whisper to Harry. "That's a first. Usually when you're in the doghouse with Aunt Anna, it's for life."

Anna Watson turned to the woman in the bed, tears in her eyes. "May, it's just that I was so worried!"

As she leaned down to kiss her cheek, May smiled and patted the back of her head. "I know, my dear, I know. I love you, too. Peter and I accept your apology."

When Anna rose, May's steely eyes turned toward Peter's friends. "And you, all of you, I don't ever want to hear any of you call Peter a coward! He's sacrificed more than any of you know. In fact, you should all take him to dinner, or throw a little party, to show him how sorry you are."

Harry and Flash looked at their feet as they nodded.

Mary Jane beamed. "Hey, I'm always up for a party. And with you feeling better, Mrs. Parker, there's plenty to celebrate."

The elder Parker smiled warmly. "What a nice girl. Isn't she, Peter? And how wonderful that you're all here. I feel very cared for. Now, if you don't mind, I'd like a minute with my nephew."

Mary Jane led the others toward the waiting room, turning briefly back to wink at Peter. "Catch you later, Tiger."

As soon as they were gone, Peter sat back down beside the bed, a wide grin of relief beneath his furrowed brow.

"Aunt May, what was that all about? You never asked me to promise anything."

He put the back of his hand to her forehead. *She's being a tiger herself. The barbiturate's probably still in her system.*

"Hush. I'm not addled. I know exactly what I did and didn't say."

"Aunt May, I want you to know…"

"I don't have to know anything, Peter, except that you are the best thing in my life, and as long as I'm here, I will love and defend you."

He put his head down on her shoulder. She twisted her lips to his ear and whispered, "That treatment they gave me cost a lot, didn't it? That awful Spider-Man didn't have anything to do with the money, did he?"

He didn't look up. "Do I have to answer that?"

She tugged his hair. "No, I suppose not. I *was* worried about what would happen to me, you know."

"Me, too."

"Until I saw your uncle."

"You saw Uncle Ben?"

"Oh, yes, standing right by my bed, bold as you please, next to a very beautiful woman."

"That rascal. Were you jealous?"

She chuckled. "No, it wasn't like that. He wouldn't come visit all the way from the afterlife with some floozy on his arm. She was more like an angel—a very, very sad angel."

Is she remembering Vanessa Fisk?

"What's important is what he said, that *you* are his future. It made me realize it's the same for all of us. I'm the living part of those who loved me and passed on, and now you're my future, too. After that, I wasn't worried anymore, because I realized that while death comes to us all, so does life."

"I just got you back. Can we not talk about death now?"

"There, there. I know you've been hurt, but you're not a child anymore. It's high time you tried to see the good side. Spend the rest of your life mourning the past, and what does that say about Uncle Ben, me, and poor Gwen? If you're going to be the part of us that lives on, it seems to me that the least you could do for us is to *live*. Anything less than that would be irresponsible. Don't you agree?"

"Yes, Aunt May. I do."

THE END

ACKNOWLEDGMENTS

HEREWITH, I present my hardy, heartfelt thanks to my editorial triad, Stuart Moore, Sarah Brunstad, and Jeff Youngquist. Lest anyone think these action-packed tomes spring whole-hog from the author's head (yeah, yeah, *aside* from the fact that I didn't exactly create any of the characters), I want to make it clear that the too-often unheralded editors do a lot of heavy lifting.

In this particular instance, that includes bearing with my crazed efforts to create a dizzily nostalgic love letter to Stan Lee & John Romita's classic Spidey work from the sixties.

Along the way, our back and forth has covered everything from the scarcity of Manhattan alleyways, the behavior of security guards, what exactly constitutes over-the-top dialogue, the adhesive qualities of webbing, the nature of cowardice, bullying, guilt and mourning, and the proper capitalization of the Power Cosmic.

Throughout, they've consistently managed to not only appreciate and support my work, but to make it better. This in spite of my occasional addict-like adherence to phrases such as *guru*, *man-o-mine*, and *hot cup o' java*. Their commitment to character, story, cadence, common sense, and yes, grammar *itself*, does them proud.

It has also all been terribly fun.

This is our third Marvel novel together (check out *Deadpool: Paws* and *Captain America: Dark Designs*!), so I assume we're doing something right.

ABOUT THE AUTHOR

STEFAN PETRUCHA has written over twenty novels and hundreds of graphic novels for adults, young adults, and tweens. His work has sold over a million copies worldwide. He also teaches online classes through the University of Massachusetts. Born in the Bronx, he spent his formative years moving between the big city and the suburbs, both of which made him prefer escapism. A fan of comic books, science fiction, and horror since learning to read, in high school and college he added a love for all sorts of literary work, eventually learning that the very best fiction always brings you back to reality—so, really, there's no way out.